DOWN FROM THE SKY

A NOVEL BY M.W. DUNCAN

SEVERED PRESS
HOBART TASMANIA

DOWN FROM THE SKY

Astronomy compels the soul to look upwards and leads from this world to another.
Plato

For Orla

CHAPTER 1

Doctor Isambard Stone, 10 Miles from Uriah's Hope, Esworth.

Dr Isambard Stone of the New Seattle Institute for Off World Archaeology was a gambler. People often said only fools partook in the habit. They were of course correct, but Stone had no need for the opinions of others as he felt himself to be quite the expert on the matter. He no longer gambled hard nor lost harder as he once did in his youth. Lessons learnt transformed him into an astute risk taker, and only when he knew the deck was stacked in his favour.

It was the gamble that brought him to Esworth, a winter-riddled planet recently announced as the Terran Cooperative's newest colony. The tantalising prospect of making a profound discovery on the mostly unexplored planet, one to shake the very core of what was known about Esworth, would mark him as one of the most preeminent academics of his generation.

And so, there he found himself, walking a rough roadway cut through difficult terrain and compacted by security patrols, and, until recently flattened further by heavy mining teams.

"Remind me, why are we trudging through a storm this bad?" came his assistant's high-pitched voice.

Winds strong enough to knock a weak man backward brought thick waves of snow, and Tanya was a lithe young woman with exercise not being her choice of enjoyment.

Uriah's Hope was a new city built with high ambition and low morals. It was a place where money went far and bribes were what made this whole endeavour possible. And if there was a price to immortality, Dr Stone paid a small fortune for the privilege.

Both Tanya and Stone wore the latest survival gear, enough to ensure they didn't freeze to death in the minus thirty-eight-degree weather. Stone wiped the visor of his protective mask. He checked his wrist mounted device, a PWD or Personal Wrist Device, which not only linked them him to the Fleet Net service, but also accessed diagnostic tools and maps, and provided recording and communication

1

capabilities. He brought up the map indicating their current location and their destination. The two dots were achingly close, but he knew it would be another hour before they arrived. Their destination was a mining camp. The camp was abandoned three weeks ago and designated as off limits due to unconfirmed reports of 'unusual unidentified activity', and those three words were music to Stone's orchestral curiosity.

"Not far, Tanya. I promise. We're almost there."

"Why here? Why did it have to be out here?" A hint of humour played on her voice. She was used to accompanying him to remote and difficult locations. Siberia was bad. Luna worse. But she never flinched from following him, after all she was an astute young woman in love with an older, educated man.

Stone blew out a breath. "If archaeology was easy we'd just kick over the stones and find what we're looking for."

Stone had first met Tanya back in New Seattle, and that meeting wasn't by chance. A relationship with the daughter of the director of Uriah's Hope project was bound to be beneficial to his purpose. And he was correct. Tanya accepted a research position, and her presence opened many doors.

Money enabled Stone to bypass rigorous checks and vetting processes, and gained easy passage to Esworth, all with the assistance of well entrenched gangs.

"This is the coldest I've ever experienced, and I thought nothing could be worse than our dig in Siberia."

"Think warm."

"Think warm," she repeated with a good dose of sarcasm. "Think warm."

Snow battered the lonely pair of travellers. Small, rolling hills capped by thick snowdrifts surrounded their route. Lonesome stalks popped through the snow, dotted with leaves of ice. Thick coils of rope flanked the length of the road, kept upright by metal pylons. They ensured no traveller or vehicle would become lost in the near impossible weather.

The landscape changed and dark shapes appeared in the unending white. Heavy machinery lay idle, almost buried under snow. Stone checked his PWD again. Only a few more minutes and he'd be upon the test shaft sunk into the ground two months earlier to discover what wealth lay beneath.

"Almost there," he yelled.

"What?" Tanya yelled back.

Stone simply waved her forward. The wind hit them at an angle and slowed his footsteps further. Stone wiped the snow from his visor and checked that Tanya followed. She gave him a thumbs up sign and onward they moved. Ahead and to the left of the road lay a dark mound.

"Over here." Stone moved quickly with his excitement.

Drilled into the side of a hill was the opening of the shaft, the passageway twelve feet wide. Stone grabbed Tanya's gloved hand and pulled her through the opening. The wind whipped past the entrance creating a vortex behind them.

"Let's move in further, away from the wind," suggested Tanya.

"This is it." Stone looked up and around. The rock face was a dark red, typical for Esworth.

"Come on," said Tanya.

"Lights on," Stone ordered.

The shaft slopped downward almost immediately. His PWD indicated the temperature had risen marginally and continued rising as they ventured further down.

He removed a glove and felt the shaft walls. Cold and like wet clay. He pushed his fingers into the wall half an inch before finding resistance. "Amazing," he breathed and returned his glove to his hand.

As they walked downward the temperature rose more and the passageway shrank. They could no longer walk side by side. Stone's PWD blinked red and he tapped at the screen.

"What's wrong?" Tanya asked.

He gave it another tap. "Fleet Net is unavailable at this depth. As of now we're cut off from the outside."

"That's bad."

Stone shrugged. "Not necessarily. It just means we can't be traced if anyone was looking for us."

Tanya unzipped her thermal coat and giggled. "You know what my father would do if he caught us out here?"

Despite the layers of clothing still remaining, the shedding of Tanya's coat combined with the thrill of climbing down into the hill caused a stirring in Stone. Despite being many years her senior a sexual relationship had developed between the two, and he never tired of Tanya's youthful body. Her father raged at the relationship and blows were exchanged. Neither man was seriously hurt but Stone won in the end. He always did.

"He tried once and only got one punch in."

Tanya pealed the gloves from her hands and sent Stone a quizzical smile. "Out here he's an important man."

"And yet here we are doing important research."

Their voices echoed through the tight tunnel.

"You know his position," she said. "He only needs to snap his fingers and I'd be holed up, grounded like a teen."

"Nobody realises the possibilities that lie here. Nobody. If they did, we wouldn't have to sneak around like criminals."

Tanya did not offer a retort. She was a long-time subscriber to his speeches.

"Everything you see here, Esworth, is possible because we got lucky. Humanity, I mean. We can trace it all back to the Night War."

"So you've said before."

"How many years ago did the war occur?" asked Stone, knowing the answer.

"One-hundred-and-sixty-two years ago," replied Tanya.

Even the most basic of students knew the history of the Night War. At a time when humans had only started exploring neighbouring planets, The Nights landed near Seattle, Washington. So technically advanced they overwhelmed the paltry defences of the fractured nations of Earth. After three years of savage warfare Seattle was wiped from the map in an orbital bombardment. And then The Nights suddenly disappeared.

And in the one-hundred-and-sixty-two years since, scientists and technicians poured over the technology left behind. A generation of the best engineers tore apart, digested and repurposed The Nights' machinery to propel humanity to the stars. It was this which led to the set up of the Terran Cooperation Council with the purpose of countering any future alien threat as well as delving into the mysteries of their technology.

"Millions died in the war, Tanya. But their deaths brought a progress the likes of which we could never hope to have achieved on our own." Stone turned to find Tanya mimicking his speech.

She shrugged and apologised with little sincerity.

"Tanya, we're pretenders to the throne, undeserving of our status in the cosmos. The war was terrible, yes, and even to this day, we watch against their return. In all of this nobody has gotten close to the reason why The Nights did what they did. We don't understand them."

"I know," she said flippantly. "Because they wouldn't communicate."

"And I will bridge the gap between mystery and understanding."

Deeproot Drilling had sunk the shaft and unexpectedly breached a chamber. Workers suffered sudden vomiting, severe headaches, hallucinations and if the rumours were true, voices were heard to speak in whispers. Stone's curiosity was piqued beyond control, his need to discover the secrets of the chamber paramount.

They rounded a corner, ducking as the shaft ceiling lowered.

"Maybe all they found were empty tunnels and bored ghosts." Tanya halted suddenly and placed a hand against the wall as if struck be a sudden exhaustion. A vein pulsated through the middle of her forehead. "I don't feel good."

"Are you trying to be funny?"

"No."

"Feeling a little claustrophobic?"

"When have I ever suffered that?"

"Can you continue? Just a little further down."

"How much further?"

"Can't be too far."

Their progress was slow. Beads of sweat trickled from Tanya's forehead. They stripped themselves of some layers. The air was full of the smell of a room that had been untouched for years.

Stone's light flashed on a crack in the rockface. "There it is."

"It's small," said Tanya.

The opening was three feet in width and five feet in height.

"Isambard, don't go in there. I can hear something."

"Hear what?"

"Things."

"Your imagination is playing havoc."

"No. I hear whispers. I don't know what they're saying but you can't go in there. And ... and it hurts." She patted her chest. "It's hurting me."

"Tanya, there's nothing here that can hurt you."

"Please, Isambard." Tanya placed her hands to her ears and closed her eyes.

Stone was not so removed from emotion to not pity Tanya, but he would not allow a thing to interrupt his work. He sent her a smile. "Stay here, my lioness. I'll go alone."

"Isambard."

Stone tapped the record button on his PWD and operated the camera mounted by his flashlight. "I won't be long." He stepped through the fissure.

The first sensation was the temperature. It dropped considerably, his breath misting.

The space was huge, vaulted and clearly not a natural formation. The walls were smooth, a fading blue metallic hue, and when his light hit them it was like an electrical current travelled vertically over the surface. Stone reached out to touch, but a feeling like a hundred pins stabbing his palm made him withdraw his hand. He blew on his hands and rubbed them together until the stinging sensation disappeared.

"Amazing," he uttered, and powered the flashlight to full.

Steps, far larger than what most adults could comfortably use, led down to a plaza. Stone carefully negotiated each one, sometimes sitting and sliding, until he reached the bottom.

"My God. I never could've hoped ..."

His light illuminated six statues some twenty-foot in height, all made from the same substances as the walls. They stood on golden plinths. The torsos retained a humanoid similarity, heavily muscled and torsos bare of clothing. But the heads, their grossness caused an equal measure of amazement and disgust. The faces snarled a demonic cruelty, the jaws wolflike with teeth, and all other features bovine including intricate horns protruding from the heads. Orbs sat in hands and a baleful green reflected from those curved surfaces as his light moved left to right.

"What are you? Gods? Leaders? Myth?"

No markings indicated any form of identification.

He laughed. "Well, nothing in archaeology comes easy."

He never expected any worthwhile discovery to be easy.

"Am I the first human to gaze upon these faces?" The question felt redundant, considering the sculptures so closely resembled the concept of demons on Earth. Stone reached out to touch one of the plinths. "Perhaps. Perhaps not. But I'm an explorer of the past, looking to unlock the mysteries of the present."

A blast of pure ice shot into his arm, a freezing cold that contorted his muscles for a full second before releasing its control.

"Fuck!" Stone clutched his shoulder and his arm fell limply at his side. His arm burned with an intense frost. He pulled up his sleeve. His skin paled to a peculiar white, a deep black vein snaking up his arm.

The floor vibrated, a soft tremor as if the beginnings of a minor earthquake. The orbs in the hands of the statues pulsed their bale green. The shaking grew in intensity. Stone struggled to keep his feet and made an awkward dash for the exit. Up the great stairs he clambered, only one arm capable of reaching and pulling him up. Tremors loosened the ground. Smalls stones bounced at his feet. He looked back. The statues flashed a glittering spray but did not move as the floor beneath them did.

"Tanya! Tanya!" He clambered upward, his feet slipping with the crumbling rubble. "Tanya!"

Two more large steps and he reached the top and dived from the chamber through the fissure. On hands and feet he caught his breath and coughed dust from his mouth. "Tanya?"

Tanya screamed words, indecipherable for the most part. She was covered by a mist of distortion, her arms flailing like an injured bird trying to take flight.

"Tanya!" Stone tried to grab her, but his hand was pushed away by an unseen force.

"They're here! Isambard, help me!"

He stood and felt a push to his chest. "I can't. I can't. It won't let me."

Tanya screamed and punched at her ears. The noise of the shaking chamber seemed to lift him from the ground. He ran.

***

Agustin Garcia, Command and Control Hub - Uriah's Hope.

Agustin Garcia sipped his black coffee and watched the storm blowing outside. The Command and Control Hub was perched above Uriah's Hope. An impressive tower with a circular top, an observatory allowing an unobscured view over the city. The unusually thick windows kept the cold at bay. He often came up here to think, watching nature's tricks while perfectly safe. He searched for a reassuring feeling, one that told him he knew what he was doing here on Esworth. The little comfort he got on this forsaken planet was Tanya. His daughter shipped in on the last intake when The Gate was open, and despite his misgivings, if she was here in Uriah's Hope, she was away from that dammed archaeologist.

Uriah's Hope — the first city and only city on Esworth — stretched out beneath him like a detailed model he built in his youth. Agustin took another sip and made a face. Coffee didn't taste like it did back home.

The centre was the hub of operations for the fledgling city. If it were up to him, which it wasn't, Agustin wouldn't have set the facility far removed from the rest of the population. As it was, it produced a sense of elitism. It wasn't quite an ivory tower, but he understood how it was perceived by those below. Even his staff didn't live in the habitation complexes underground, for they had apartments separated from the general population. It was an empty dream. The architect of the city, Uriah Simmons, laid out the plans long before Agustin ever dreamed of being in the position he was.

Director of Operations. A grand title for someone that essentially spent his time managing one disaster after another. They said there would be teething problems. The teeth were rotten and in the process of being replaced. Agustin and his staff did their best, and to date nobody had died on Esworth.

He didn't linger too long. The air was eerily still and the temperature uncomfortably cool. It felt like a mausoleum. Agustin took a final look outside and started down the stairwell. The Hub was occupied day and night, rotating staff ensuring the continued running of the city. So far, they had fought off a half-dozen minor disasters and Agustin was braced for another. He fathomed that a lack of disasters voided the need for a man in his position.

Agustin's return to The Hub attracted little attention. Rows of consoles and workstations housed operators all linked in with headsets. He sat into his swivel chair and pulled his tablet over his knee. One more hour of work and then he'd retire for some sleep. Tomorrow, he and Tanya would join for their weekly breakfast in his apartment. It was an event he never missed, no matter how in demand Agustin was. Tanya's childhood favourite, eggs Benedict, was the meal he always served up.

"Nobody makes these like you, Dad," she would often say with her mouth full, then smile in such an unguarded way that all he could see was his little girl.

Agustin scanned through the latest shipping manifests detailing supplies which needed to be shuttled down from the orbital stations. Food, medical provisions, electronic equipment, uniforms, industrial bins and lining. All looked on the up and up except for the request for an excessive amount of pillows. A typo? One too many zeros? He'd have that looked at before giving his approval. The latest weather report was in, too. The current storm was expected to last many weeks.

"More fucking snow," he said to the tablet, watching the storm's projected movement from orbit.

"That's the one thing we have in abundance. All the bloody snow in the world," said Assistant Director Dale Twomley, a smile on his face.

"And pillows, allegedly."

Twomley frowned quizzically. "I'm sure there's a reason for that announcement, but I'm not sure I want to know."

Twomley was a hawkish man who spurned vision correction procedures in favour of wearing circular lens glasses. Agustin suspected a phobia of surgical tools too close to the eyeball kept Twomley away from any optometry specialist.

"You should get some rest, Agustin. There's nothing here I can't deal with."

Agustin pushed his tablet aside. "I was up at the viewing platform. Have you ever wondered what the first humans thought as they came through The Gate? What made them think a ball of ice like this would make a secondary home?"

"You know history as well as I. It was the only Gate to open when we came knocking. By chance or design, here we are. You're thinking too much. Sleep. That's an order."

"Ah, Dale. I don't think an assistant director gets to order a director around. But I happen to agree with you." Agustin climbed from his chair.

"Tomorrow's your day with Tanya?"

"Yes. Eggs Benedict times two."

"Pass on my best, won't you?"

An alarm sounded before Agustin reached the elevator.

"Go, I'll deal with it," said the Assistant Director.

Agustin ignored his friend and rushed back to his chair and pulled his tablet close again. He hit the flashing alert symbol and read the brief message. Twomley did the same on his.

"Shit in my coffee," he cursed. "There's someone outside the perimeter. They've activated an emergency PWD beacon."

Agustin streamed the picture to his monitor, manipulating the map to identify the exact location. "He's nine miles outside of our perimeter. What's out there?"

"Nothing's out there," said one of his operators. "One of the mining camps that was abandoned because of the storms is close by but it was evacuated weeks ago."

"Someone we left behind?" suggested Twomley, an eyebrow raised.

"Not possible," replied the operator. "Everyone was accounted for."

"If they had access to a PWD they would've called for help before now," reasoned Agustin. "Whoever it is won't last long out there. Find the closest Red Aquila team and get our trespasser intercepted. Fast."

Twomley carried out the order.

Agustin threw a quick look at the elevator door. Another late night of work with the possibility of not hitting his pillow until late morning. He almost laughed to himself at the thought of wanting a pillow.

"When they find him nobody else is to speak to him. Understand?"

"Yes, Director," came the replies.

"Now, let's see if we can identify who it is before I have the privilege of meeting him. Get me a list of those with a permit."

To leave the safety of Uriah's Hope without a permit was a criminal act. External security was outsourced to Red Aquila, a private army which conducted patrols ensuring nobody left. It was for their own good. Esworth was untamed. Without the proper training or equipment, it was a death sentence. To get nine miles from the city was almost impossible.

"Let's go, people. And I want all the information on the Deeproot Mining Camp."

***

Red Aquila guards stepped aside as Agustin marched their way. The prison was a separate complex connected to the rear of the UHMP Precinct building, officially under the jurisdiction of the Uriah's Hope Municipal Police Force. He'd showered, eaten a quick meal and managed to grab a few hours in his apartment before the call came to say the trespasser was ready for interrogation. Agustin left a message for Tanya indicating he'd be late for their breakfast. He hated it. He'd missed a lot of Tanya growing up and was determined to make that up, even with something as mundane as cooking breakfast. It counted, at least to him.

"Open the door," he ordered two straight-faced guards.

The doors opened and Agustin stepped through. The guards followed. The corridors were lit brightly, white walls reflecting the fluorescent lights above. It was a fortress of heavy doors, security cameras pointing at their every move. And bored guards. To this date, the venue had been sparsely utilised. Crime had yet to take root in the fledgling city. Or rather it had, but the effects were yet to be fully felt. The next level of security doors parted and he was led to a cell.

"I'm Ramirez, sir. It was my team that found him out there." Ramirez was unshaved and emanated a strong body odour.

They briefly shook hands.

"Hell of a job out there, Ramirez. You do your company proud. Did he say anything?"

Ramirez rubbed his chin. "He was barely conscious, sir. We almost ran him over. If it hadn't been for the PWD beacon we'd never have found him. He wore the right gear to be out there. Kept him alive long enough."

"Did he say anything?" Agustin repeated.

"Sir," Ramirez said apologetically. "He said a lot of things and nothing. You know how it is when the cold gets to you. You jabber nonsense as much as sense."

"You'll have a report sent to me. Don't leave out any detail."

"Of course, sir. He's weak from being out there. We've sent for our medic to check him over."

Agustin moved to enter the cell, then added, "Thank you. The report can wait 'til you've had some food and rest."

Agustin pushed his thumb to the reader and the door slipped open silently.

"Hello, Agustin. Fancy seeing you here." Isambard Stone sat at a table, a thermal blanket draped over his shoulders, hands and feet shackled by restraints. His face was pale and drawn. Blood clung to his cheeks and nose. He spread his wrists and the handcuffs jangled. His arms shuddered and his teeth chattered. "I'd get up to welcome you, but, as you can see I'm unable."

"You!" The word came out as a half roar dripping in venom. Agustin's anger readied him to propel over the small table and land twenty punches.

"You know him, sir?" came Ramirez's voice from behind. It appeared Ramirez's curiosity was piqued enough to ignore exhaustion and hunger.

"What are you doing in my city?" said Agustin.

Stone tilted his head. He blinked twice as if trying to work out where the voice came from. "Your city?"

"Answer me!"

Stone frowned. "I wasn't in your city. Well, I was before my expedition."

"Expedition? You shouldn't be here," he said, finger pointing at Stone.

Stone shrugged, then another chill made his shoulders shudder again. He looked to Ramirez. "I'm not feeling too good. I'd like to see a doctor."

Agustin stepped forward and fumed, "You're breaking three laws by even being in this room."

"I told you, Agustin, I'm not well."

"You're not registered to be in Uriah's Hope. You're trespassing outside the perimeter. And bribery."

"Bribery?"

"That's the only way you could've gotten here. Have I missed anything?"

"We found him with a hacked PWD," volunteered Ramirez. "It's encrypted. We can't access it."

"You've all missed something," said Stone. "None of that matters, Director Garcia. I'm here because I need to be. I've found something that will change the course of human history."

"Another of your unfounded chases?"

Stone sneezed. "No. This might even alter what we already know of it."

Agustin suddenly realised what Isambard Stone's presence might mean. "Where's Tanya?"

"There was an incident, Agustin. Something happened out there that I did not foresee."

Agustin grabbed Stone by the collar. "Where's my daughter?"

He shook his head. "It's the cold. Thinking straight is difficult."

Agustin lifted Stone from his seat until the restraints halted further movement. "Where is my daughter, you piece of shit? Answer me!"

Stone grabbed Agustin's wrist. The sudden sensation of cold was shocking. Agustin threw Stone back onto his seat. He looked to his wrist and forearm. Where Stone had touched sat a perfect imprint of fingers burned into his flesh.

"What did you do to her? Tell me or you're dead!"

The hands of Ramirez pressed at Agustin's shoulders. "Director?"

"I'll kill him!"

Red Aquila guards were suddenly pulling Agustin from the cell.

"Where is she?" Agustin roared.

"Agustin!" called Stone. "I can help you find Tanya but I need assurances. You need me. You hear? You need me."

The cell door sealed.

"Let go of me." Agustin shrugged off the restraining hands.

"Director?" said one of the guards.

"I'm alright." Agustin straightened his shirt, then rubbed the burn and the cold at his wrists. "Stay with him, Ramirez."

"Yes, sir." Ramirez drew his pistol and returned to the cell.

Agustin tapped his PWD and called Dale Twomley. Within seconds the Assistant Director's face appeared on the screen.

"Dale, send someone to check on Tanya."

Twomley pushed his glasses up his nose. "Trouble?"

Agustin looked away from the screen and back at the cell. "Could be. You remember Isambard Stone?"

"Tanya's archaeologist friend?"

He hated when Twomley referred to Stone as that. "He was the one outside the perimeter."

"That's impossible."

"Seems not."

"Security is too tight. Getting in and out of the city … how'd he get out?"

"We'll worry about that later."

"Onto it. I'll get back to you."

The screen fell dark.

Agustin pounded on the cell wall. Ramirez came back out.

Agustin looked at the guards. "It's all fine here, thank you."

The guards exited.

"Ramirez, ready your team to take me out to where you found him. This has to be off the record."

"You give the word and we'll go, sir."

The chime indicating a call connecting sounded in Agustin's ear. He pressed a finger to the bud in his ear.

"Agustin, she's not there and the bed doesn't look slept in. They found her PWD in the room."

"Tell them to keep looking."

"She's a smart girl, she wouldn't have gone with him out there."

Yes, Tanya was a smart girl. Smart and obstinate and curious.

Agustin turned to Ramirez. "I'm giving the word."

***

Agustin paced in his apartment. Large and luxurious by Uriah's Hope standards, but sparse if judged by Earth expectations.

"And if it was your kid, Dale? Tell me you wouldn't be going out there yourself."

Agustin stopped and stared at his friend and colleague on the screen. Twomley removed his glasses and pinched the bridge of his nose.

Agustin blew out a loud breath and nodded. "You'd be going."

"I'm not saying I wouldn't. But I'd expect you to try to convince me to let the professionals handle it."

"Professionals? Yes, I suppose they are that." Agustin moved from the screen and pulled out his insulating suit, a thin jumpsuit. He stepped into the legs, pulled up the waist and wriggled his arms into the sleeves. It was a civilian grey and red. He'd worn it once since arriving and it was then uncomfortably tight. The zip whistled its expected sound as he secured the suit from hip to neck. It was still tight. He plucked at the crotch trying to create a little room. "But you and I both know they're the ones responsible for smuggling in contraband and people."

"Speculation," scoffed Twomley, waving a hand.

"It's more than speculation. How are we progressing with his PWD?"

"Techs tell me the level of encryption is … well, challenging."

"Then they need to work harder."

"We need to face the prospect we may not gain access to his data. Unless he willingly opens it up for us."

"I'd happily rip off this tight …" Agustin gestured down his leg, "and march back into that cell and thump Stone until he spills."

"You and me both, but the guards may not—" Twomley looked from the screen. "Looks like Red Aquila's ready for you. You must have done some fast talking."

"Command wasn't too easily persuaded."

"There's reasons for that."

"And Tanya's the best reason for them to agree."

"Many of the patrols are being ordered back here. The weather's looking bad. If something goes wrong, I don't know how long it will take to reach you."

"I'll be back with Tanya before you know it." Agustin grabbed his survival overalls, stepped into it and pulled it up his body, stalling at his midsection. He heaved it a couple of times and slipped his arms into the sleeve, moving his shoulders until it sat properly. "Might look at losing some weight when I'm back. Tanya will be pleased to hear that."

"We'll monitor you from here. Good fortune to you, my friend."

The screen blinked off. Agustin pulled the zip up to his chest and sucked in two slow and deep breaths. He already felt like he wasn't getting enough air. He strapped his mask at his neck, then pulled an antique box from the cabinet by his bed. Inside was a relic from a time long past. A revolver handed down through his family. Impeccably maintained, it hadn't shot a bullet in anger in many lifetimes. He kept it loaded and while there were newer weapons available, he favoured this family relic. Agustin placed the weapon in his pocket and left his apartment.

***

A large portion of Uriah's Hope had been constructed underground, subterranean by necessity. The climate was too fierce to expect the inhabitants to brave the weather daily. Long transit tunnels linked each part of the city to the next, and one could walk the entire route if you had three hours. For the most part, Uriah's Hope was ten-thousand people cowering beneath the ground, hiding from a hostile planet. Command staff had access to a separate transit network, smaller, designed for only a handful of people to use at a time. Agustin took it from the apartment complex to the Red Aquila motor pool. It reminded him of a great hangar. Large blast doors kept the weather at bay.

Ramirez waited at the disembarkation point with a fellow Red Aquila operator who looked none too pleased.

Ramirez had showered and shaved. He held out a hand to assist Agustin from the train. "We're ready to go, sir. Myself and eight of my men."

Agustin stepped from the train without the offered help. "Good, Ramirez."

The men wore TAL45 assault rifles on tactical slings at their chests. These were favoured by the Private Security Company and The Hope's Municipal Police. Above their whiteout camouflage survival suits they wore torso armour which extended over their shoulders, bulking both men noticeably.

"And you are?" asked Agustin.

"Dan Coil, sir. Director, can you confirm we'll be compensated for this?"

"For this?"

"This," Coil replied with a weak gesture to the air. "We're exhausted, been out there a long time, you know?"

Ramirez shot Coil a warning glance.

Coil frowned. "What?"

"You've showered and eaten," said Ramirez.

"Doesn't lessen the exhaustion. And don't get me wrong, sir, I don't mind long hours of work. But just like to know we'll be compensated."

Agustin flashed a diplomatic smile. "I've squared it all away, soldier. Your help is being recognised at the highest levels."

Coil looked confused. "Recognised?"

"Let's get this project moving," ordered Ramirez, and Coil didn't protest again.

Agustin was led to the patrol vehicle, The Esworth Track. Impressive machines, easily twenty tonnes, armoured and sealed against the weather. Esworth Tracks. They had the power to plough through huge snowdrifts.

Agustin climbed down through the open hatch. Along the length of the interior were short benches on each side. The driver's compartment was completely separate from the crew.

"Your seat, sir." Ramirez gestured to the seat furthest from the entry point.

Agustin strapped himself in while the soldiers deftly swung into their seats and secured their weapons. None acknowledged Agustin. Two sat at operating consoles and tapped at keyboards. Ramirez whispered to each of the soldiers. The interior light turned to red and the vehicle powered up, engines rumbling to life. Agustin looked for ear protection, but the noise wasn't overpowering.

"We're insulated from the noise of the engine, sir," explained Ramirez.

But the interior shook enough to set his teeth to chattering.

"Can't help with that," said Ramirez with a laugh.

Screens lit up displaying information from outside and real-time images from the external cameras. The lights transformed from the red to a pale ambiance.

The Red Aquila operative sitting across from him smiled and nodded. "It's good to have you along on this one, sir. Don't worry. We'll get your daughter back."

"I hope so."

Another said, "You've got a set of balls on you, mate. I mean, Director. Most people in your position would send us out while they stayed safe on The Hope." He gave a thumbs up, closed his eyes, and seemed to fall asleep in seconds.

Others broke into quiet conversation. It was only then Agustin genuinely appreciated the risk these men took every day for others, and they seemed relaxed, unconcerned, chilled even. Much like Tanya. Always excited about the next adventure with focus speared to her passions, never heeding the inevitable risks. It was just like the time she disappeared with Stone to Siberia, chasing some half-heard rumour, no prior warning, worrying him sick and only making contact when they had run out of money.

Agustin fired up his PWD. Filed reports from mine's site manager, Byron Thomas, suggested before the order to abandon the mine came, the drilling teams struck a fissure causing a minor collapse. No injuries. A small gap in the rockface opened revealing a chamber beyond, not like the rest of the shaft. Workers fell ill within an hour. Migraines, light and sound sensitivity, vomiting. Byron Thomas ordered the drilling teams out of the shaft.

Further down the report, 'Like ghosts standing at your shoulder, whispering in your ear. We could not understand the words but knew something was near,' and 'Teams refused to return, and the mine was closed.'

Agustin read the lines again and made a note to speak with the site manager on his return to the city.

***

Progress through the snow came to a halt. The digital screens showed mountains of white.

"Looks like we're stuck," said Ramirez. "Even the Esworth Track is susceptible to unbeatable snow blocks."

"We'll continue on foot." Agustin unstrapped himself.

"Impossible, sir. The temperature's dropped to minus forty-four. We'd be dead in two hours."

"So what do you propose?"

"Turn back to The Hope. Wait for a break in the weather and try again."

The wind howled outside, strong enough to rock the super heavy machine. Agustin knew the weather was worsening. Over an hour ago he lost connectivity to Fleet Net.

"I won't return to the city without my daughter. If none of you will come with me, I'll go alone."

Ramirez released his safety restraints, ducked his head and moved closer to Agustin. "You know I can't let you do that, sir. I won't allow the director of Uriah's Hope to die out here. We need to turn around, sir, before we become snowbound."

"Are these vehicles not designed to ride out storms?"

"We get stuck here, we die," said Coil.

Ramirez moved closer to Agustin. "He's right. We have to be smart about this."

He wanted to open the door, stride out into the snow and find Tanya. It's what any father would do, no? Agustin studied the monitors. Huge, rolling banks of snow blanketed the road. Seven miles. That's all they'd travelled.

Agustin let out his captive breath. "Then get us back home."

Perhaps Tanya was more like her father than he realised, for his passion to find her was prepared to ignore the risks to himself and others.

***

Agustin marched to the interview room and halted at the door. He adjusted the revolver at his hip, tucking it into his belt at the back of his waistband. Deeproot Drilling had to have the answers he needed. Answers Tanya needed.

"Mr Byron Thomas?"

Byron sat with his back to the door but climbed to his feet when Agustin spoke. He was a large man, with wide shoulders which hinted at a lifetime of manual work. The stench of stale beer was strong, yet Byron Thomas didn't appear drunk. Perhaps he was a seasoned drinker who had crawled into a bottle and hadn't started to think about climbing back out.

"Thanks for coming in with such short notice. I'm Director Garcia." They shook hands and Agustin took a seat on the opposite side of the long table. "Please sit."

"Your assistants were very vague about why I'm here, sir. I was ready to turn in."

A knock came at the door and Dale Twomley entered carrying two steaming mugs.

"Don't we have people to get the coffee?" Agustin asked Twomley.

Twomley shrugged and handed the mug to the Director. "Thought I'd make myself useful."

Agustin lifted the mug to his mouth and inhaled. "I don't know about you, but the damn coffee doesn't taste the same out here."

Byron sidled closer and fixed a baleful gaze on Agustin. "You didn't bring me here to talk about fucking coffee."

Agustin sipped his coffee, did not break eye contact then returned the mug to the table. "Like ghosts standing at your shoulder, whispering in your ear."

Byron sat back in his chair.

"You locked your report away well enough. One thing about being Director here, you can access a lot more than most."

Byron shifted uncomfortably. "And?"

"Officially the mine closed due to the severe weather front moving in. Your report suggests otherwise."

Byron did not offer a retort.

"Help me understand."

"I thought that was buried," said Byron.

"Not deep enough."

Byron blew out a heavy breath. "I was told if I repeated that information I'd lose my job. Unfit to work."

"Not under my watch," said Agustin.

"Shit." Byron raised his hands. "Have you ever had a sensation where it feels like somewhere you weren't supposed to be?"

Agustin nodded, a gesture to continue rather than an acknowledgement.

"Well, imagine that feeling multiplied by a hundred. There was some … some physical presence pushing us out. Whatever it was wanted us gone." Byron rubbed the back of his thick bull neck. "I know how this sounds. Even talking about it now, it feels like it was a dream. But it wasn't. We all felt it."

"What did you find down there?"

"A room. Some kind of chamber. Through the crack in the rock I could see blue walls. Metallic or so they appeared. I didn't get closer. Trust me, if you saw it, you'd not want to get closer either."

"What about the voices?"

"The voices. God, the voices. When they started I made the decision to pull back. My guys, they're hard workers. They ain't afraid to work. A few of them fell to the ground, grabbing their temples, complaining of headaches, migraines, the worst they've ever had. One of my guys spewed his guts up. Nobody knew what the hell was going on. And they all looked to me like I could give them answers. Me!" The tough worker had melted to a frightened man. "I didn't know what to do other than get out. Those unaffected carried those too sick to walk. They were scared. I could tell. Not ashamed to say I was, too. That place. Fuck that. We don't get paid enough."

Dale and Agustin looked to each other with unspoken questions.

Byron continued. "None of my team really spoke about it after that. And to be honest with you, Director Garcia, if anyone else asked me what you're asking, I'd have told them to go fuck themselves rather than talk about it."

"Why?" asked Twomley.

"Because if the rumour gets out that we cut and run, spooked out of a job, people look at you different, like you're all fucked up in the head, that you can't do the job no more. I've got family. I can't afford that. None of us can."

"I appreciate your honesty, and for taking this time to see me. I'm sorry you had such a … difficult experience out there."

"A difficult experience? You haven't believed a word I've said, have you?"

"No. Not so. I'm very interested in what you have to say."

"Bullshit. I can see it in your face. You're gonna put people back out there, aren't you? That will be one huge mistake, mark my words." Byron stood from his chair. "Am I free to go?"

"This is not a prison."

Byron Thomas didn't wait for further conversation. He left.

"Do you believe this nonsense about ghosts?" asked Twomley.

"Here? In these forsaken worlds, I don't dismiss anything."

"Yuji Sanada of Red Aquila is waiting for you in my office."

"Remind me who he is?"

"They call him The Colonel. He's the ranking operator on Esworth, not one of their suits and ties."

"I'm to be reprimanded for hijacking their patrol?"

"I expect so," said Twomley with a smirk.

***

21

"Yuji Sanada of Red Aquila." Sanada stood straight and proud. He wore the uniform of Red Aquila, the crimson bird on his shoulder proudly standing in contrast to the darkness of the rest of the uniform. He was powerfully built, despite retaining a slight frame. His dark hair was slicked back.

Agustin managed a smile as he moved around the table and shook the offered hand.

"Is that a genuine Night Blade?" asked Agustin, nodding to the relic of legend Sanada wore at his belt.

The weapon was a foot and a half long, constructed by the Nights for close combat, with a lethally sharp blade. Aside from that, an energy charge could be activated along the length of the blade. Agustin had seen archived footage of the blades in combat. The weapon was ill-fitted for human hands, the handle too long and poorly balanced, but they remained the source of great pride for the owner. And they traded well on the markets back home.

"It is. Won by my family many, many years ago during the Night War at the battle of Tokyo." Sanada's hand rested on the pommel. His English was perfect and only a faint accent hinted at his Japanese origins. "Director Garcia, I apologise for this unannounced visit."

Agustin waved away the apology. "It's good to finally meet you."

"Actually, we've met before."

"We have?" asked Agustin, eyebrow raised. "You'll forgive me. It's been a long and tiring day."

"Yes, a gala celebrating the opening of one of the habitation blocks."

"Ah, of course," said Agustin, not quite remembering the specifics of the encounter.

"I've been informed you ordered one of my units out of the city when all others were pulling back due to the weather?" The question wasn't voiced in an accusatory manner, rather a statement. "I understand that some in the bureaucratic side of my organisation authorised the action with the promise of some form of compensation. This did not go through the proper channels and could create an embarrassing issue between your office and my organisation."

Agustin raised his hands. "Guilty as charged."

"Your daughter, Tanya, she's missing?"

"Yes."

"I have family. I'm not heartless. But you see, Red Aquila is not just a private army. You understand?"

"I understand. And as you said, you have family, so you understand."

"The organisation comes with lawyers. The costs of your adventures are exorbitant."

Agustin reluctantly nodded. A tense silence followed.

Sanada looked out the window and sniffed heavily. "Your daughter faces a trying time out there. It's not impossible to survive but her chances are slim."

Agustin's jaw tightened. "Not if we're out there looking for her."

Sanada snapped his attention back to Agustin. "Do not overstep your authority. You have influence on Esworth and I'm sure with Fleet. But that does not extend to Red Aquila."

"Just like all Red Aquila's activities only extend to their legal duties on Uriah's Hope?" It was an open secret that Red Aquila was complicit in smuggling people known as the Unwanted, those without homes and resources who took to living in the natural tunnels under the city.

"Director—"

"I've become aware of certain anomalies in my city. Individuals are here when they shouldn't be. Goods on the banned list show up on the black market. One does wonder how they get here."

"Careful, Director Garcia. I am not a man to threaten and I resent your implication."

"You know I was motivated by love for my daughter. Had it been you who lost a daughter out in this godforsaken place, you'd have done exactly the same. If it's monetary reimbursement you need, you'll get it. And out of my own pocket. But do not come here hypocritically to lecture me on the difference between right and wrong. Never make the mistake that I'm ignorant of what happens in my city."

Sanada lifted his chin high.

"Does it still work?" asked Agustin.

"Does what still work?"

"The Night Blade."

Sanada touched a hand to the Night Blade again and smiled without a hint of friendliness. "I'm unsure. I've never had cause to activate it. But, Director, I believe a more suitable response to your transgression might allow us to continue our fruitful relationship."

"A fruitful relationship," Agustin repeated easily.

Sanada nodded. "A fruitful relationship. And so, you have been officially warned." Sanada left.

***

Agustin stripped off to his underwear before the mirror. He ached from tiredness and his arm still burned where Stone's grasp had burned. The imprints on his wrist and forearm had dulled.

He would see Stone in the morning, go hard on him if necessary and extract the information he needed. But for now, he needed sleep to ensure a clear head tomorrow. By the bed was a picture of Tanya. He picked it up and sat on the edge of his bed. It was taken after she completed voluntary work in Korea. It was a passion of Tanya's to work in nations and states outside the Terran Cooperative. He'd been reticent to let her go, but her mind was made up. She was beautiful, intelligent, wealthy and extremely independent. Why did she have to fall under the spell of Isambard Stone?

Being a father was one of the most difficult experiences of his life. The surrender. The surrender that came with being a father. Agustin had to surrender to Tanya, allow her to make a life of her own, make decisions, make mistakes. And he had no one to share the burden for Tanya's mother passed too young. For much of the time Agustin felt like he was whistling in the dark when it came to being a parent.

Had the mistake of Dr Stone cost Tanya her life? Had he not done his job of fathering well enough?

There were hundreds of pictures of Tanya stored digitally but he loved the physical ones more. It made things a little more real to him. He returned the picture to its place, rolled into bed, then kissed the tips of his fingers and stretched over and touched Tanya's face. "I'll come for you, Tanya. I promise."

Agustin slept but no dreams came. In his mind, behind closed eyes, all he saw was the relentless whiteness of the untamed wilderness of Esworth.

CHAPTER 2

Doctor Isambard Stone, Uriah's Hope Prison, Esworth.

Stone rolled back and forth on his sleeping pallet. Since being out there, heat seemed like a thing of the past. Twice he'd asked the guards to increase the temperature in the cell. They obliged him on both occasions, and he could feel the sensation of heat prickle at his skin but his core remained chilled. He sniffed loudly, wiping his nose with his sleeve. He was thinking clearly now, more than before. If he wanted out of the cell, he knew what he had to do.

Tanya was a bargaining chip. She would ensure his release, and his dislike for Agustin could not interfere. He asked the guards to summon Agustin. They were noncommittal. By rights, prison was Stone's future for the next year. He committed too many offences to pay a fine and walk away.

Was she still alive? Stone hoped so. He was fond of her. Not many would've been brave enough to follow him out there on Esworth.

The cell door chimed and slid open soundlessly. Stone sat up and threw off his blankets.

Two Red Aquila guards entered. One armed, weapon not quite pointed at Stone, the other carrying a breakfast tray. It wasn't that they considered him dangerous, Stone was sure. He wasn't physically intimidating and had shown no aggression since his incarceration. He suspected the rumour of his burning touch had spread among the operators, a touch that caused chilling coldness. Even Stone himself didn't understand what occurred.

"Breakfast," uttered the female guard, throwing the tray down on the table. They both backed out and the door slid closed again.

A small bowl of cereal with a carton of milk, a banana, and ham and eggs. Not restaurant quality but extremely appeasing in his state of hunger. Stone ate greedily.

"Charming," he muttered, his mouth full of the ham. It was a lie, but his grumbling stomach was eager to be filled. He had made his money on food, outside of academia. He invested large sums of money in the process of growing meat. Lab Farmed Meats. The process had been refined to the point it was profitable. The hindrances to farming, coupled with the increasing outrage of the treatment of animals, Stone sensed an opportunity and invested wisely. It always did strike him that people cared more for animals than they did for their fellow humans.

Yet.

The warm meal did nothing to relieve him of the constant chill. He looked around his modest cell. It boasted a small sleeping pallet, toilet, sink, and a table and chair both bolted to the floor. Other than that, Stone was confined to his own mind.

The door chime sounded again and the door opened. A flurry of Red Aquila guards entered and behind them, Director Garcia.

"Stand, Stone. Keep your hands at your side." Tanya's father's words were clipped, and spiked with impatience.

A guard stepped forward to shackle Stone.

"That won't be necessary," said Agustin.

"Sir," he protested. "It's for your own protection."

"I know the rules, but it won't be necessary."

The guard barked at Stone. "Sit. If you get out of the chair, we'll be back in a heartbeat. Got it?"

"Got it," said Stone, sitting back on his bed.

The guard nodded to Agustin. "We'll be outside should you need us, sir."

The guards left.

"I thought I'd have to bang on for days to get a message to you. Yet here you are."

Agustin leaned against the wall and eyed him slowly from head to toe. "You look better."

"I feel better, albeit marginally."

"Food okay?"

"If I'd paid for it I'd be requesting a refund."

Agustin sniffed heavily. "Yes, you are indeed on the mend and close to being your old self again."

Stone smiled.

"Our last meeting was unfortunate. I regret some of what happened."

"I don't remember much of it. How's your arm?"

Agustin rolled his sleeve up and shrugged. "Almost gone, but it's of little consequence."

"I'm sorry about that. I don't know how it happened."

"I spoke with the doctor who examined you. He can't offer a reason either."

"I've a feeling that a lot on Esworth will be a new experience. We've not yet scratched the surface, so to speak."

"Whatever our past differences, Isambard, I hope we agree that we both care for Tanya. That is a commonality which we can build on, I believe."

So, Agustin was prepared to partake in a diplomatic dance, too. "I agree, Director Garcia."

"And I'm sure you don't want to rot in here until The Gate opens again and you're carted off to Earth."

"You are correct."

"All I care about is Tanya."

"That's not all you should be caring about, Director Garcia."

Agustin tweaked his brow. "And what do you mean by that?"

"Out there is something completely beyond our ability to explain. It's monumental. Perhaps dangerous. Perhaps glorious, but it's waiting to be discovered."

"The chamber?"

Stone stared at Agustin. He knew of the chamber? How?

"I've accessed the mining reports," said Agustin, as if reading Stone's mind.

"I need to go back there." Stone could not disguise his passion.

"And I need to get Tanya back here."

"Of course, of course," said Stone with a sympathetic frown. "Agustin, whatever is out there will most definitely affect your city, the people here. Even the people back home."

Agustin sneered. "Then we can work together. Help me get Tanya back and you walk out of these cells today."

"And the chamber?"

"If we can get back there, you have my word you'll be on the crew."

"Your word?"

"A man's word is all he can really give these days. I think you know I'm good for it."

"I'll work with you, Agustin. But I also want a full and permanent residency permit. And proper accommodation. I wish to be integrated into society here with no limit to my stay."

Agustin rubbed at his wrist. "You ask a lot."

"Nothing that's not within your power to grant, I'm sure."

"And I have one more demand. When I get Tanya back, you stay away from her."

In that moment, Stone understood that Agustin knew what type of man he was. Stone didn't understand it fully himself, but he could not have anything in this world, or any other world, interfere with his desire to discover. But he was looking at a scared father, and desperation opened the door of opportunity like nothing else.

"Agreed."

"I'm not sure your word is worth anything."

"Damned be your thoughts about me, Agustin. They don't matter. You have my terms. I'll be here when you've made up your mind." Stone lay back on his bed. "And tell your techs they'll never break the encryption on my PWD. I paid a lot of money to make sure of that."

Agustin sprang forward and kicked the bed. Stone raised his arms to block any forthcoming blows. But then remembered no one would touch him.

"Goddamn, Isambard. Stop playing your fucking games. Enough. My daughter. Is she alive?"

He sat up. "She was when I last saw her."

"What happened to her?"

"Believe it or not, if I could have saved her, I would have. When I ran she was behind me. Agustin, something monumental is on Esworth, but it's not for the faint of heart. We need each other."

***

Agustin Garcia, Uriah's Hope, Esworth.

"You look tired," said Twomley, his hot mug of coffee twisting as it warmed his hands.

Agustin nodded, then sipped from his own mug. "I didn't sleep well."

Agustin and Twomley had taken to the habit of breakfasting together. It gave them a chance to talk outside The Hub. The challenging work environment had the propensity to destroy friendships and breed animosity if not negated by some social interaction.

Twomley seemed to not register his reply.

"Something on your mind?" asked Agustin.

"There's always something on my mind."

"A contagious virus then, you and me both."

"I don't sleep well at most times, but last night was strange."

"How?"

"I slept, I guess, but my eyes felt like sand. I didn't dream. Not that I dream every night but it felt like ... I don't know. I'm just extra tired, I suppose."

"And that's not making everything better?" Agustin gestured to the heaped plate of bacon, eggs, mushrooms and thick sourdough toast in front of Twomley.

Twomley smiled, then stuffed his mouth with a forkful. "It's helping," he mumbled then chewed loudly.

It never failed to astonish Agustin that his friend did not possess the girth of a house with his food choices and meal sizes.

"You met with Isambard Stone before coming here?" Twomley said, with the last of the food in his mouth making his pronunciation only minorly skewwhiff.

"I did."

"And?"

"Bastard's making demands before he'll talk."

"Demands? Such as?"

"He wants residency here. He wants out of the pen. He wants to work on Esworth, and, most important to him is being the first to return to the mine."

"You know you can't grant what he's asking, and every decision here has a paper trail."

"I know."

Twomley took his glasses from his nose, sipped his coffee, and replaced his mug to the table. "Agustin, I hate to say it but we need that guy. If we're going back to the mine and there is something there, something dangerous, we need to know as much as we can. Yes, we can send drones when the weather clears, but he knows things. You need to weigh up what to do. If it goes tits up, you're on the next rotation back to Earth, fired or facing charges."

"I know that, Dale," snapped Agustin. "It's my daughter that's out there. I'd risk everything to get her back to me. Everything. You think I really care what they'll do to me if I screw it up?"

"Then do it off the books. Give him one of the vacated apartments. Have some of our staff attached to him at all times. Give him a little but provide him with the illusion that he's won, that he's in control."

Agustin ran a hand through his hair.

"If the UHMP scan him for ID, our staff can be there to defuse the situation. It's a risk but it keeps you safe and gets us what we need from him. And no matter what we need done, there are people in Uriah's Hope who'll do it for the right fee."

Agustin blew out a loud breath. "I know what you're saying."

"They're predicting a break in the weather in five days."

"Five days?"

Could Tanya survive out there for five days in those temperatures? She was smart. She was fit. And Agustin ensured Tanya was fitted with the best survival equipment the moment she had arrived, knowing his daughter was likely to wander impulsively. There were mining camps and research stations out there in the wilderness. She might have stumbled across one, found shelter. It was possible. It had to be possible.

"The day of the next gala," suggested Twomley.

The gala was to be the official opening of Uriah's Hope, a grand celebration of all that humanity had achieved. Of course the city existed on Esworth for many years but the Cooperative wanted to make it official that Uriah's Hope was open for business. Agustin did not feel like there was much to celebrate. Without Tanya safe, it felt like a piece of his chest had been ripped out. She had planned to accompany Agustin to the gala. At Tanya's insistence they'd shopped together for outfits from one of the finest outlets on The White Way for the event. The White Way was a vaulted subterranean thoroughfare that relied on artificial light. It was an area of commerce, business and restaurants. A transit system ran high above the street.

"What about this one?" Tanya had asked, selecting a flowing sapphire blue dress with an incredibly low neckline.

Agustin typically had little interest in women's fashions, but played the dutiful father, and encouragingly suggested the colour suited her and she should try it on.

Tanya disappeared behind a curtain and returned barefooted, twirling with a huge smile. "Well?"

Agustin was astonished. Those eyes, that smile, the way her hands opened in invitation. "You look so much like your mother. You know that was her favourite colour?"

"I know, Dad. That's why I picked it."

Agustin kissed his daughter on the forehead, and for one moment thought he caught the scent of his wife, a floral scent mixed with the freshness of a recent shower. "I couldn't be more proud of you. It pleases me to no end to have you come out here to The Hope to be with me."

Tanya looked at the price tag. "Whoa. It's expensive."

"What's the point of me coming shopping if I can't treat you?"

Yes, he wanted her back.

"Red Aquila cannot be involved, Dale. Not after what's happened."

"Won't work. You're going to have to speak with Fleet. The road will be buried and we'll need to plough it. Fleet can have a shuttle down here and fly us out. If they provide some marines as security, so much the better."

Agustin slipped his PWD onto his wrist and fashioned it in place. "I agree. They're our best shot. We should get to work."

High above the large monitors on the far wall, a digital timer counted down: *38:12*. Less than two days until The Gate would open to welcome new arrivals, just in time for the gala.

Stone. Fucking Stone. He hated the doctor.

***

Captain Olivia Scott, Terran Cooperative Fleet Ship (TCFS) Eris.

Captain Olivia Scott stood in the stateroom of the battle cruiser Eris, the flagship of the Esworth Defence Fleet. She gazed out from one of the many viewing ports. Her reflection appeared in the darkness beyond. Orbit above Esworth was a hive of activity. Small automated repair drones buzzed around two mighty defence platforms in stationary orbit. Romulus and

Remus were super massive rail cannons capable of taking down capital ships with their lethal salvo. The two halos that seemed to hover around the long cannons were hangars, storage areas for weapons, a communication centre and crew accommodation. It was from there that Esworth was declared safe whilst under the watchful eye of the Romulus-pattern. Captain Scott knew better. Those defence platforms could be outmanoeuvred and destroyed. They needed her ships to truly protect Esworth.

Beyond the stations, cluster satellites providing access to Fleet Net blinked silently. Freighters docked at orbital facilities, delivering cargo for shipping to the planet. Her ships lay further beyond, in formation. Fifteen ships. Two battle cruisers, one battleship and twelve destroyers. The mightiest fleet the Terran Cooperative could muster. It swelled her heart to be part of it.

Far below, Esworth gleamed like a pearl in the black. Storms raged on the planet and Eris was close enough to see those storms in some detail with the naked eye. Rolling, flashing and churning cloud cover moved as if in slow motion. It looked so alien compared to Earth, more intense than any storm on the home world, or any of the other planets in the system. Esworth was unique.

Captain Scott was born into a fleet family. The Scotts suffered worse than most during the Night War, and since then each generation was expected to serve. Olivia Scott enrolled when she turned of age. Expectation was high and as assumed, she surpassed all elements, rising through the ranks until achieving her own captaincy. And Eris was the finest ship in the fleet with the most durable crew. Yet for all she achieved she had not been in combat. Since the Night War there had been no further contact with alien life. No opportunity to prove she was worthy of the prestigious name. It felt like her rigorous training had been a waste.

Scott took a final look in the direction of The Gate, an elongated structure of Night design interfaced with human technology, allowing a measure of control. With no faster than light travel capabilities, The Gate was the only method of travel to and from Earth. It needed to be activated and powered on both sides for travel to occur.

"Lost in thought, Captain?"

Jan Holopainen, her executive officer was bearded and quick to smile. He'd been on Eris for almost two years. He tugged at his uniform, pulling it into place.

"A little, XO. A lot of time to think at the moment. Have you ever wondered how long all this will last?"

Holopainen joined her at the viewing port. "I'm not sure I follow?"

"How much longer do you think the Terran Cooperative will fund all this? We've had no threats."

"The Nights disappeared. They could come back at any time. Watch the night," said Holopainen, quoting the common phrase.

The Nights, so called for their skin pigmentation, were a warlike and uncommunicative race. They stood between six and eight feet in height and possessed what could be described as four arms and two legs, though variations were known. Within the head sat a cluster of eyes, like that of a spider, small obsidian orbs that lit up when they caught the light. A small nasal passage sat in the centre, but no mouth. They breathed oxygen and seemed to sustain themselves on a liquid diet. Their ships were sleek in design, customarily dark-armoured and reliant on powerful beam weaponry. They travelled by The Gate and so far nobody traced them back to any region of the known galaxy. They were as much a mystery now as they were at the first attack.

"You sound bitter."

"No, I'm not bitter, Jan. I'm worried."

"Well, I have something that'll cheer you up, Captain. A message arrived from Esworth. You've been invited to the gala."

Scott made a noise like she tasted something extremely bitter. "Why me?"

"Might be short of females for the dances," he laughed. They would never be so informal in the presence of their crews.

"I don't dance."

"You're captain of the Eris. Flagship in The Fleet."

She returned her focus to the planet below. "It doesn't look all that inviting."

"No. It's not what I imagined the new home for humanity would be."

"You should take my invitation."

"I have two left feet, and you'll need me to keep things running here."

"Any word on Admiral Hastings?"

"No word. That's sixteen days he's been down there."

Informally, Admiral Hastings was called Whiskey Hastings due to a historic battle with alcohol. For whatever reason, sixteen days ago, he lost his current battle with sobriety, took a shuttle to the planet below and disappeared into Uriah's Hope. The sailors of The Fleet spent their free time in the city but remained shy of the areas still under construction and not activated, those areas waiting for the next lot of settlers to arrive through The Gate. Those areas were controlled by the gangs and the desperate. If someone wanted to disappear in Uriah's Hope, there was an abundance of locations to do it.

"Nobody saw it coming."

She nodded. "I should have. Nobody was closer to him than me."

"We'll bring him back. Even if I have to go down there myself."

Scott looked to those storms, swirling and churning. She sure felt a long way from home.

***

Agustin Garcia, Eris, Esworth Orbit.

The combat shuttle rocked and jumped. His two marine companions seemed quite relaxed in response to the violent shaking. Agustin grasped the edge of his seat and every violent movement threatened to empty his stomach of its contents.

The shuttle gave a final lurch and pulled away from the icy grip of Esworth. The turbulence suddenly lessened and they accelerated toward the Esworth Defence Fleet. The shuttle sported several long and narrow windows on both sides of the craft's hull. The Fleet was arrayed in battle formation with the lumbering battleship at the centre, and the smaller ships positioned around like satellites. All along their dark hulls pinpricks of light blinked in the dark. The engines burned a fantastic blue to the rear. A small collection of long freighters waited near for the return journey to Earth, bulky vessels that brought in supplies to Esworth and then conveyed materials home. Import and export was big money business when it came to Esworth. It also kept the colony fed. At present, Uriah's Hope couldn't produce the food needed to keep the entire population fed.

They passed Romulus and Remus, their size awe-inspiring. They were two magnetic cannons, each capable of destroying a capital ship with their fire. The two stations were the forefront of defensive technology, long barrelled superstructures with a ring of habitable, smaller structures around the base. Five-hundred men and women were stationed on each platform, well-trained, well-disciplined.

The ship turned and approached the rear of the battle cruiser Eris. Earlier, Agustin had requested to be aboard the flagship to witness the opening of The Gate. It was an innocuous request, one that avoided the expected red tape if he had requested an audience with Captain Scott.

The shadow of Eris fell across the shuttle plunging the interior into darkness. Only the small internal lamps periodically placed along the roof made it possible to still see. A feeling of insignificance fell over Agustin as they sped into the cavernous docking bay of Eris. He had forgotten the sheer size of the warships.

The engines throttled down, pushing him back into his chair. The shuttle twisted and hit the landing zone. The engines cut and they were plunged into momentary silence. The rear hatch opened on the shuttle and the marines unbuckled themselves, then Agustin followed. A squad of marines in full battle gear waited in the hangar, their weapons shouldered in salute.

"If you'll follow us, Director. Captain Scott is expecting you."

Agustin pushed himself from his chair and swayed a little before his equilibrium returned. It was always the same when he travelled on a ship. He followed the marines from the shuttle, their footfalls heavy, booming on the metal walkway of the hatch.

They passed through the corridor of the warship. Nobody paid him much mind. The corridors were long, well lit, yet still felt minutely claustrophobic. They entered a lift and stood in silence as it ascended. The doors opened revealing the bridge. Two marines stationed on the inside came to attention.

"Please proceed, sir," boomed one of the erect marines, and the doors closed behind Agustin.

The bridge of the battle cruiser Eris reminded Agustin of The Hub back in Uriah's Hope. To the front, a large screen showed the scene directly to the prow of Eris. Above it, the digital countdown clock, just like The Hub. A bank of workstations lined the front of the viewer. Lights flickered on screens and intermittent beeps sounded a high pitch. To his right, navigational aids took up an entire wall. The captain and first officer's chairs stood in the middle of the bridge on a raised section of decking. To the right, crew manned a weapons station and all staff were focused on the coming task.

Captain Scott rose from her chair, smoothed down her uniform and saluted crisply. Scott was pretty. Perhaps a few years into her thirties, with mousey hair tied back into a tight bun. She was slender, the uniform possibly concealing a strong body, and she radiated strict professionalism.

"Director Garcia, welcome aboard Eris. It's a pleasure to have you. May I introduce my XO, Jan Holopainen?"

A tall officer stood to her left, a smile on his face.

Agustin threw out a hand and shook Scott's hand first, then Holopainen's. "The pleasure is all mine."

"I trust your trip from the surface wasn't too uncomfortable. The weather is particularly difficult at the moment."

"A little bumpy, Captain, but your crew got me here in one piece. I have to admit, I'm not much of a flyer."

Scott waved her hand to one of three observer chairs toward the rear of the bridge. "The Gate will open in a matter of moments. Please, sit and enjoy."

"I was hoping we could speak after the completion of the transfer, Captain."

Scott raised an eyebrow then nodded. "As you wish."

Holopainen guided Agustin to one of the observer seats and parked himself next to Agustin. "Is this your first time seeing The Gate open, sir?"

"The first from a ship, Commander."

"It leaves me amazed every time."

The digital counter cycled rapidly toward zero. Travel time between Earth and Esworth ranged between twelve and fourteen hours. The Gate operation was mostly automated with intense human oversight to ensure nothing went wrong. The Gate could only be powered for seventeen hours, twenty-two minutes before the need to recharge. Each Gate opening was carefully synchronised with Earth, for both ends needed to be open at the same time for the travel to occur. The space between The Gates was known as the Starless Sea.

Agustin's original transition through The Gate had been a difficult experience. He and everyone else on board were rendered unconscious. Agustin woke with a migraine and a sensation he'd been somewhere nobody should go, and the nightmares that followed for months were horrific. No one could explain those curious experiences.

"Here we go," said Holopainen, as he turned his head away from the sight.

Agustin wasn't quick enough. The Gate burst to life producing a flash of pure light. It blinded Agustin momentarily. He rubbed his eyes. Where there had been the black of space in The Gate structure, it was now replaced with a swirling miasma of purples and reds all churning like the contents of a witch's cauldron.

The freighters powered up and accelerated past Fleet and approached The Gate. The long haulers lined up, accelerated to full and plunged into the mysterious Gate. One moment they were there. The next they were gone.

And that was it. Nothing to do now other than to wait for the arrival of the next round of ships from Earth.

"Nothing happens fast in space." Holopainen shrugged then stood.

"Director Garcia, shall we?" said Scott with an impassive expression. She pointed in the direction of her office just off the bridge.

Agustin followed the captain to her office. The room itself was plain enough, a work desk with two chairs at the front and one behind for the captain. A glass jug of water and two cups sat beside her personal workstation. A photo frame, quite ornate, was the only personal touch to the room. He couldn't see the photo. He checked her finger for a wedding ring. None. For a quick moment he wondered if the frame contained a photo of a family member, just as photos of Tanya could be found in his room. Scott moved around the desk and sat, indicating Agustin should take one of the two in front. He sat, finding the chair too rigid to be comfortable. That was the military way.

"So, Director." Scott leaned onto the desk and made a pyramid with her thumbs and index fingers. "You've seen The Gate opening. Now what do you want?"

"Excuse me?"

"You've overseen many Gate openings, Director. All from a distance I'm sure, but enough to not need to travel this distance to see yet another."

"Very direct, Captain."

"Honesty ensures we do not waste each other's time."

"May I have some water?" He nodded to the jug and glasses.

"Be my guest."

Agustin poured himself a cupful and sipped. He crossed his legs and grinned. "Deeproot Drilling, one of the mining corporations, was sinking shafts and breached an underground chamber."

"The place is full of them. We've seen the terraforming reports. It's a honeycomb maze underground."

"Some of the mining team got sick. Vomiting. Hallucinating. Headaches."

"And?"

"Some claim to have heard whispering voices, voices close to them. I've spoken with the team leader. I like to think I'm a decent judge of character. He was honest. And he was scared. The weather has halted further exploration of the surface."

Scott leaned back into her chair, reclining slightly. "So what's your concern?"

"I think there's something there which warrants further exploration. We, both of us, have a duty to protect the people living and working on Esworth. I don't have the resources to do it alone."

"Why not just seal the mine and ensure nobody goes there?"

"The thought had crossed my mind, Captain, but as I'm sure you'll appreciate I don't want to simply ignore something that could be a problem in years to come."

"You suspect a …"

"A phenomenon."

"A phenomenon?"

"Captain, for all we've achieved on Esworth, it's still a mystery. We can breathe the air, drink the water but what else is out there? The Nights built a Gate here. What else is here?

What we think we know, and what we actually know may be two very different things."

"Some miners getting scared and abandoning a mine does not warrant a military response." Like a skilled fisherman, Captain Scott poised herself to draw more information. She was no fool and likely realised Agustin hadn't disclosed the full story.

"Captain Scott, we don't know each other well. Trust is a thing that is earned, not given flippantly."

"I agree."

They stared at each other over the no-man's-land of her desk. Scott's workstation beeped every twenty seconds; the sound irked Agustin.

"Two civilians recently left Uriah's Hope after the mine was abandoned. They made it to the mine. One, an archaeologist with the New Seattle Institute of Off-World Archaeology. Doctor Isambard Stone and his assistant Tanya Garcia. My daughter. We've got Stone in custody. Tanya is still missing."

Scott tapped the table. "Your daughter —"

"This isn't about her," Agustin interrupted with his lie.

"No?"

"I want her back, Captain, but I'm not allowing that desire to colour my decision-making. Since his return, there's something not quite right about Stone. His hands, cold to the touch, he held my wrists briefly in the prison and it felt like I'd been burned. He won't tell me what happened down there but he's alluded to the presence of something important. Dangerous or not, all he's focused on is the discovery that awaits, not the pitfalls, nor my daughter. And for the moment, he's not divulging anything more unless he gets concessions."

"What does he want?"

"Permits, residency, and to be the first person to return to the mines. He knows something."

"Are you of the mind to grant him his demands, Director?"

Agustin nodded. "I am."

Scott pushed away from her desk and crossed to the viewing port. The eerie lights from The Gate pulsed nearby, distorting her reflection in the glass. "You're dealing with a curiosity, not a threat. Why not seek the assistance of the UHMP?"

Agustin threw his hands in the air. "Because they're too busy looking for your alcoholic admiral!"

"Do you often get your way with rudeness, Director?"

Agustin calmed. "I'm sorry, Captain. I've not been sleeping and every avenue I travel for help presents me with a closed door. Are you a parent?"

"No."

"Well, with Tanya out there, I'm not myself."

Scott studied Agustin for a long time. She returned to her desk and tapped at a keyboard. "Give me the coordinates of the mining facility. I'll request one of the destroyers to conduct orbital scans of the location. You'll need to find me evidence of a perceivable threat if you want this door to open, Director."

"Thank you," said Agustin on a sigh.

"And on the subject of Admiral Hastings, I'm sending Holopainen back with you. I think it wise to have a member of Fleet on Esworth to liaise with the UHMP. I trust you'll find him suitable accommodation and ensure he has the support he needs. And now, you'll stay on board and dine with us. We'll shuttle you down after the arrival from Earth."

"Of course."

Scott tapped at more keys. "I understand you, too, are invited to the gala. I was privy to the guest list."

Agustin rolled his eyes. "It's not good timing."

"You're looking forward to it as much as I then?"

***

Dr Isambard Stone, Red Aquila Prison, Uriah's Hope, Esworth.

Stone lay under a blanket on his bunk, legs crossed at the ankles, running through the narrative of his journey to the mine with Tanya.

Asking Tanya to join him on Esworth was something he now regretted, a remorse he would not share with another's ears. She had been reluctant at first and he lured her, courted Tanya with promises of financial reward, excitement and adventure. But it was not those that won her over. It was the implied promise of requited love that was the winning lure, and Stone was prepared to polish that morsel of bait to a mirror finish. And so he had decided his love for Tanya would be a non-traditional type. He cared for her welfare, enjoyed her company, laughed at her anecdotes, and sometimes craved her body with a passion that even surprised himself.

He had not kept his end of the bargain and now his mind and body were restless. His every being yearned to go get back to that mine, to that chamber and its secrets.

The door alarm buzzed and opened. Stone threw back the covers and pulled on the thick gloves provided earlier by one of the kinder guards.

The new arrival wore round glasses and walked without fear into the cell. A guard lingered at the door.

"Ah, Director Garcia's tea lady."

"Mouthy for someone without too many options," said Twomley.

Stone nodded his false apology. "Assistant Director, you have news?"

"I'm here to grant you your release."

"Garcia is giving in to my requests?"

"Director Garcia asked me to impress upon you that if you try to fuck us over, the consequences will be dire. And I'll see to that myself."

"Threats are unnecessary, Assistant Director. I made the offer genuinely and will hold my end as long as he holds his. When do we leave?"

"You've been granted provisional residency. When the storm subsides, plans will be made to return to the mine. For the moment, you'll be confined to your apartment, under supervision and you'll work with our people sharing what information you have."

"Bravo," he said, clapping his hands together. "Sense prevails. I'll ignore the fact that I'll still be a prisoner. But it's enough for the moment. Tell Agustin I said that. Tell him I'm a reasonable man."

"Does a reasonable man leave his partner out there in the element to fend for herself?"

Stone wanted to scream he had been terrified and didn't understand what he was seeing.

He had tried to reach her, hadn't he? He reached out in a genuine attempt to save her?

And the most honest part would be to say that something in that chamber didn't want him to save her. He couldn't explain it. Stone wasn't religious, in fact he looked at religion as one step from mental illness. But those statues undeniably held a power when he looked upon them. Fear and wonder seemed to mix in equal measure as if the inspiration was lifted directly from the Bible. Stone needed to get back to the chamber. It was like being underwater, needing to break the surface.

"We're all human, Assistant Director."

CHAPTER 3

Director Agustin Garcia, Henrietta Hall, Uriah's Hope, Esworth.

The day to celebrate Uriah's Hope and its achievements arrived. The monolithic Henrietta Hall was a flurry of activity, a hugely expensive endeavour financed by corporations. It was a tribute to investment, money and the willingness to succeed in the harshest conditions. Unlike most of Uriah's Hope, a large portion of the hall was constructed above ground inside the city's defensive wall. It required a huge allocation of energy in to keep it warm and powered. It dwarfed all other buildings in the city with the exception of The Hub. Its spires reached high and looked like a cathedral lacking any hint of religious iconography. Clad in granite shipped from Scotland, it spoke of the old world contributing to the new.

Henrietta Hall was bedecked in finery with drapes of warm colours and the flags of the Terran Cooperative nations on the walls. Guests mingled. Six-hundred drawn from Uriah's Hope, Earth and Fleet. Many had shipped in from Earth just for this event, and they would remain on Esworth until The Gate opened again. Politicians, military personnel, celebrities and academics congratulated themselves on achievements and progress. They sipped the finest champagne, ate delicacies prepared by preeminent chefs from Earth and transported to Uriah's Hope for the sole purpose of this event. Classical music by the New Seattle Symphony provided the backdrop to the celebrations. Another expense as the musicians would play for one night and return to Earth on the next rotation home.

Agustin's suit was too small. With the press of bodies, the temperature felt insufferable. He tugged at his collar then grabbed a glass of bubbly from a polished plate passing by on the hand of a slick-haired waiter. Another plate passed dotted with tiny mountains of crepes beneath stringy dill and thinly sliced smoked salmon. What was Tanya eating? She was very resourceful. For all his mistrust, the New Seattle Institute provided her with weeklong training camps, drilled her with

43

survival techniques and taught her how to use and craft essential equipment.

At the time she protested. "I look like I've been living on the streets outside the Cooperative for a month."

Agustin preferred that look. No makeup, skin flushed by an influx of fresh air and healthy activity. She looked like a young girl again, the one that would giggle and twirl when he held out a hand and asked her to accompany him in a dance.

"Lost in thought, Director Garcia?" Chief Constable Reid of Uriah's Hope Municipal Police wore her dress uniform, dark blue shirt and trousers with a tie of red around her neck. Her blonde hair was loose, shoulder length with a dyed black streak hanging provocatively to the left of her face. A side-arm was holstered on her hip.

"While my body may be off duty, my mind never is." He drank heavily from his champagne flute.

"You've given me a logistical nightmare, Agustin. Not to mention the influx of residents for this party. At least the food and wine are good," she said, taking a sip of her own glass. Reid stopped a passing waiter and selected a small bundle of grapes on the vine. "You know how much it costs to get grapes here?"

Movement came at the head of the hall near a small platform.

"Looks like the speeches will begin soon, Chief Constable."

"Would it kill you to call me Bex?" She popped a grape into her mouth, and thick lips made hard work of the chewing.

"How goes the search for the Admiral?"

"Uriah's Hope is a big place. There are many places someone could go if they didn't want to be found. Let's hope to God he hasn't gone into the Undercity. We're searching when we can, but my people are overstretched as it is."

"Sightings?"

"Not since the White Way four days ago. And the witness couldn't be a hundred percent sure it was him. You'd think that in our city, with all its hi-tech surveillance and facial recognition programs, it'd be quite impossible to simply disappear."

"His chip?" All members of the Terran Cooperative Fleet were implanted with a sub-dermal chip on the back of their left hand which allowed tracking while serving aboard vessels.

"His chip was found aboard Eris."

"Cameras?"

"Security cameras identified him walking along The White Way. We'll get him. He'll surface when he runs out of food."

"My daughter could be in a similar situation, though not by choice."

"You have my sympathy. I wish the UHMP could do more but we don't have the resources to mount any kind of search outside of the city."

The music came to an end, and there followed polite applause.

"Isn't that Captain Scott of the Eris? By the woman in the red dress," asked Reid, deftly changing the subject.

Agustin looked across the heads of people. He was taller than most which made the task quite easy.

"Yes, that's her. And Commander Holopainen."

The two stood as an island surrounded by a sea of well-wishers. An aura of distinction was attached to those in The Fleet. The smart burgundy dress uniform, shiny epaulettes, boots highly polished to create a reflection. Medals weighted Scott's shirt, honours awarded to her forebears who died in the Night War. Such was the honour and distinction the Scott family won. And the elite of society hovered, hoping to be bathed in that aura.

"I should save them from the gauntlet of well-wishers. I'll speak to you later, Bex."

Reid placed a hand on Agustin's shoulder. "Enjoy yourself. It'll do you good to take your mind off things."

"May I borrow the young Captain for a moment?" said Agustin on reaching the two. Agustin guided Scott from the mob and to a moment of calm. "I thought you could use the break from all that."

"Thank you. I've had my fill of their dull questions. How do you do it?"

"I have observant staff, quite clever at herding and appeasing."

"I didn't know half their names."

"If you can remember a quarter you're doing well." Agustin smiled, and the small gesture caught him off guard. "How are you enjoying my city, Captain?"

"The weather's been too severe to stand on the surface. Can you really say you've set foot somewhere when you're far below ground?"

"It still counts."

Taps at a microphone drummed from speakers at all corners of the room.

"What do you say to a group like this?" Agustin said.

"You have nothing prepared?"

"I've been a little preoccupied."

Scott's mouth tipped to a half smile. "You're the figurehead of everything that's right with Uriah's Hope. Just get up there and start talking."

"And so I shall."

Video drones lifted from the floor, ready to record what was to come for posterity. Another tap at the microphone brought a partial silence to the room. The podium was draped in the flag of the Terran Cooperative. The speaker, a beautiful woman with short black hair and a tight-fitting dress, climbed the few steps to the podium. A voice booming out announced Zara Dean as the speaker.

"Who is she?" whispered Agustin.

"Zara Dean. She's an actress."

"Ah! The actress." Agustin wondered what her fee was for today's festivity.

As if hearing his silent ponderings, "And Zara has donated her fee to help the orphans outside the Terran Cooperative."

Fifteen nations on Earth were not part of the Terran Cooperative. At the conclusion of the Night War, when the organisation was formed, several nations remained clinging to the old ways, mostly Muslim or those already isolationist to the extreme. The Cooperative territories prospered, and those outside crumbled. With a failing economy and aging infrastructure, life in those places was harsh and brutal. Aid flowed regularly from the Cooperative but only enough to keep widespread famines at bay. Several Islamist insurgencies waged jihad against the Cooperative, bombings and small-scale infiltrations. Several crime syndicates operating outside the Cooperative sponsored armed groups to create tensions. There was a war raging, but one that was far away from cameras.

"Generous."

Zara Dean spoke briefly about how proud she was to be in Uriah's Hope, how impressed she was at the progress made and announced that her production company would be purchasing property in the city, creating five-hundred new jobs. She remained on the stage playing emcee, introduced each guest, smiled broadly and planted a kiss on both cheeks when the guest arrived at the podium. It was a procession of nattering delegates and political figures, lauding humanity's progress here and their hopes for the future.

And then, "It's my pleasure and honour to welcome Director of Operations for Uriah's Hope, Agustin Garcia."

The crowd parted for Agustin. Hundreds of eyes turned his way, hands clapped, heads nodded. Agustin climbed the steps to the podium deftly, and like all previous guests, a kiss was planted on each of his cheeks. Zara Dean smiled and nodded some encouragement. Encouragement to provide words appropriate to the event was not necessary, but encouragement to not tear off his tie and march out to find his daughter certainly was.

Agustin grasped the edges of the podium. "Ladies and gentlemen, and honoured guests."

***

Captain Scott, Henrietta Hall, Uriah's Hope, Esworth.

"Ladies and gentlemen, and honoured guests, I'd like to welcome you to Uriah's Hope and Esworth. It is our wish that …" Agustin paused mid-sentence, his focus speared to the rear of the room.

One in the crowd chuckled. But the director did not look like he'd forgotten his speech. He looked confused.

"Admiral Hastings?" said Agustin.

A din erupted. Heads swivelled. Foreheads frowned. Three UHMP officers rushed past. Scott followed in their wake. Penetrating the last of the crowd, they suddenly halted. Admiral Hastings was on his knees, uniform filthy and tattered. His sleeves were rolled up, and his arms were horridly blistered and bleeding. The Admiral's eyes, once dark and full of reassurance, were pale orbs.

"Hal!" Scott rushed to the Admiral's side. "What happened to you?"

Hastings' unseeing eyes fixed on Scott. "Olivia, is that you?"

Holopainen appeared at Scott's side. "Get those out of here," he ordered, pointing at the drones humming overhead.

"It's me, Hal," said Scott.

"Olivia. I can't stop the voices. They're too much. They're with me all the time."

"You need help."

"At first I couldn't understand the voices. Too much noise on Eris. I had to leave. But here, they're clearer." Hastings' hands shot up to his temples and he moaned, his face twisting in pain.

"We need to get you back to Eris, Hal," said Holopainen. "Doctor McCormack will know what to do."

"No!"

"Admiral, listen to Captain Scott. Back to Eris," urged Holopainen.

"The voices, they're here. And they know we're here. The Fleet is yours. Save it." He winced, then pulled a thin bladed knife from his belt. "We shouldn't have come here. God, the pain. We shouldn't have come here. All of us are lost."

Hal Hastings thrust the knife into his neck and twisted. The crowd screamed. Many ran. Hastings fell to the floor.

Commander Holopainen went down to Hastings' side. The dying Admiral spoke to Holopainen, but his words were not heard by Scott. Admiral Hastings' eyes glazed over.

"Shit," mumbled Holopainen.

"What did he say to you?"

Holopainen shifted uneasily. "They're already here."

"Get something to cover the Admiral. Contact Eris and have a shuttle sent immediately. I want his body examined by McCormack, and I want a Captain's meeting aboard Eris in four hours." Scott wiped away a tear.

***

Agustin Garcia, Command Hub, Uriah's Hope, Esworth.

Agustin and Twomley sat in The Hub conference room, Agustin at the table and Twomley perched on the edge. Hal Hastings' death had been broadcast to the entire city, and now the frozen image of Hastings' body remained on the conference screen.

"Was he sick?" asked Agustin.

"Does he look like a well man?" replied Twomley. "I hear Fleet won't allow our medical staff to examine him?"

"No. Chief Constable Reid had something to say about it but … this is a disaster." A crippling tiredness threatened to bring Agustin undone. He wanted to crawl away to some dark place and sleep. "You know what Reid said? She's so dammed logical about things. She said she told me Hastings would turn up."

"A little bit of gallows humour doesn't go astray."

"A little early, don't you think?"

"I've instructed our PR team to confer with Fleet and come up with some response to what happened. Hastings had demons. We all know the rumours of the drink problem."

"Have you seen a drunk man stab himself in the neck over and over?"

"Do you have a better idea?"

A knock at the door halted further discussion. One of the junior operators stepped into the room.

"Sorry to interrupt, Director. Captain Scott of the Eris has arrived."

"Thank you, Sally. Show her in."

"Well, I'll leave you to it," said Twomley, hopping off the table. "We both need sleep after this. Captain," he said, greeting Scott as she entered, then he left.

"Please, take a seat, Captain," invited Agustin.

Scott took a seat.

"Fleet lost a great man today. Even us in the civilian authority had respect for Admiral Hastings. His navel reforms made for interesting reading."

"Yes, and if I can be permitted to return your previous directness, what do you want?"

Agustin suspected he saw more grief in Scott's eyes than he expected and immediately regretted his forwardness.

"I've heard you've cancelled all passes for Fleet and marines to be in Uriah's Hope."

"Yes. In a few hours we'll have lifted them all from the surface."

"Hal was my mentor. He meant more to Fleet than I could possibly tell you."

"So why did he take his life?"

Scott shook her head. "Hal hadn't been drinking for some months. He complained to me about being unable to sleep, but it was just a comment made in passing. Then he just left, somehow cut the chip from his arm and disappeared in your city."

"Did he have family?"

"A wife and three adult kids." Scott stood from her seat. "Hal Hastings wouldn't commit suicide."

"I believe there may be a link between Hastings and the mine."

Scott frowned but before she could offer complaint, Agustin cut her off.

"Hear me out. I've watched the recordings and he mentions voices. For someone in such a trusted position in Fleet, he must've been evaluated regularly."

"We're evaluated every month."

"What did he whisper to Commander Holopainen?"

"Nothing. The musings of a great man driven from sense."

The door of the conference room burst open.

"You need to come to The Hub," said Dale Twomley. "Both of you."

***

The giant display dominated the front facing wall in The Hub. Twomley used his PWD to interface with the screen and it switched from displaying an external view of the city to a topographical map.

"And this is the area surrounding Uriah's Hope?" asked Agustin.

Twomley nodded. Three communication officers sat watching the display, headsets on, talking quietly to whoever was on the other end of their microphone.

Ricki, a twenty-two-year-old senior communications officer, looked to Twomley. "When the storm hit, two Red Aquila patrols became snowbound."

"Are they still out there?" asked Captain Scott.

"Yes, ma'am. The most westerly patrol stopped broadcasting an hour ago."

Agustin stepped closer to the screen.

"The Esworth Tracks are designed for survival out there, sir. Even in the harshest of conditions," explained Ricki.

"And the second crew?" asked Scott.

"We can't make contact," said Twomley. "Last we heard from them was a few minutes ago. This was the last we received. Ricki, play the recording for Director Garcia and Captain Scott."

The Hub was quiet, the usual low chatter gone. The recording started with a burst of static then a harried female voice materialised. "This is Red Aquila patrol seventeen east. Snowbound. There's things, or ... something outside our Track."

More static came.

"We can see them moving. Two of my patrol are dead, collapsed holding their heads in pain. We've fired warning shots to drive the creatures away."

A jumble of shouts and a scream.

"They're coming. They're breaking in. I'll—"

The audio clip ended abruptly.

"We've been unable to get them back on Fleet Net." Ricki pulled his headset from his ears and let it rest around his neck. "There's something out there. She called them creatures."

"Speculation," cautioned Scott.

"There's more." Twomley sat heavily into his chair and pointed at the screen. "Show them."

Ricki cleared his throat. "As part of Uriah's Hope defence system, there are cameras around the city at certain points. They don't run a constant feed. They're motion activated and smart enough to differentiate between a natural movement, say, the wind blowing a branch on a tree as opposed to the movement of an animal or person. And this is a still from the east side."

The screen was frozen, a display of white of varying shades, the picture lacking resolution.

"What am I looking at?" demanded Agustin.

"Top right." Twomley almost whispered the words.

In the top right of the picture, dark smudges. Ricki tapped at his keyboard. The image was enhanced as the screen zoomed in and out. The dark smudges resolved to be human-like shapes. Two arms, two legs, a body and head.

"Could it be the Red Aquila team tracking back to the city?" asked Scott.

"No, ma'am. This was ten miles from where the snowbound vehicles were. It's impossible for someone to walk that distance in conditions like this."

"They look tall," said Agustin.

"There's no reference for size," said Twomley. "We don't know what we're looking at."

Agustin turned to Scott. "Captain, do you now concede we need to work together on this?"

Scott pursed her lips. "How much has Doctor Stone revealed so far?"

"Very little," answered Twomley. "He's cooperating but perhaps not as fast as he could."

"Get him talking. I'll return to Eris and we'll have a mission ready for the morning."

Agustin grabbed Scott's hand. "Bravo. Thank you, Captain."

"Agustin, your orders?" asked Twomley.

"Activate the defence grid. Anything outside our walls not broadcasting a friendly signal is to be considered hostile."

Uriah's Hope was bristling with defence platforms, automated turrets and parapets where men could walk and watch beyond the wall. Heavy artillery pieces were mounted at regular intervals along the wall. Anti-aircraft batteries were dispersed between them. This was the first time such an order was made.

"What about the Red Aquila patrols? As unlikely as it is, there's a possibility they could be moving back toward the city," Twomley pointed out. "If they've lost equipment, they may not have the ability to identify themselves."

"We don't want to be killing our own," interrupted Scott. "I advise positive ID on any potential engagement. I'd be happy to attach some combat system operators to assist."

Agustin rubbed at his forehead. "Of course." *Of course. Of course. Think straight!*

"Let me know when the defence grid is activated." Scott turned away from the screen and stepped closer to Agustin. She lowered her voice. "Your earlier question, what Hal said to Holopainen. He said, they're already here."

***

Captain Scott, Eris, Esworth Orbit.

Via the communication conferencing system, the waiting Captains looked like a box of toy soldiers. Captain Goodsir of the battleship Erebus, Captains Keeler, Ito, Chao and Khatri of the destroyer squadrons, and Captain Shellenberger of the Aberdeen.

Colonel Hopkins sat behind Oliva Scott, out of view of the cameras. Scott expected the coming conversation to be challenging. Hal Hastings often spoke of his frustrations with these captains who were many years Scott's seniors, and a real mix of contentious and short-tempered climbers. Cliques had developed with undeserved loyalties, and unwise pacts, and Hastings had said that only another Night War would kill off the factions.

Scott wore her crisp uniform, her hair tied back tightly. "I'm sure by now you've seen the footage from Henrietta Hall. Admiral Hastings is lost to us. And so, I'm taking command until such a time as Fleet Command appoints another. Any objections will be noted and included in my report to Fleet Command." The fingers on her right hand played with the written decree made by Hal Hastings only six weeks earlier, a decree placing Olivia in charge should Hal become unexpectedly unable to perform the duties himself.

The expected objections did not come. The toy soldiers on the screen did not move.

"Good," she said.

Captain Shellenberger of the Aberdeen cleared his throat. "Captain Scott, I believe I speak for all captains present in wishing you good fortune in your new command. You'll have our full support."

Scott nodded her thanks but knew not to celebrate the suggestion of collaboration from all. "Director Agustin Garcia is of the belief there is something potentially dangerous on Esworth, something that's gone undetected in the years since we've been coming here. You've all received a copy of the data burst detailing the most relevant and recent intelligence?"

Heads nodded.

"We've scanned the planet over and over." Captain Goodsir of the Erebus had a round face and ruddy complexion. "Outside Uriah's Hope there's nothing. No energy signatures. Nothing to indicate a presence."

"And yet the intelligence suggests otherwise," said Scott. "We have two objectives. The first is a search and rescue. Two of the PMC Red Aquila patrols are snowbound and we've lost all contact. I'm sending a company of marines down in five shuttles. One-hundred-and-fifty marines. Two platoons in two shuttles will travel to a mine ten miles outside of Uriah's Hope. The marines will provide protection to a civilian team. Doctor Stone of the New Seattle Institute of Off-World Archaeology will lead the investigation of the mine."

Captain Goodsir protested. "It seems to me all our resources would be better spent in finding the patrols, not chasing ghosts in the tunnels and mines."

"Nothing has been said of ghosts, Captain Goodsir," said Scott. "Once we've located the missing patrols, the first marine element will travel to the mine and set up a defensive perimeter, holding until the civilian team concludes its investigation. Director Garcia has suggested this location may provide answers."

"Watch the night," Captain Chao uttered the old mantra of warning. "Have the Nights returned?"

"I see nothing to suggest these anomalies are anything to do with the Nights." Colonel Hopkins moved into frame.

"And best we don't allow such a rumour to flourish," said Scott. "Idle talk like that will cause panic. The mission is scheduled to take place at six-hundred hours. Our most recent weather report suggests current storm conditions will have abated enough to make travel achievable. When The Fleet is brought into combat formation, we report this as simply a drill to test the readiness of our forces. Speak to your XOs but nobody else is to know of our plans, not at this stage."

"Why the secrecy?" asked Captain Goodsir.

"Secrecy breeds disaster," said Captain Keeler. "Why not be transparent with the crew? They'll do their jobs."

"Yes," said Goodsir. "They'll do their jobs even if we send our people down there chasing ghosts."

"It's been decided," said Scott. "For the time being, this is a rescue and a drill."

"You're making a mistake, Olivia," said Goodsir with little cheer. "Our very purpose out here is to ensure the security of Esworth and protect against enemies known and unknown. Tell the crews, be honest with them."

"There will be no further debate on this."

"Hal Hastings would've listened, taken the wisdom of the other captains." Goodsir had worked closely with Hal Hastings for a long time, and many believed it was their friendship which led Goodsir to commanding Erebus.

"And I have listened. But my decision stands." She paused. "And Hal is dead. This meeting is over."

She touched a button on her PWD. The faces disappeared into darkness. "It could've gone better."

"That is the struggle of command. They'll look to you for direction yet criticise you at every decision." Colonel Hopkins moved to leave. "Get some rest, Captain. We need our head in the game tomorrow. I don't know what's down there but I'm preparing for a shit storm."

***

Dr Isambard Stone, Uriah's Hope, Esworth.

Stone's apartment was modest but adequate. Better than the cell. The shiny kitchen appliances would remain shiny for the term of Stone's residence. He possessed no particular penchant for cooking and was pleased to know food outlets on The White Way were aplenty. The bathroom consisted of a tiny porcelain vanity, a toilet, and a shower with a sliding glass screen. A large bed and a workstation were tucked into the far corner of the main room. With no windows in the underground accommodation, large portrait screens displayed images of forests in spring which could be changed to any landscape of his choosing.

He was not under house arrest, but two members of Agustin's security team were stationed outside his apartment. Dressed covertly in plain clothes, they would be his shadow and he'd been told in no uncertain terms any attempt to ditch the dour men would see to a return to his cell, and a short wait for a newer cell back on Earth.

The chime rang at the door. A more pleasant sound than the one in the prison.

"Come in," he called. The door had already opened before the words left his throat. "Director and Assistant Director. To what do I owe the pleasure?"

"We're here to collect on our offer," said Twomley. "The footage from your PWD."

"Very well. Please sit." Stone gestured to the one chair at his workstation.

Neither of the directors sat. Twomley handed Stone the PWD.

Agustin frowned. "Show me what happened to my daughter, Isambard. Tomorrow we go out there to find her. Together."

"Fair enough." Stone sat onto the bed and tapped at the PWD's screen. He cast it to the workstation. He did not watch it himself. Instead, he watched Agustin. The director stood tall, his arms crossed. His jaw worked hard as the footage rolled. Twomley split his attention amongst Stone, the director and the screen. Stone half expected Twomley to reach over and punch him in the nose. But no blow came.

They watched the footage in silence. Agustin cried.

CHAPTER 4

Director Agustin Garcia, Uriah's Hope, Esworth.

As expected, the storm abated in the hours before Agustin woke. The small party waited on one of the many landing ports, this one just off The Hub, and exclusively used by command. Chief Reid allocated two UHMP minders, Alison Burton and Tommo Henning, to keep Stone in check and Agustin alive.

Agustin yawned heavily, having suffered a restless night with little sleep. He looked to the grey skies wondering if all was prepared by Captain Scott and The Fleet, their invisible guardians. It should have been comforting knowing that powerful warships prowled the space above the planet. But it wasn't. It made him feel vulnerable. Problems on the planet were his to deal with.

"I still think you shouldn't be going," muttered Twomley, looking ill-at-ease in his survival gear. Neither man's regular duties required them to be outdoors.

"Tanya is out there," said Agustin, simply.

A light wind whipped up, blowing flurries of snow. Armed officers from the UHMP stood watch, looking to the sky.

"There," shouted one of them, pointing upwards.

Twomley touched his ear and nodded. "Clear the pad."

The group repositioned to behind the safety rails. Automatic flak turrets moved. Chugging cogs grinded noisily as the weapons tracked the new arrivals. Two groups of shuttles descended rapidly. They were larger than commercial shuttles, armoured and designed to insert troops into a warzone. Their wingspan alone was wider than the length of the pad.

Agustin held up a gloved hand to ward off the downwash from the engines. The shuttle hovered, then rotated slightly before landing. The rear hatch opened with a thud and two marines in full combat gear beckoned the group to the craft.

Twomley shook Agustin's hand. "Keep yourself out of trouble," he yelled. "Listen to the marines and get back here. I'll be keeping tabs on the live feeds."

Agustin nodded.

Twomley turned to Stone. "Don't fuck this up."

Agustin waved Stone toward the shuttle, and the UHMP officers followed. The hatch closed and he was ushered into a chair.

A marine pulled a belt tight around his chest. "Private Akerfledt, Director," she said, introducing herself. "Snug as a bug."

A marine seated opposite Agustin said, "Director, I'm Captain Geary of the Terran Cooperative Marines. I'll be with you out there. Any questions, direct them to me." Geary looked far too young to have been made Captain. He was fresh-faced, not a hint of stubble. "Don't worry, we'll watch your back."

The shuttle powered up and lurched forward. Agustin gripped his harness restraints, and suspected his stomach was about to be left on the pad below. Everything around him shook. He closed his eyes.

"Not used to it, Director?" came Private Akerfledt's voice, struggling to be heard above the chaos.

"Unfortunately no." Agustin's reply came out as a grimace.

It didn't take long for the flight to calm. Agustin opened his eyes. Smiles were aimed his way. And one set belonged to Stone. Agustin craned his neck to look out the closest window. The shuttle passed through sporadic and heavy cloud. Mist whipped past the window and was gone. Another shuttle moved into view, skimming the clouds as they did.

"You're all going to be part of history," said Stone. "Today we're doing a great thing and you'll all be recognised. All you brave men and women here with me, we're flying to immortality."

"Shut up, Stone," said Agustin.

"The future of archaeology lies out in the stars, Agustin. On planets like Esworth. The further we push, the closer we get to unravelling our own history."

Tommo Henning gave Agustin a look asking if the Director would like Stone forcibly silenced. Agustin was tempted.

Silence was their companion for the remainder of the journey.

Captain Geary moved through the shuttle, hand on the rail that snaked along the roof. "Check face masks and weapons."

The captain found a seat and strapped in. The shuttle reduced its speed, descended and landed with a bump. Akerfledt unclipped Agustin's belt then formed up with the other marines at the ramp. They carried TAL80 assault rifles, long barrelled weapons with a ballistic scope and heavy stock. A long magazine protruded from the underside. Three carried shotguns and heavier machineguns. Agustin stood from his seat. Burton and Henning kept Stone seated with a hand on his shoulders.

Geary sidled next to Agustin. "What do you make of the chamber we're headed to?"

The chamber was a mystery. Even someone not well versed in history or archaeology could notice the striking resemblance in the Esworth statues to those which would have been found on Earth in the distant past.

"I think there's more to Esworth than we thought possible."

"Let's find your daughter." And then to the rest of the group, "Masks on!"

The marines snapped their masks in place and readied their weapons. Geary moved up the line of his troops and checked the cameras strapped to each shoulder. Only then did he snap his own mask into place. As Agustin fastened his, a sudden sense of claustrophobia threatened to swoop. He breathed in heavily, convincing himself there was ample air.

The hatch lowered and the marines stomped out. They split into squads and moved in combat formations to secure a perimeter around the craft. The signal was given to proceed. Agustin followed Geary from the shuttle and on to the cold planet's surface. The mine was to the north. He now shared the same surface as Tanya. Hope danced with dread.

The wheels of abandoned machinery were hidden deep beneath snowdrifts. Cabin roofs peaked through the white. The second shuttle touched down a short distance away and more marines emptied from the hatch. Drones prowled overhead. Drones were notoriously unreliable on Esworth. The weather often knocked them out of the sky, or the signal became so scrambled any information they provided was unreadable. But on a day where the weather broke like today, they had their uses.

The marines used their own secure network for communication, but also had access to the general channel Stone and Agustin used.

"It's clear, Director," reported Geary.

Stone appeared at Agustin's side. "It's good to be back. Looks a little different."

"Let's do this," said Agustin, his words seeming to circulate within the mask.

"Follow me."

Geary signalled and marines followed Stone. Agustin tracked behind, his two UHMP minders in tow.

"Wait at the entrance," said Geary through the communications system.

A drone flew past and straight into the entrance of the mine. The men were still a distance away, lifting legs high to move through the unploughed snow.

"I must go first," demanded Stone. "I know the way."

"This is happening one way and one way only, Doctor," came Geary's voice. "My men will lead, you'll follow."

"That's not what we agreed on," complained Stone.

"Shut up, Isambard, or I'll happily pull that mask off your head," said Agustin.

Twomley's voice appeared in Agustin's ear. "We're patched into the live stream. Our cameras are showing what the marines can see."

"We've lost contact with the drone," said Geary.

"Expected," said Twomley. "Colonel Hopkins warned we'd lose telemetry the deeper we go."

There was silence on the radio for a moment. Agustin suspected the marines were busy on their own communication system.

"I know the way," said Stone.

Agustin was no more than ten steps from Stone and wanted desperately to tackle the man to the ground and pound his head until it bled.

"Stand by," warned Geary, and more silence followed.

With TAL80s raised, the marines entered the mine. Strong tactical flashlights flicked on. The beams illuminated the tunnel well enough. Agustin was the last to step into the entrance. Out of the wind, the temperature rose greatly. Geary removed his mask, sniffed the tunnel air and motioned for the others to do the same. Agustin took in a huge gasp of air as if he had been holding his breath the whole trip. The consistency eerily reminded him of a storage room in his parents' house back in Iowa, an attic room storing the culmination of a lifetime. Rarely did anyone enter that room, and when Agustin did, it felt strangely criminal to disturb its peace.

He wanted to call out Tanya's name, but Geary motioned for everyone to continue. The ground was blissfully smooth and allowed for easy passage. Each step took them down, and down further into the earth. Henning and Burton were busy slowing Stone. They'd place a firm hand on his shoulder and keep him from overtaking the marines.

Twomley's voice popped in his earpiece. "Did you take that thing we discussed?"

Agustin touched the pocket in his survival overalls. The revolver was there, but he didn't want to broadcast the fact. "I've got company," he said cryptically.

Light from outside quickly disappeared and the darkness behind the group felt like it was chasing fast, ready to swallow them up. Agustin flicked on his flashlight and clipped it to his belt. He pulled off his glove and touched the wall. The rockface felt damp, clammy and sunk at his touch. This section of passageway was smooth, both the walls and ceiling, like someone had cored a section of Esworth's rock. Three beeps sounded. Agustin checked his PWD. Fleet Net was no longer available.

The marines halted, signalled to each other, dropped to one knee and made ready their weapons. The UHMP officers forced Stone down and drew their own more modest firearms. Both carried standard issue UHMP side-arms. Agustin knelt too, searching wildly to identify the threat. No gunfire. The passageway became entirely still, so much so his own breathing seemed to rumble.

Captain Geary's name was called. The lead marines had spread out, their weapons aimed forward, their flashlights highlighting a small pile of clothing, backpack and survival gear.

"What have we got?" asked Geary.

Agustin was a step behind. A small pile of clothing and a backpack sat ahead.

Stone pushed past Captain Geary. "It's Tanya's."

Agustin rushed at Stone and snatched the backpack away. There were no signs of blood, no signs of damage to the exterior of the bag.

"How do you know it's hers?" Agustin rummaged through the backpack. He pulled out a notebook. So like her. In a digital age she enjoyed the simplicities of the past. At the bottom of the bag he found a foldable hairbrush. Hairs were entangled on the bristles. It reminded him of the times he had to clear the shower drains. And there were many. Agustin sniffed the brush. He smelt his daughter.

"I bought the backpack for her as a gift before coming out here."

The marines lowered their weapons.

"Keep moving," ordered Geary.

Stone's eyes were speared at Tanya's clothing, a thick jumper which always swamped her slender frame and a pair of worn jeans.

Henning took hold of Stone's arm. "Let's go, Professor."

"It's Doctor, actually."

"Director Garcia. We have to keep moving," said Geary.

Agustin put the hairbrush in his pocket and hurried to catch up. They continued on, dropping deeper into the mine. Fifteen minutes later the chamber narrowed and the ceiling lowered, leaving no more than four inches clearance for the tallest in their group. It felt like Esworth was swallowing them whole.

"The entry to the chamber should be close," shouted Stone.

"How …" Captain Geary touched his forehead and stumbled a step to the side.

"What's wrong?" asked Agustin, holding onto the strong marine's arm. "What's happening?"

Down the line, three more marines fell out of step, holding their heads. They pulled their helmets off, and rubbed at their eyes with force.

"It's like a pressure behind my eyes. Fuck, it hurts." Geary vomited and fell to his knees.

Another marine grunted and pressed fists to her temples. "I can hear their voices. Oh, Jesus. The pain."

It was just like the miners reported. Not everyone suffered from whatever the hell was in the tunnel. Not everyone fell victim to the voices or the pains.

"Get back up the tunnel, Captain. Take your marines," said Agustin.

"Sergeant Major Hart," gasped Geary, then clasped his hands over his ears. "Take command. Get us the hell out of here." Geary vomited again.

"Retreat! Everyone back to the surface!" Hart wrapped an arm around the fallen female marine.

"My daughter is down here!" protested Agustin

Hart shook his head. "We're combat ineffective. I can't let you go ahead."

Henning was helping Stone's other minder from the ground. The archaeologist slipped further into the tunnel.

"Get him," said Burton. "I can get out myself."

Henning looked to Agustin and pointed his flashlight in the direction Stone decamped. "Follow me, Director."

While most of the group escaped the tunnel, Agustin and Henning took off in pursuit of Stone. After a left turn in the tunnel, Stone's flashlight could be seen bouncing from wall to wall, and then disappeared as he eased through a fissure in the rockface.

***

Dr Isambard Stone, Esworth Chamber, Esworth.

Dr Stone could still hear the shouts and cries of the marines far behind, as he once again stepped into the Esworth Chamber. Esworth Chamber? Such a bland name. Perhaps when officially named, his own name would be attached and celebrated. The chamber was poorly illuminated and eerily still. The vibrations that caused him to run in fear the first time were not present. He tapped at his PWD and the camera mounted to his pack clicked into operation.

"This is Doctor Isambard Stone of the New Seattle Institute of Off-World Archaeology. I am taking the first step toward communication in the name of humanity."

Stone removed his gloves, and balled his fists over and again. The constant chill which had plagued him was a mere background irritation rather than a constant complaint.

He sat, dangled his legs over the first descending step, and his boots found the second. He continued in the same cautious fashion. Three steps. Four steps. Five. The flashlight was intuitive, linked into his PWD and moved automatically to ensure the most beneficial beam. Six steps and more until he would reach the floor of the chamber.

The beam of his flashlight widened. "It would be a shit of a time for my camera to faulter."

The large statues of the human-demon hybrid standing on gold plinths were wreathed in the green, bale light. Long tendrils from each snaked and conjoined creating a circular dais. Within the conjoined vortex of green was a figure, a flesh and blood reproduction of the idols. It was easily ten feet tall, powerfully built, raging silently caged within the confines of the light. It struck at the restriction, hammering talon tipped fists against the light. With each blow it struck, its hands were forced back by the energy shield. Yet all was utterly silent.

Stone stepped closer. "I have no idea what I'm seeing here. It appears the figure in the centre of the light is confined. I'm sure it is aware of my presence and I am positive this is not a Night. I've seen preserved corpses in person and the ratio here is disproportionate. What I'm looking at is a previously unknown life form. Fascinating. Absolutely fascinating."

Stone's chest thudded and his heartbeat thumped in his ears. He moved just out of arm's reach. The creature made no movement but the red eyes followed him as he moved. He could hardly conceive that such a colossal specimen could have been naturally birthed. Its arms were long, reaching down to its knees. The torso reminded him of carved Greek marble, muscles impeccably defined with snaking veins over the chest. The legs were covered in a ruddy hair, like that of a Highland cow. The head seemed oversized for the body. Its mouth sat wide with an array of dagger-length teeth. An impressive set of antlers crowned the head, sweeping back in an intricate, twisting design.

"Without further understanding of the life form before me, and I am sure this is a life form, I'm stumbling in the dark as to how to communicate."

Stone moved left then right, and those angry eyes followed his every movement.

"My name is Isambard Ossian Stone, of the New Seattle Institute of Off-World Archaeology. I am, um, from Earth. Terra. In the Sol system. I am human. Can you understand me?" Stone stepped closer and outstretched a hand.

"Isambard! Put your hand down and step away."

Stone did not turn to Agustin, but dropped his hand. "Leave if you must."

"You don't know what you're dealing with, Isambard. Come away from that thing."

The creature's focus did not leave Stone.

"Leave me to my research."

The creature's mouth stretched as if roaring, but no sound came.

"Isambard!"

Stone turned. Agustin stood at the bottom of the steps, a revolver aimed. Officer Henning was at his side, likewise armed, but gazing open-mouthed at the creature.

"Now!" said Agustin. "I order you!"

"Do not shoot. You have no authority here, Director Garcia."

"You've no idea what you're dealing with."

Stone turned back to the creature. "I've crossed the Starless Sea for moments like this. Tanya may still be in this cave system, Agustin. Go find your daughter."

The creature moved within its prison, and suddenly pressed its head against the shielding light. It pushed harder, eyes never leaving Stone.

"Stone, the statues. Look!" shouted Agustin.

The tendrils of light which connected the six statutes to the nimbus prison, flickered and dulled. By the plinths, shadows moved but stayed beyond the reach of the light. The energy field flickered again and faded to nothing. The creature bellowed at the intruders, the sound loud enough to shatter glass. Its eyes darted back and forth, then returned to Stone.

The thing reached out and grabbed Stone by the backpack, snaring the camera and flashlight. Gunshots rang out. The creature was stopped but not downed. Agustin appeared at Stone's side, grabbed the straps of the backpack and unhooked the clasps. Stone dropped to the floor and felt Henning dragging him.

"Get up!" yelled Henning.

"Leave me," urged Stone.

"Move, or I'll kill you myself," said Agustin.

"After everything I've done to you. Leave me."

Henning hauled Stone to his feet. The creature looked to the chamber's ceiling and then its eyes searched for Stone.

"Run!" said Henning.

The three men started up the stairs. The creature was slow but began its pursuit. Henning fired. The creature stopped momentarily, but there were many steps to yet climb.

"Give me the gun." Stone held out his hand. "You get out of here."

The creature roared and moved forward, its stride lengthy and nimble. A torrent of gunfire erupted from the chamber's entrance. A line of marines opened up at the creature with their TAL80s. The beast shrunk back, holding up its arms to protect its face.

"Climb," urged Agustin.

***

Captain Scott, Eris, Esworth Orbit.

Scott turned to Holopainen. "Get our link back, XO. We need to know what's happening down there."

Holopainen moved to the communication panel. The Fleet was arrayed in battle order, the Erebus at the centre, battle cruisers on each flank and a screen of destroyers. The formation appeared as a long diamond. The disposition ensured the best possible environment for retrieving the shuttles and providing orbital support should it be required.

The live feed for the search party was re-established. Vision from drones showed sheets of snowfields. So much of what was happening disturbed Scott. Admiral Hastings' suicide was proving to be a prelude of what was to come. Figures in the snow at the edge of the Uriah's Hope defences. Missing patrols stranded in the storm. The Esworth Chamber and possible evidence of a previously unknown alien race. All of this, and she had to keep Fleet from fracturing.

"That's Private Akerfledt's body camera," said Holopainen.

"Give me the audio," said Scott.

The marines guarding the shuttles and perimeter broke from their tasks. Marines spilled from the mine entrance shouting for medics. Some were dragged.

Akerfledt dropped to her knees and removed the helmet of a prone marine. "What happened down there? Where's Captain Geary?"

The marine's face was twisted in pain, eyes shut tight. He hadn't put his face mask back on when exiting the mine. None of them had.

"Leave him to me," came another voice.

Akerfledt moved toward the mine entrance. She halted a marine who was running toward the shuttles. "Where's Captain Geary and Sergeant Hart?"

"There's something horrible down there. We need to prep for launch."

"Geary and Hart?" she yelled.

"Geary's injured and Hart went back for the civilians."

Akerfledt continued toward the mine entrance.

"Captain?" One of the watch team turned to Scott. "I'm detecting something unusual from Esworth. A huge heat source. It wasn't there a moment ago."

Scott pulled up the diagram of the world below, jumping to the highlighted sections. The area of the mine and chamber was red, indicating heat. "What the hell am I looking at? Identify the source."

"Trying, Captain."

"Contact Colonel Hopkins. Get those marines out of there."

Holopainen pointed to the live feed. "My God! Captain, the mine."

**

Agustin Garcia, Esworth Chamber, Esworth.

Religion had not touched Agustin since he was eleven years. Yet right at that moment he prayed, prayed to any God, any Saint that might listen while he ran through the tunnel like the flames of hell chased at his heels. Henning ran ahead, pushing Stone forward, and Sergeant Major Hart and his four marines ran directly behind.

"What the hell was that in there?" Agustin shouted to Stone.

"I don't know."

"You don't know? You knew something otherwise you wouldn't have wanted to come back here."

"I don't bloody know, okay? I was going back for the statues, not to see one of them come to life and kill us."

A tremor shook the tunnel. Agustin stumbled then righted himself.

"Shit, this is what happened just before Tanya disappeared," yelled Stone.

Their progress slowed as another tremor followed.

"But I don't hear voices. Anyone?"

"No," came multiple replies.

"What's different about us?"

"I've never heard voices," said Stone. "I don't have answers."

Agustin clambered the last few metres from the tunnel and met with natural light. It blinded him momentarily.

"Move, move, move," ordered Sergeant Major Hart.

Agustin moved away from the mine entrance. He passed a squad of marines with rifles raised, laser sights set on where he'd just come from.

The shuttles were in prelaunch mode, their engines warm and ready to ignite. Medics knelt over four injured marines. One medic gestured wildly and the injured were transported on stretchers into the shuttle.

Tremors from below the ground grew in force. Agustin, Hart and Stone fell to their knees.

"This is worse than last time," said Stone.

Two marines hauled Agustin to his feet. He fumbled for his mask. He turned to find everyone on their feet, masks in place. The earth shook again. Rocks around the mine entrance dislodged and swallowed two marines. A second tremor struck. It dislodged a chunk of the mine's entrance. Rocks tumbled and two marines were buried. Henning and Hart ran to the entrance.

"How many people have to die because of you?" Agustin yelled at Stone.

He ran at Stone and punched him hard in the chest. Stone stumbled back and fell into the snow. Agustin jumped on top of him and threw two more punches.

A rumble sounded from the mine, an echo so terrible it made Agustin clamp his hands over his ears. The thing from the Esworth Chamber squeezed itself from the mine entrance and stood tall. Its red eyes took in every detail.

Marines opened fire with their TAL80s. A ferocious hail struck the creature. It staggered back, raising its elongated arms up to ward off the attack. When it roared, Agustin believed if all hopelessness could be collected into a single sound, that would be it.

"Back to the shuttles and take off. Now!" ordered Hart on an open channel.

The marines pounded the creature with all the firepower they had at their disposal.

"Move, sir!" Henning pushed Agustin toward the shuttle and pulled Stone to his feet.

It was only two hundred metres to the shuttle, but it felt like a marathon. His legs were heavy, clumsy, and he fell again and again.

The sound of gunfire thinned. The demon leapt forward, a distance no human would ever be capable of, and landed amongst Hart's marines. The monster swung left and right, tearing at the marines within its reach. Its talons cut through flesh and bone, severing arms and crushing heads. Hart and six remaining marines continued to fire.

More creatures spilled from the mouth of the tunnel. All were the size of a large bull, covered in ruddy hair, heavily muscled, with strong forward limbs and the same burning red eyes sitting over stunted snouts. They charged.

"They'll be slaughtered," Agustin wept.

"And we will be, too, if we don't get out of here."

***

Captain Scott, Eris, Esworth Orbit.

One by one the body camera relays started to blink out.

"Get them out of there! Now." Scott could not fathom what she was seeing on the screen.

"I want a firing solution for the target area," Holopainen said to the weapons team.

"Sir, if we fire, we kill them all," advised one.

Sergeant Hart's body camera was the last to show evidence of what was happening. Hairy creatures, muscular and fast, were slaughtering everyone in sight. And his was the last to blink out.

Scott called Colonel Hopkins at Marine Command and Control. "Launch the Leviathans!"

"Leviathans? They're still experimental, Captain."

"Launch them now!"

CHAPTER 5

Clive 'Atlas' Drinkwater, Erebus, Orbit of Esworth.

The alarms sounded as they sometimes did, warning Atlas of impending deployment. He jumped from his bunk, snatched up his clothing and raced the short distance to the Leviathan Bay. The massive war machines waited, suspended by heavy chains. Support crew hurried making final preparations. Something suggested it wasn't a drill. Atlas pulled on his pilot overalls and zipped himself up.

"Powered up and ammo full, Atlas." Chief Hanks gave Atlas the thumbs up. It was Hanks' job to ensure the machines were prepared for war.

The Terran Cooperative paid big bucks to the Singh-Frederick Corporation to develop the next generation of killing machines. The Leviathans were humanoid weapon platforms, piloted from the inside by an operator. Fifteen-foot and boasting cutting edge weaponry, they were the pinnacle of battle development by humanity, a true game changer when it came to ground warfare.

Neural interfaces were implanted in the body of every Leviathan pilot, and they also underwent extreme bone density and gene therapy. The result was that Atlas became something more than human. He was stronger, taller and prone to anger quickly. It was a true honour to become a Leviathan operator. The selection process was vigorous and mortality rates high. Atlas, quite literally, was one in ten-thousand.

Atlas slapped Chief Hanks' shoulder. At seven-foot he towered above Hanks, and too often Hanks made jibes about Atlas' physique, often calling him Freak.

"Is it a drill? You heard anything?" asked Atlas.

Hanks shrugged. "Heard nothing."

The other two members of Atlas' team, Sheona *Owl* Armstrong and Luna Pale, entered the bay and raced to their own war machines.

Atlas scrambled up the ladder to the pilot's compartment and carefully eased in. The pilot's hatch closed, plunging the claustrophobic compartment into darkness. His armour closed around him and the clasping mechanism clicked loudly. Within seconds, neural interfaces at the base of his skull and back connected, bringing the machine alive. Atlas closed his eyes, waiting for the pain. In battle situations the speed of the connection could be forced, bringing the Leviathan online in a fraction of a second, but the consequence was extreme pain for the operator. So far, no lasting damage had been identified to the operator, but Atlas knew it was only a matter of time.

A bolt of hot iron sizzled through Atlas' eyes and travelled to the back of his skull. Every muscle in his entire body contracted. Another click indicated pain relief medication was being injected via his wrist, but his jaw clenched and he growled, cursing until the pain subsided.

Atlas and his Leviathan were now one. He saw the world through the Leviathan's optic systems. His Heads Up Display (HUD) provided a trail of scrolling information. The routine tests were conducted, arms moved and weapons were raised. "Owl? Luna? Systems check?"

"Systems nominal," replied Owl, her voice clear and confident.

"All good. Ready to roll," Luna replied.

Atlas was armed with a Reaper Cannon, a multi-barrelled rotating weapon that could produce such a heavy rate of fire it could tear through a building.

The HUD indicated it took five minutes and sixteen seconds from alarm to test completion. He was not pleased. Under five minutes was ideal. Four and a half minutes, optimal. A series of lights blinked along the floor giving guidance to the launch point.

"Let's get this done," Atlas said over the communication system.

The Singh-Frederick support crew moved aside to allow the three titans passage.

The two other Leviathans left their support struts and marched toward Atlas. Atlas turned his Leviathan. The support chains dropped away and he led his team to the launch point. They were slow, cumbersome and with each step the machines swayed a little. The heavy armour came at the cost of speed and nimbleness.

The bay itself was a large platform with bell-shaped drop pods berthed beneath. The three Leviathans lined up at the precipice. A loading crane swung around securing Atlas'

Leviathan, lifted him from the platform and deposited him into the drop pod. Heavy clamps secured the machine to the wall of the pod.

"You think this is real?" came Owl's voice on the internal system. Her soft speech belied the many strengths the woman possessed, both physical and mental.

Atlas had once inquired as to the source of Owl's nickname. Owl had replied, "Mind your own fucking business." He did not ask again.

"It's bullshit," snorted Luna Pale. Luna had too often tried to bestow himself a nickname. He tried Bruiser, Hammer and Lancelot, but none stuck. Both Atlas and Owl considered his real name too hilarious to be silenced. "We'll be back in our beds in an hour."

"There's something different about this," said Atlas. "No one's given me a bullshit brief yet."

"Curveball?" suggested Owl.

"Maybe. Maybe not," said Atlas.

"Maybe it's aliens?" suggested Luna, ever the joker. "Or the Nights. Oh, the Nights are back and we're being shot down there to save the day. We'll be known as local superheroes soon. Caped Crusaders."

"You'd look pretty in a cape, Luna," quipped Owl.

The interior lights of the drop pod turned to red. External struts moved the craft into launch position.

"Um, we're ready for the announcement, people," said Luna. "Drill over. You know? Time to go home."

"Looks like this shit's real," said Owl.

Atlas' HUD flashed. *Marine team on Esworth surface under attack.* Pictures followed, stills from body cameras.

"Fuck," said Luna Pale. "You seeing what I'm seeing?"

"Yep," said Atlas.

"What the hell is that? And are we the only ones going in?" asked Luna.

"Doesn't matter," said Owl. "There's marines dying down there."

The drop pod tilted. *Warning* flashed red on the interior display.

"See you on Esworth," said Luna.

This was it, thought Atlas. The first true test of the Leviathan Project in a combat situation. They were drilled to perfection but simulations never gave the same experience as actual combat. The display monitoring his heart rate and vitals showed an increase in beats per minute, up to one-hundred-and-twenty-two beats. He regulated his breathing, concentrating on taking regular controlled intakes. This was it, him and his team were the first of the Leviathans to go into battle.

The drop pod fired from Erebus like a bullet. Atlas, Owl and Luna were simply powerless passengers. As G-force hit, Atlas closed his eyes. The craft rumbled as it entered the atmosphere, thrusters fired, steering their descent to planet. Navigation and control were handled by operators back on Erebus.

"Brace! Brace! Brace!" warned the operator on Erebus.

"Brace? What the fuck do they think we're doing in here?" Luna's voice shook with the movement of his craft.

The Leviathan suits were filled with gel compartments, designed to protect the pilot but it didn't stop Atlas from tensing his body. The drop pod impacted with bone-jarring force. Warning alarms blared, detailing damage to the pod. Atlas did not give the list one moment's thought. It was someone else's problem. The drop pod was a one-way ship.

"Hey, Owl? How's your hair?" said Luna, groaning.

"Saddle up," said Owl. "Let's go see these things for ourselves."

The clamps holding the three warriors in place released and the side of the pod opened in an explosive burst.

Atlas stood, the suit performed the same action, perfect synergy between man and machine. He was the first to step onto Esworth. The integrated systems scanned for targets and provided atmospheric information. The optics display on Atlas' HUD lit up, directing him to their objective.

"Let's go save some marines," said Atlas. "Follow me."

***

Agustin Garcia, Above Esworth Chamber, Esworth.

The shuttle engines ignited, the heat so intense Agustin felt it through his mask. Henning pushed Agustin and Stone up the ramp, the officer's mask no longer on his face. He strapped Agustin into place and did the same for Stone, then headed back to the ramp.

Agustin pulled off his own mask. "Where are you going?"

"Getting the marines up here, too. Stay here." Henning disappeared.

Stone's eyes closed and he mouthed words to himself. Was he praying?

"All this is your fault, Stone. You hear me? Before you showed up things were fine and I still had my daughter. You're taking everything from me. I should beat you, drag you out of here and leave you to those things."

"Maybe you should." Stone dropped his chin. "Maybe that's what I deserve but I didn't start this. You know that. They were here and if it hadn't been me it would've been someone else."

Henning dragged a marine into the shuttle. The marine's vest was torn around the stomach. Intestines bulged. Agustin unbuckled and helped Henning. The marine looked young, Tanya's age. His brown eyes were rolling back into his head. Another wounded marine was dragged aboard, screaming, his left arm missing at the shoulder.

Tanya. Please don't have ended up like this.

***

Atlas Drinkwater, Esworth.

The three Leviathans crested a mound. Atlas cycled through the optic enhancements. One shuttle was airborne, another grounded. Bodies of dead marines were strewn over the short expanse of snow, while the wounded were being dragged away by comrades.

The Leviathan's systems marked each of the strange creatures as a target. Two-hundred-and-twelve, including one colossal creature in the centre of the horde. None of the operators had faced actual combat before. This was trial by fire.

"They're eating the dead," said Luna.

An order came over the comms. "Leviathan Control to Leviathan Actual. Proceed and neutralise hostiles. Secure area for medical evacuation and recovery of the KIAs."

"Are they seeing what we're seeing?" asked Owl.

"They see better than we do." Atlas zoomed in on the nearest creature. Its hide looked like that of a bovine, its face was that of a bear with a longer snout, and short antlers protruded at uneven points from the head. It could move standing on two legs but was more effective utilising all four limbs like an ape.

"Can those things even be killed?" said Luna.

"We need to hustle. They'll be on the shuttle before we know it." Atlas raised his Reaper Cannon, the chamber rotating ready to spit out its volley. "I'll draw them away. Be ready."

Target locks blinked all over his display, calculating the distance of the enemy to be five-hundred metres. The Reaper Cannon was a fearsome weapon, one that without the augmented strength of the Leviathan Suit would have been impossible for a man to wield.

"Good hunting," said Luna, his voice filled with a little uncertainty.

Atlas opened fire. High calibre rounds thudded into the mass of creatures. Spent cartridges flew all around. Creatures lost arms, heads, and some were bisected completely. Marines retreated fast, firing as they went. The creatures cleared away some metres. The HUD calculated thirteen dead targets and two wounded enough to unlikely be a further threat. The downside of the Reaper Cannon was the limited amount of ammunition it stored. Atlas ceased fire.

As the marines closed in on the shuttle, the unharmed collection of demons regrouped and turned as one toward the Leviathans.

"Well, you've gotten their attention, Atlas. Now what?" Owl was at Atlas' side.

"Leviathan Control to Leviathan Actual. Larger creature is now priority," came the order through the comms.

The largest demon stood apart from the throng of the lesser. It seemed to be holding back, an overlord of sorts shielded by its smaller brethren.

"He must be the Pied Piper," said Owl.

"Then let's blow up his flute," said Atlas.

A wave of the creatures charged. They were fast. Two large fuel tanks sat on Owl's shoulders, and fuel lines snaked down her arms connecting to firing nozzles. Two flames ignited in anticipation of firing. The creatures bounded into range. The arms of Owl's Leviathan straightened and thick jets of flame engulfed the creatures at the lead. Their screams were wails, and those charging behind caught fire quickly and dropped to the ground.

"Yee-haw," yelled Luna like an excited cowboy.

"Well, they sure feel pain," said Owl.

The burning hair and hides gave off black smoke. Six of the beasts raced around the group that Owl toasted. Atlas opened up on the flanking force, ripping through them with complete accuracy. More advanced.

"I can get a shot at the big bastard." Luna's Leviathan brandished an L-Cannon, a direct energy weapon designed to obliterate armoured vehicles. A huge battery pack was mounted on his back, and two twisting power cords coiled from the battery to the weapon.

Luna started forward. He backhanded one creature and it flew through the air. Luna fired and a brilliant blast of red disintegrated two. He fired again and obliterated another two. One creature charged at Luna's side. He punched and missed. The creature leapt onto the Leviathan and held tight. The Leviathan moved left then right but could not shake off the creature.

"Ah, a little help would be appreciated," said Luna.

"I'll go," said Owl, like she was offering to do a coffee run. She thundered into Luna and squashed the creature. It fell to the ground, and Owl grabbed it and tore its neck from its torso.

Atlas fired at the coming onslaught. "Get the Pied Piper, Luna!"

Luna moved as fast as his suit would allow. The larger demon started back to the mine entrance.

"Now!" yelled Atlas.

Luna fired, but not before the demon shrunk back into the tunnel. As if a silent yell of retreat was signalled, the surviving creatures disappeared back into the mine.

None of the operators said a thing for some moments.

"Fuck! I was gonna be famous. Luna Pale kills giant fucking devil monster on Esworth. That'd get me a lovely, young lady with big tits and I'd marry her, retire and never leave Earth again."

"You're a pig, Luna," said Owl.

"Yeah, and I was gonna be a rich pig."

Atlas zoomed his optics in. "Leviathan Actual to Leviathan Control—"

"We can see, Leviathan Actual. Provide cover and the dead will be gathered," said a sombre voice from Leviathan Control.

When Atlas first signed up he had envisioned deployment against Jihadist Islamists and corporate militias. And when sent out here he believed battles to be a thought of the past. After all, who was there to fight out here?

It was a bad fucking day. Worse for the marines. There would be an extensive debrief session. He hoped that someone smarter than him had answers. And he knew if the creatures had attacked with their full force, the three Leviathans wouldn't have stood a chance either.

**

Agustin Garcia, Uriah's Hope, Esworth.

Hell was a word tossed into conversation casually. Flippantly even. Agustin had witnessed hell. He rolled the glass tumbler between both hands. Ice cubes knocked at the sides, and he sipped from the best of Twomley's private stash of scotch. Tanya was dead. There was no way she could've survived that hell.

Agustin knuckled away his tears and poured another as the conference room door opened.

"Jesus, Agustin." Twomley inspected the scotch bottle. "I said one to calm yourself down."

Carafes of water, hot-water urns, and platters of fruits and fresh pastries sat on a side trestle.

"Try some of that," said Twomley.

"My daughter's dead, Dale."

"Oh, Agustin." Twomley poured himself a shallow scotch and swallowed. "A father shouldn't have to go through what you're going through."

Agustin emptied his glass and held it out to Twomley for a refill.

"Pull yourself together. At least for this meeting. After that, take a day or two off. Let me handle The Hub."

"I don't even have her body to bury. I couldn't even do that for her."

"Agustin, I need you sharp. Fix your shirt. The others are arriving. Once this is out of the way, you can sleep. I'll have the medics prescribe something to help. Okay?" Twomley handed Agustin a packet of mints. "And chew on these."

Twomley locked the bottle away in his cabinet. Agustin dropped his empty glass onto the table and looked out the window. It had snowed again, piling the slanted roof of Henrietta Hall with snow. He popped two mints into his mouth and chewed. The massive circling walls of Uriah's Hope used to give him comfort, but now, after today, the mighty walls of the city seemed insignificant and redundant.

Agustin turned.

Twomley handed a black coffee to Agustin. "What would Tanya want you to do?"

"What would Tanya want me to do?" She was always the one to build Agustin up when he was down. He didn't have anyone else he could rely on for that. One time, when Agustin was passed over for the administration of one of Earth's orbital habitation facilities, it was Tanya who picked up the pieces of his shattered ego and reinstalled hope. "She'd want me to make sure what happened to her couldn't happen again."

"I think she would, too."

Agustin stood, buttoned up his shirt, rolled his sleeves down and fastened the cuffs at his wrists. He had changed his clothes since returning from Esworth but not showered.

"Dale, I'm going to ask you for a favour, and you have to do it, okay?"

"Anything but another scotch."

"If the melancholy takes me like that again, you need to shake me out of it."

Twomley slapped Agustin's shoulder. "We don't just do this job, Agustin. We live it. We'll get through this meeting and talk, okay?"

A soft knock came at the door and a hub assistant poked her head in. "Directors, they've arrived."

Captain Scott and Captain Goodsir of Erebus walked in. Then Chief Constable Rebecca Reid of Uriah's Hope Municipal Police. Dr Stone followed, a screen tucked under his arm, thick gloves on his hands. Then came Colonel Hopkins of the Terran Cooperative Marines and last, a giant of a man with a Mediterranean tan, perfectly white teeth, and muscles bulging beneath his flight suit.

"I don't think we've met." Agustin extended a hand to the last arrival.

"This is Clive Drinkwater, team leader of the Leviathan Squad," said Twomley.

"I prefer to be called Atlas, sir."

Atlas' hand swamped Agustin's.

"Well then, Atlas, you and your team did a hell of a job out there. You saved a lot of lives, mine included. Please accept my personal thanks."

"Was our duty, sir."

"We've all heard of the prowess of the Leviathans. I was humbled to see them in action. Please," he said to everyone, and gestured to the trestle. "Help yourself and take a seat."

Scott and Goodsir were the only two to indulge, made themselves coffees, and all sat around the large table.

"All of you have played a part in the events of this morning. You each hold a privileged position with full access to information and recordings of what happened at the Esworth Chamber. So, let us come together as a collective and plan ahead for what is to come."

"And what is to come, Director Garcia?" Captain Goodsir inspected the imprint of Uriah's Hope emblem on his coffee mug. "Shall I tell you what I know?"

"Please," said Agustin.

"I know that a lot of marines died on Esworth to indulge the curiosity of a fringe academic."

Stone refused to meet anyone's stare, and instead activated his small screen and focused his attention downward.

"And one could argue," continued Goodsir, "that the curiosity stirred about this Esworth Chamber was a ruse to solicit a rescue mission for your daughter."

"How dare you, Captain!" spat Twomley.

"Oh, I certainly dare, Assistant Director. What has occurred could be considered a gross misuse of power."

"Captain Goodsir has raised a point." Scott looked to Twomley. "And his service and honour allow him the privilege to question Director Garcia. If we're to foster a productive working relationship then all here should be free to state facts and ask difficult questions."

"Then let him state facts and pose questions rather than spit ridiculous accusations," said Twomley. "And be mindful that Director Garcia is grieving the loss of his daughter."

Agustin raised a hand, requesting calm. "Let's speak facts. Doctor Stone entered Esworth illegally, left the city and trespassed on private property. He came here hoping to find a truth. But he was right that there was something more than Uriah's Hope on Esworth. And what was uncovered has changed our situation. We thought Esworth a planet of extremes. Extreme cold and extreme loneliness. We've found it to be a planet of extreme mystery." It pained Agustin to provide that minute measure of support for Stone.

"We've stirred up a hornet's nest with our blundering down there," said Chief Constable Reid. "How many marines died, Colonel?"

"Thirteen dead," said Colonel Hopkins quickly. "And two still fighting for their lives."

"A heavy price to pay," said Scott.

"Nobody likes to lose people under their command," said Rebecca Reid.

"So let's think logically," said Twomley. "Right at this moment, it doesn't matter how or why the Chamber was explored. What matters is what happens now. Companies are expected from Earth soon. They'll be sinking hundreds of shafts into the ground. How long until they disturb the Esworth Chamber, or even one like it? There's an enemy out there. Imagine the slaughter if unarmed miners and crews were set upon?"

"You use the word enemy to describe these, um …" Goodsir struggled for a word.

"Demons," supplied Colonel Hopkins.

"Well, I prefer creatures," said Goodsir. "And these creatures may not be our enemy."

"What are you saying?" asked Twomley.

Goodsir shrugged. "What if Stone poking his nose down in that place roused them from some sort of slumber, or hibernation, or simply a peaceful existence? What if their attack was just a defence to our intrusion?"

"Captain Goodsir." Twomley stood from his seat and walked to the table of refreshments. "I feel I must remind you that before the expedition to the Chamber, two Red Aquila patrols were lost and our security perimeter was probed by unknown persons. One would assume that the demons, or creatures, were aware of our presence."

"I'm not convinced," said Goodsir.

"They may not be our enemy," said Stone.

All eyes looked Stone's way.

"Perhaps we could hear from the architect of the expedition." Twomley returned to his seat with two coffees, one for himself and one for Agustin. "Doctor Stone?"

Stone straightened. "When I went back to the chamber, I saw the creature as a discovery. Perhaps a life form I could communicate with. I now believe it intended harm. We breached the chamber and perhaps that was enough to earn its hostility."

"If it's hostile, it's our enemy," argued Twomley.

"Atlas, perhaps you could give us your understanding of those creatures," suggested Scott.

"Yes, ma'am," the big man began. "My team and I dropped to planet and immediately engaged the creatures to allow the marine shuttles to take off. We detected no threats of firearms or projectile weapons. The smaller creatures advanced, perhaps fearlessly, and my hunch is they were protecting the one huge creature. Two reached one of our Leviathans and their claws proved to be capable of great pressure. Yet they did not penetrate the armour, and rather, they retreated."

"They retreated why?" asked Scott.

"I perceived no reason. I suspect we were being tested."

"Tested?" said Agustin.

"It's just a feeling, sir."

"Tested," repeated Scott softly, her eyes taking in everyone at the table.

"Could we deploy all our Leviathans, send the whole complement to the mine?" asked Agustin.

"If I may?" said Atlas.

"Of course," said Agustin.

"If those creatures didn't retreat, I wouldn't be here. Our ammunition is limited and we would have been overrun. You'd need a powerful attack from overhead."

"I will not allow Fleet to open fire on Earth's first colony world," said Agustin.

"And we need to consider the heat source under the surface," added Twomley.

Dr Stone stood from his seat. "I have something." He tapped as his PWD, casting what he was looking at to the large screen on the wall.

The creature was imprisoned behind the green light bars.

"This is the chamber. Watch the very top left of the screen when it breaks free and reaches for me."

The creature moved from his prison. Dr Stone rewound the footage three times and allowed it to play at a slower speed each time. The light in the chamber was dull and as such made everything appear in grey.

"What are we looking at?" asked Agustin.

"See the figures cloaked by shadows?"

"The lesser demons?" asked Reid.

"That's what I thought initially. Watch as I scrub the footage." Stone played the footage again, rewound, slowed, rewound again. The footage grew clearer and the flashing green light illuminated what was originally hidden in shadows. Rows of hundreds of grey shadows were lined up like pawns on a chess board against the wall, all with heads bowed and hands held reverently before them. Stone moved to the next frame, where a burst of the green tendrils illuminated the section of the chamber.

Agustin leapt from his seat. "Tanya! It is Tanya, isn't it?"

"I believe it is," said Stone. "If I'm not mistaken, to the left and right of her, three of the missing Red Aquila soldiers. Look when the light flashes again. You can just make out their uniforms."

The light flashed and the soldiers' uniforms were confirmed.

Agustin ran a hand through his hair. "Why didn't she scream or call out for us? We were so close."

"Who are the others standing there?" Reid joined Agustin and squinted at the screen.

"I haven't been able to clean the footage enough yet," said Dr Stone. "But, if the entire back section of the chamber is full of people or whatever they may be, it would hold, what? How many?"

"Hundreds." Twomley removed his glasses. "It would hold hundreds."

"So who are they?" asked Captain Goodsir.

Twomley rubbed the bridge of his nose. "We have a problem with undocumented arrivals in the city, and for the most part, they're not known to us. We, and I'm sure Chief Constable Reid would agree, have assumed they've all gone to the Undercity."

"But hundreds?" asked Reid.

Twomley took some time to answer. "We couldn't account for that many."

CHAPTER 6

Atlas swiped his card. The door to his team's apartments silently slid open. Luna was head banging, throwing devil horns in the air. The heavy metal music was loud. Damned awful stuff to Atlas. He sent Luna a frown. The volume was turned down.

"Beer?"

Atlas nodded.

Leviathan teams bunked together, sharing confined quarters within Erebus. An orbital facility was planned, but until then, Atlas endured Luna's music choices and the long list of his other annoying nuances.

Luna returned to his dancing, an open bottle of beer in each hand. The quarters they shared lacked personal charm. None had close family, wives, husbands or serious partners, so no faces smiled from shiny frames or hung on bedheads.

The men clinked the bottles together. A little froth spilled over Atlas' hand.

"So, are we the toast of the town, Atlas?"

Owl appeared from the shower room wrapped in a towel, her hair dark from the water. She turned the music off.

"It was a strange meeting." Atlas sipped from his bottle. The beer was most welcome.

"Do they know what it is down there?" Owl unwrapped, and wiped her hair with the towel.

"Shit, Owl," said Luna, looking away. "You're like a toddler wanting to be naked more than dressed."

Atlas wasn't so quick to avert his eyes. He enjoyed seeing Owl naked with a true admiration. She was powerfully built, lightly tanned, athletic with defined muscle masses. Her toenails were polished with a pearl enamel. She usually chose dark colours.

"No, Owl. No one has any idea."

"They sending us back down there?" Owl grabbed a beer.

Atlas averted his eyes. "Get some clothes on. We need to talk."

"We can't beat those things," said Luna.

There was never any actual silence on a warship like Erebus. While Atlas waited for Owl to return, the pause in the conversation was filled with the battleship's mechanical and rhythmic heartbeat. At times it felt like a lullaby to Atlas, a soothing sedative of sorts.

Owl returned in a flimsy wrap-around nightgown. "It would be unwise to put the Leviathans down there."

Atlas sat on their sofa and the two followed. Owl crossed her legs and one thigh and knee escaped the cover of that gown. Her skin held a sheen like she had just oiled her entire body, and fragrance convinced Atlas his suspicion was correct.

"There's something else you guys should know. Turns out when they were in that chamber, they found hundreds of people and turns out one was Director Garcia's daughter."

"Hundreds of people?" said Luna.

"They thought they were statues. Didn't twig to the truth until we returned and Doctor Stone went over the bodycam footage."

"Who are they?"

"Some are missing Red Aquila, but the others," he shrugged, "they can only guess."

"Fuck," said Luna, peeling the label from his bottle of beer. "And a rescue mission?"

"No," said Atlas.

"No?" said Owl.

"No," repeated Atlas. "They've decided the best scenario is that those things stay down that hole."

"That's not a problem for us then. Not tonight anyway," said Owl.

"Not tonight," said Atlas.

***

Atlas woke from a dream, and in that horrid moment between sleep and wakefulness he was still on Esworth battling a swarm of giant demons, firing until his ammunition was spent. His death was imminent.

Atlas threw the sheet from his body and wiped sweat from his forehead. He took a few deep breaths, pushed himself from his bunk and splashed cold water on his face. It was 0200 hours. Not tonight, he had told Owl. But today would be a new day.

Atlas dried his face, pulled on his clothes and boots, and closed the door behind him, leaving the sounds of Luna's snoring locked away.

Atlas made for the contemplation room as it was informally known, a viewing platform on the underside of the ship. He often made his way there when sleep was impossible to trap. Yawning guards nodded as he passed. It was quiet, the ship's heartbeat keeping him company for the five-minute walk. The doors were already open, the lights dim to provide a better view of outside. But he was not the first to attempt solace early that morning in the contemplation room. Captain Goodsir stood at the viewing platform, hands clasped behind his back. Paris Quinn, Captain of the destroyer Renown stood likewise. Both looked out to distant Esworth. As beautiful as it was terrifying, it appeared an orb of pristine whiteness.

Atlas sidestepped into the shadows of the room.

"We all miss Admiral Hastings. But it should have been me," said Goodsir. "Captain Scott's lack of experience leading anything other than a squadron doesn't make her the natural choice."

"Hastings put too much faith in her," said Paris Quinn. "But don't discount Scott's name. If you move against her authority, you might find yourself alone."

"She's timid. That makes her weak."

Captain Quinn shrugged. "Perhaps. But look for the dangers."

"We're dealing with a threat to humanity the likes of which we've not seen since the Night War. We must be decisive, and Director Garcia and his gaggle of yes men won't do what needs doing."

"And what do you propose?"

"What do I propose? Action. Will you follow me, Paris?"

Paris Quinn turned to Goodsir. "I will not support action that will result in bloodshed in The Fleet. I will not fire upon another ship."

"You won't need to, Captain. It can be done without bloodshed."

Paris Quinn returned her attention to the world outside the ship.

"Captain Scott will be removed. Recce Tyler on Colossus will have to be dealt with. We'll do what needs to be done and sort this mess out later."

"You know the consequence if this fails?"

"I'm acting in the best interests of the Fleet, humanity and the Terran Cooperative."

Silence fell in the room for a long time.

"Tell me more," said Captain Paris Quinn.

***

Atlas arrived back at his team's quarters. Luna's snoring was still loud.

"Couldn't sleep?" Owl stood at her door.

"Nor you?"

"I keep dreaming about dying. They're bloody nightmares, Atlas."

"And yet here you are, alive and well."

Owl looked beautiful silhouetted in the doorway. Her light nightwear was almost see-through. They often had sex. Owl and Luna would occasionally share a bed, too. It was just a thing that happened. No promises and nothing more.

"Why don't you come in here?" Owl began to unbutton her top. "Maybe we can tire each other out and finally get some sleep?"

Atlas hesitated, so much on his mind.

"I only bite where people can't see." Owl reached out, a rare smile painted on her face.

For the next hour Atlas lost himself with Owl forgetting about Esworth, the creatures and Captain Goodsir. And after, Owl curled into his side, her head on his chest and quickly found sleep while thoughts spun through Atlas' head.

***

Agustin Garcia, Uriah's Hope, Esworth.

Agustin sat on the edge of his bed, staring at last night's empty bottle of whiskey. He had planned to drink himself into oblivion, keen to forget who he was. But oblivion had not been obtained. Before sleep, an image of his daughter, a statue in the Esworth Chamber, blurred and cleared and blurred and cleared again and again. Nothing made sense.

The clock displayed 0743 hours. The sleeping pills Twomley had procured sat untouched on the table.

A celebration was scheduled, one to welcome the birth of the first native to Uriah's Hope.

He plodded to the toilet, relieved himself, then Agustin checked himself in the mirror. "How are you going to deal with the day?"

His apartment door opened.

"Morning, Director. Sleep well?" The UHMP officer smiled pleasantly and offered Agustin a travel mug. He was young and his hair was cropped army style.

"I rang a few times, but you didn't answer, and I was worried …"

"And you are?"

"Assigned by Chief Constable Reid, sir."

"To do what?"

"Protect you."

"Protect me from what?"

The officer looked uncomfortable. "Did you sleep well, sir?"

"Do I look like I slept well?"

"Well, shall I leave you to dress, sir?"

Agustin looked down at his stomach, his hips, his legs and to his toes. Totally naked. He sipped from the travel mug. "Coffee. Do you think the coffee tastes different here than back home?"

The cop shrugged. "I don't really like coffee. To be honest with you, I don't like hot drinks."

"I don't think we can be friends." Agustin began his morning routine of dressing. "What's your name?"

"Joshua Brooks."

"You come all the way to the coldest place humans inhabit and you don't drink coffee?"

"Correct, sir."

Agustin finished dressing. "Shall we?"

The two men took the metro system. They rode in silence. Agustin flicked through the secure reports on his PWD. One detailed a wave of sleep related issues, a report compiled by the Chief Medical Officer of Uriah's Hope. It included headaches and hallucinations within the city. Agustin marked the report as urgent, and made a note to discuss the issue with his Medical Administrators. Possibly Fleet, too.

"We've arriving, sir," said Brooks.

He shut off his PWD. "Let's get this over with."

The metro pulled into the stop. The doors opened. Citizen Liaison Officer Harris Potter greeted him with a gruff nod.

Potter was on Agustin's staff and wore the required sharp suit and tie, looking every part the government stooge.

"Christ Almighty, Director. Did you think about having your clothes pressed?"

"I need an advisor to greet me as soon as I step off the transit, Harris?"

"Yes, Director. I'd say you do." He hiked a thumb over his shoulder. "The vultures are circling. Shall I brief you?"

A crowd of reporters waited behind the security gate. All eyes were speared at Agustin. Small camera drones hovered overhead.

"No need, Harris. Just watch my back out there. Those birds look hungry."

Potter looked to the UHMP officer.

"This is Joshua," explained Agustin. "There's something wrong with him. He doesn't drink coffee."

The three men marched through the security gate into the main public area.

A small, blonde woman with a wolfish grin was the first to reach Agustin. "Director Garcia? Some words regarding what happened with Admiral Hastings?"

"It was a tragedy and we all mourn the loss of such a stalwart servant of the Terran Cooperative and Fleet."

"Director, does the UHMP accept any responsibility for the events that led up to Admiral Hastings' suicide? How could a mentally unstable man simply stroll into one of the most secure events we've seen in Uriah's Hope?"

"Director Garcia will not be answering questions at this time," said Harris Potter. "Official statements from the Director's Office have been made available. Thank you."

UHMP officers in uniform created a funnel for Agustin to escape. "Move aside! Move aside!"

Agustin climbed the steps of the habitation complex. The Hab Zones were built like a ziggurat, each level holding many apartments of various sizes depending on the make-up of the family.

"This apartment, Director." Potter pointed at an open doorway. "Miss Reike Neumann. Arrived on the last rotation from Earth."

The apartment was spacious. The bedroom and living room were one. Through a doorway he spied a small kitchen and beyond that, a bathroom with a bath. Baths were quite a rarity for The Hope.

Reike Neumann stood by a small crib, one hand resting on the edge. She was a pretty woman, in her early thirties. Her business suit was a little tight, and her dark hair was swept into a dishevelled bun. Agustin remembered well the first months of Tanya's life. His wife detested her weight, cried with the endlessness of exhaustion, and cuddled their baby daughter like she might float away with the slightest breeze.

Reike smiled. It was the radiant smile of a new mother.

"Thank you for welcoming me into your home, Miss Neumann. It's my pleasure and absolute delight to be here and welcome the newest citizen for Uriah's Hope."

In the crib slept a tiny baby, wrapped tightly in white blankets, oblivious to the fact she was about to become the most famous person on Esworth. When Tanya was born, Agustin was afraid to hold her, fearful of breaking such a fragile gift. It was only at the encouragement of his wife that he found himself sitting in a rocking chair for hours, cuddling his new daughter and watching her every breath in sleep.

"Thank you for doing us the great honour of coming here personally." Reike spoke with a tinge of a German accent.

"Have you decided on a name?"

"Hope. Her name's Hope."

"A beautiful name for a beautiful child."

Potter pointed to a static camera set up in the corner of the apartment and gave Agustin a nod to the device.

"Reike and Hope are perfect examples of what we will achieve here in Uriah's Hope and on Esworth. We will create a place where every child is limited only by the scope of their imagination. We will provide each and every citizen the means to reach their full potential. Uriah's Hope will be the shining example of what humanity can achieve when we're mobilised toward a common and righteous goal." Agustin looked to the camera. "That, my friends, is what we're building here. It gives me goosebumps to just be part of it."

Reike giggled.

"From myself and Uriah's Hope's newest resident, I wish you good day."

Potter waved his hand over his throat, indicating the feed ended.

"Thank you for putting up with us here," said Agustin. "I hope you've found it not too much of an imposition. The little one did so well."

"Can I make you or your assistant some refreshments?"

"No thank you. We won't stay long. Tell me, what area of employment have you taken up?"

"I'm a third tier technician at Hydroponics."

"Ah, keeping the city fed. A very important job. I'm thankful for your contribution."

Reike touched Agustin's hand. "This must be difficult for you, Director. I want to offer my condolences at the loss of your daughter."

"There's an urgent message, Director," interrupted Harris.

"Excuse me please, Reike."

Agustin tapped at his PWD. Twomley appeared on the small screen.

"The automated turrets are firing. The demons are on the move."

***

"Show me," ordered Agustin, dropping into his chair in The Hub.

The large screen flashed a topological view of the city. Four miles outside the city walls, green and red dot-markers formed a circular periphery. Each depicted the location of automated turrets. Red indicated firing and all were on the northern side, the lineal attachments on the screen indicating each had used twenty percent of their ammunition.

"What's happening?" asked Agustin.

"The creatures are close enough to set off the automated systems."

"They're not moving toward the city?"

Twomley shook his head. "No."

"So where are they headed?"

"No idea. There's nothing out there."

"Or there's something out there we don't know about."

"Couldn't agree more. They wouldn't migrate like that for no reason."

More dot-markers flashed red.

"Red Aquila's scaling back their patrols to the four-mile mark and will conduct resupply missions to the automated turrets," informed Twomley. "We've suspended all commercial passes until a full risk assessment has been completed. Fleet deployed fifty-two marines to man the city's defensive weapons out on the wall."

"Good." Agustin pointed to the map. "The UHMP and marines acted quickly."

"I feel like we're sitting on a huge powder keg." Twomley pushed his glasses up to his forehead and rubbed his eyes.

CHAPTER 7

Atlas Drinkwater, Erebus, Esworth Orbit.

Atlas found the marines' mess hall. The long room was filled with tables and attached stools. Marines moved along the chow line, holding out trays. The day's meal was beef stew with a heavy dose of garlic. Marines and the Leviathan Teams seldom interacted outside of training exercises and combat simulations, and his presence received ill-favoured and curious looks.

He spotted his target sitting with another marine in quiet conversation. Jenny Styles looked different. Her usual blonde ponytail was gone, and in its place was a shaved head with a thin layer of stubble which hinted at the dark colour of her natural hair.

Atlas climbed over Jenny's stool and sat. It was a tight squeeze. He felt like an adult sitting at the kids' table. "I need to talk to you, Jenny."

Jenny frowned then played with her stew. "You shouldn't be in here, Atlas."

"I thought we were friends?"

Jenny was a Lance Corporal in the Terran Cooperative Marine Corps. They had a sexual relationship which lasted two weeks, screwing in concealed alcoves and Jenny's apartment in the scant downtime they shared. To Atlas it was simply a consensual shedding of clothes and groping, but Jenny's words had hinted at something a lot more serious, and something not wanted by Atlas. Jenny did not accept the rebuff and badgered Atlas for a period.

"Friends? We screwed for a few weeks, and you put an end to it, Atlas." Jenny's left eye was heavily bruised.

"What happened?"

"To us?" she asked with a harsh laugh.

He pointed to her eye.

"I got careless. Now, get the shit out of here. I don't want to be seen speaking with you." She shovelled a chunk of beef into her mouth and chewed.

"I need your help."

Jenny pushed away her tray and stood.

"Hey!" He grabbed her arm. "It's important."

The mess fell silent and all eyes speared their way.

Jenny shrugged off his hold. "You've got nothing important to say. We lost people down there. Good people. And you're not welcome here."

Atlas climbed from the stool. "And you can thank my team you didn't lose more."

Two male marines started to approach.

Atlas held up his hands in surrender. "I'm not here for trouble. And I'm sorry for your loss. Our loss. We saved as many as we could."

Jenny hesitated. "What do you want?"

Atlas gestured they move away from prying eyes. They left the hall and walked.

"You marines have a separate communication system, separate from the Fleet, yes?"

"Why?" said Jenny.

"Can Fleet access the communications?"

Jenny frowned her impatience.

"I need to speak to Captain Scott on Eris. But I don't want Fleet to hear."

"You gotta tell me why."

"It's better you don't know."

Jenny tuned left into a darkened corridor and pulled Atlas with her. She stopped and looked up to him. "Then I won't help you."

"What if I said it was for the security of this place?"

"What if I said you had to pay for it?" Jenny played with the cuffs of his shirt.

Atlas contemplated taking advantage of the shaded corridor and giving Jenny what she wanted. He'd not done it with a woman with a shaved head. But he knew he would come to regret it when Jenny's badgering began yet again. "Don't do this, Jenny."

She pouted. "Well, the truth is, I don't have access to what you want. The marines run a separate communication system for command and control operations outside Fleet comms but it would be someone much higher than me who could access it."

Atlas stared for a long time. She was telling the truth. "Jenny, please don't repeat this conversation. Ever. And I like your new hairstyle."

***

Atlas decided to head back to his quarters and strode the quiet corridor lost in thought. He didn't have connections high enough in the marines who could help him. Getting to the city would let him set up a meeting with someone from the Director's Office who would at least be able to put him in touch with Captain Scott. He'd have to apply for a pass to travel to the surface but that shouldn't be too difficult to source. He'd saved up several free days to spend this month. It was the safest way he could think of to connect with Captain Scott. Sure, he could place a message and wait for her to reply but that could be weeks and would be easily traceable by Erebus.

"Clive Drinkwater?"

"It's Atlas," he said automatically.

Atlas turned around. Two ensigns stood behind him. He didn't recognise either. Both had pistols in holsters clipped to their belts. Both stood rigid, hands on their belts. The corridor behind them was unusually empty.

"I've got somewhere to be," he said.

"What's the rush?" said one.

The two men were substantially smaller than Atlas. To take them both on would still be like wrestling two cats.

"And which of you two is going to draw the short straw?" asked Atlas.

One ensign pulled his pistol and aimed it at Atlas' head. "Looks like it's me. You need to come with us now."

"You're not going to shoot me?" Atlas spread his hands showing he wasn't armed and laughed. "Put your gun away before someone gets hurt."

The second ensign pulled his pistol up, too. "Come with us and we'll explain everything."

Atlas widened his stance and crossed his arms, ensuring his biceps popped like boulders. "I'm part of the Leviathan Project. We are not under Fleet Command. So, here's what's going to happen. I'm going to keep walking and you're not going to follow me."

A sudden stabbing struck at Atlas' neck. His muscles began to feel like jelly. He turned to see another sailor holding a hypodermic driver.

* * *

Atlas woke to absolute silence. He was prone, feet dangling over the edge of a metal bench attached to a wall. The slim mattress beneath did little to fend off the cold. A single light blinked above his head. He was naked and the only piece of privacy was a scratchy blanket that covered his hips and knees. The brig!

Floor to ceiling shatterproof glass made up the wall to his right. A shadow moved from the far corner and slowly resolved into the image of a man in Fleet uniform.

"Rise and shine, Atlas Drinkwater." Captain Goodsir stood tall, his arms behind his back.

Movement evaded Atlas, his usual strength gone. His mouth was dry and when he tried to talk it was only a croak that ventured from his tongue.

"Good morning." Goodsir moved and sat at Atlas' side. "You won't be able to talk for some hours yet. But you can listen."

Atlas could not move a limb. Goodsir's greeting of morning told him his absence would now be known. But he was locked away in a critical part of the ship and doubted any inventory or record would show his attendance.

"So, let's start with the more important stuff, shall we?" Goodsir leaned in close. "Whatever you think you heard last night, you are wrong. And as you're unlikely to believe me, you'll remain here for the interim."

Atlas looked to the ceiling and the four points of the room.

"It's not luxurious, I know. But it has its purpose. I admire what you and your team did on Esworth. Without your intervention our casualty count would be greater. You're an asset to the Cooperative, Atlas. And that is why I ordered no harm come to you. We will need people like you in the times to come." Captain Goodsir stood. "Few comprehend what I'm about to do. But I have spent more years in service than anyone else here, and as the captain of the most powerful warship in Fleet, I don't need to explain myself."

Atlas couldn't follow what the man was speaking about.

"I don't seek to usurp command from Captain Scott, but it will be done if necessary, for my number one duty is to ensure the safety of Esworth. And God knows right now all we are doing is cowering behind walls and hiding. We didn't win the Night War by timidity." Goodsir walked to the wall of glass, studied his reflection, lifted his shoulders and chin. "When I have the planet below under control, I'll submit myself to naval judgment."

Atlas concentrated all effort to roll from the bench, but the only thing to stir was a grunt from deep in his throat.

Goodsir broke away from his reflection. "You disagree? History will show I am right. It will be said that Captain Goodsir displayed courage in the face of adversity. From orbit we have the means to eliminate the threat and I intend to make arrangements to do just that. And so, you, Mr Clive Drinkwater, will be here until the crisis is over. Your ID chip isn't readable here in the cells, and officially you've gone AWOL. Don't make things difficult, Atlas, and you'll be treated kindly. I'll see you on the next page of human history."

***

Dr Isambard Stone, Uriah's Hope, Esworth.

Dr Isambard Stone stood outside a busy Chinese food stall in the subterranean street, The White Way. He closed his eyes and listened to the humdrum sounds of Uriah's Hope. Footsteps, both fast and slow, adult giggles, high-pitched questions moving past hurriedly, a stall holder passing change from a purchase, a greeting, a departure. It was a comfort to be surrounded by people docilely churning through everyday life. After the events of the chamber, it was as if the collection of humanity, no matter how servile, would protect him.

He gave silent thanks for finally being left alone, his notoriety diluted so much that even his UHMP minder was reassigned.

A sharp bump and a perfunctory apology drew him from his invocations. Isambard sat on a stool at the food stall.

He nodded to a male diner to his left. "Any recommendations?"

The man wore a suit without a tie, the shirt button undone revealing a pendant of Saint Christopher.

"You could pick anything from the menu and be happy," he said between slurps of the large bowl of soup.

Two chefs worked at a frantic pace, cloths in their hands as they grabbed the handles of smoking woks. Oil sizzled. The fiery scent of garlic and chilli jumped from the stovetops.

"What's good?" he called to the chefs.

One looked up with a short smile. "For you, chicken chow mein. You'll like it."

Stone removed his gloves and laid them on the counter. "Then chicken chow mein it is."

Two well-dressed women sat to the far right end of the counter. Their eyeshadow was dark and rouge bright. He supposed they were beautiful in a way with lips that smiled as they chatted, and possessed a noticeable confidence to their posture and the tilt of their chins. They were about Tanya's age, and he wondered if they had an intelligence to match. She was focused, driven and believed in the work she applied herself to. Her will to succeed at times almost matched Stone's. He liked to believe that he infected her with that passion but suspected that it was something she maintained from childhood. What a waste to lose such talent. And it was all his fault.

"Go away!" One woman swatted at something beside her stool. "The Unwanted are here!"

The second woman moved from her seat and grabbed at something. When she turned around, Stone caught sight of the skeletal arm of a small child. Another was trying to break the woman's hold. The children were filthy, their hair matted, and their clothes mere rags.

"Call the police!" she shouted.

"Who are they?" Stone asked the diner to his left.

The man laughed. "You new here or something?"

"Well, something I suppose."

"They're the Unwanted."

"The Unwanted?"

"That's what we call people living in the tunnels under the city. They sometimes come up to the surface to pinch stuff and cause trouble."

"They're just kids."

The man shrugged. "They send the little fleabags up here."

"And if the police come?"

"Jail. They're illegals. Then they're sent back to Earth."

"Jesus!" The woman slapped the child across the face, knocking it to the ground. "The little shit bit me!"

Before the child could get to its feet, the woman grabbed hold of its arm and slapped it again.

Stone pulled on his gloves and got off his stool. "I'll take it from here."

"I want charges pressed. It bit me. See?" She tried to show Isambard her injury but the child was kicking and squirming and finally escaped her grasp.

"What sort of cop are you?" she complained. "Chase them!"

Stone didn't bother to correct the woman's assumption, but he did chase after the kids.

They moved quickly, dodging shoppers and tables and trolleys, and Isambard lost sight of the two as they passed a line of trees on the side of the street. He looked left and right. Nothing. As he turned to retrace his steps, he spotted the children hunched beneath a bench seat.

"There you are," he said pleasantly. "You don't need to run. I'm not a cop."

He knelt on the ground. Two boys, a fear in their eyes also holding a great measure of arrogance. "Come out. I won't hurt you."

A sudden coldness was pressed against his neck, the unmistakeable sureness of a blade.

"Stay on your knees, cop," came a shaky voice from behind. "I don't want to kill you."

Stone tried to turn around, but the knife was pushed harder to his skin. "Stay exactly still."

"I'm not a cop. I just want to talk."

"Talk about what?"

"The kids. You. The Unwanted. I want to understand your life. I'd like to help."

"Just stay away."

"I'm not sure I can do that." Stone reached back quickly and grabbed the hand that held the knife.

The woman squealed and the blade clattered on the ground. Stone jumped to his feet.

The woman stared at her hand. "What have you done to me?"

"You'll be fine in a day or two. I'm Doctor Stone."

"A medical doctor?" She wore an overcoat that may have been a bright colour on another day rather the murky brown it was now.

"I'm an archaeologist."

"Then I don't think you'll be able to help."

Stone plucked the knife from the ground and handed it back handle first.

The woman hesitated then snatched and returned it to a pocket inside her coat. "Come."

The children ran to her side and held her legs.

"Do you want food? I'll buy you all a meal if you'll agree to talk."

The woman's hunger was obvious in the twitch of her mouth. But she held the children closer. "There's plenty of other people in the city to talk to."

"I'm sure the children would like to eat. What's your name?"

She looked around, a frightened bird sensing cats approaching. "Salina."

"Well, Salina. I'm Isambard. Isambard Stone. And the names of your children?"

"They're not my children. They're children of Uriah's Hope. We have to get back to the Undercity before the cops arrive."

Isambard ran a hand through his hair. One boy studied his every move. The other picked his nose and danced on the spot as if he needed to find a toilet.

"No, there's another way."

***

Salina stood rigid in the doorway of Stone's apartment, a proactive arm around the two children who stared with mouths ajar.

"You'll be eating cold burgers if you stand there much longer." Stone threw the bags of burgers and fries on his table, grabbed spoons for the ice-creams, and placed the choc-chip cookies on a plate.

Salina would not move.

"How long since you've eaten?" he asked, munching into a burger. It was not to his liking. Too fatty and the cheese tasted plastic. The mixture of mayonnaise and sauce ran down his chin. "Mmm. Delicious."

The children pushed past Salina and made a beeline for the food.

"Please." He indicated to the sofa.

Salina's footsteps were hesitant, her eyes bouncing from corner to corner, but she did not sit.

Stone held out a burger. "Is it warm enough in here for you?"

Salina accepted the food and ripped open the wrapper quickly. She downed the burger as if it was a small pancake. She wiped her mouth with the back of her hand then removed her coat. "It's fine."

"Hang it on the back of the door if you like." Stone shut the door.

Salina nodded and hung the coat. Her maroon hoodie and denim jeans were as filthy as her coat. "Aren't you worried about people seeing us here?"

The closed door created a vacuum for the scent of unwashed. Isambard lit a scented candle and placed it on the small coffee table next to the sofa, hoping his intention was not obvious. "I think the authorities have bigger fish to fry than me at the moment."

"What do you mean?"

Stone smiled. "Never mind. Tell me about the Unwanted."

Salina frowned. "I thought you were kidding about not knowing of us."

He offered a sympathetic smile. "I'm just new here and not very wise to how it is in Uriah's Hope."

The kids grabbed a box of fries each. Salina followed suit.

"Come," she said to the kids, and the three sat on the sofa.

"Are there a lot of you?"

Salina nodded.

"And where do you live?"

Salina pointed down.

"Down?"

"Underground," she mumbled around chewed fries.

"There's caves?"

"And a network of tunnels." She swallowed. "It's warm at least."

"So why do you choose to live down there?"

"Choose? That's an interesting choice of words. We arrived here by alternative means, so we're not citizens and therefore can't apply for housing. Some of us live in the unused sections of the city, but gangs control those places, full of brothels and drug dens, and lots of cops. If you want to avoid them, you live in the tunnels under the main streets. So if you can call it a choice ..." She shrugged and filled her mouth with more fries.

"And what were your alternative means?"

"Smuggled in by a freight company and facilitated into the city by Red Aquila who has the contract for custom checks. There's a saying amongst us, once you're Unwanted, The Hope takes you forever."

"Is there no help available?"

"Help? Sure. The UHMP round up all Unwanted they find, and hold us in a cell until they can be shipped back to Earth. If you're a citizen of the Terran Cooperative Nations you pay a fine or spend time in jail. If not, you're sent back to your nation of origin."

"Your nation of origin has to be better than your current situation. Surely?"

"Everyone's quick to judge. But you don't know what people are running from, what brought them here."

"Hmm," he said with a quirk of his eyebrows. He filled the kettle and switched it on. "Tell me about the gangs."

"The New Worlders? They run the brothels and the drug trade. And they're slavers."

"Slavery? Here?"

"You are naïve," she scoffed. "We keep as far away from them as possible. They'll take young Unwanted, force them into addiction then whore them out or have them working in other ways."

"I've heard of the Peacemakers, but only rumours. Who are they?"

"They run smuggling rings and offer protection, but for a price. You want to get something or someone in or out of the city, the Peacemakers have a way."

Their conversation paused as Isambard made two coffees. He did not ask Salina for her preferences. He simply made another identical to his, black with two lumps of sugar.

"Thank you," said Salina hesitantly, as she accepted the hot mug. "There's a religious group, too. Preachy stuff and that. They call their leader The Pilgrim of Hate. But that's all I know about them."

Isambard grabbed the ice-creams and passed them to the kids "Have you been down there long?" He took a seat on a single sofa opposite his three guests.

"Long enough. I'm nobody." She sipped her drink, placed it on the small coffee table at her feet, then rolled up the sleeve of one of the children to reveal a black tattoo of tribal curves and crosses winding up the child's arm. "This is Olga and this is the mark of The New Worlders. I rescued her from a whorehouse three weeks ago. She's twelve."

"She's ..." Isambard was stunned at the realisation of the grubby, elfin child with hair to rival a dirty mop was not a boy, but a girl. And twelve? She looked no more than eight. But the thought of the child being sold for sex made him angry. He blew out a loud breath.

"It's people in your city who buy that trade. Boy or girl."

"I'm sorry."

"Why are you sorry? Did you make people the way they are? Did you allow the gangs to take root in the city?"

"No. I'm just saying."

"You can save your pointless words." Salina pulled up her own sleeve to reveal an identical tattoo running the length of her forearm.

"Look, why don't the three of you stay here for a few days? Get yourself back in order, fill your bellies. Maybe I can help you get assistance." Stone never considered himself a kind person, but at that very moment he felt a foreign feeling of protection tugging at his hand.

"And what do you want in return?" she said with accusation.

"No. No, you've got me all wrong if you think I—"

"I've made the mistake of accepting charity before. I won't make the same mistake again." She drank again from her mug then stood.

"At least finish the food before you go."

"We've stayed too long." Salina nodded to the children. They ran to the table and filled their pockets. "Please, don't look for us after this."

"One more question. Down there, in the Undercity, have you ever seen or heard of strange creatures, myth-like stuff?"

"All people can be monsters."

***

The need for robust leisure facilities to stave off inevitable boredom was identified some time ago, and Uriah's Hope's planners allocated sections of the city as entertainment districts to include bars, casinos, cinemas, gyms and sporting facilities. The White Way housed most of the bars. It was here Stone was confident he would find the person who would lend him the assistance he sought.

"Try the New Esworth," suggested one lonely male lost in his glass of whisky at the bar of a dark establishment with carpet that soaked up every footfall. "Red Aquila operators prefer that place."

Stone paid for the man's next drink and left.

The New Esworth looked like a tavern plucked from Tudor times. Whitewash walls, exposed wooden beams dark with stain, and a heavy oak door with serpentine hinges. Above the door sat the establishment's name in scrawling font. Inside, chandeliers pumped out light. The bar area was accessed via a small staircase of three steps. A piano tinkled soft music. Three staff in black and white busied themselves behind an impressively stocked bar. Men and women chatted on barstools. Tables were small with room for two comfortably, or four squashed. A woman's laughter seemed to hit the ceiling. She threw her head back and blew cigarette smoke into the air. A familiar man sat at a table in the corner, a hand around a pint of beer, his focus on the laughing woman's legs.

"What's he having?" Stone asked a bartender.

The barman looked past Stone. "Berliner IPA."

"Pour me two."

Stone carried the two drinks to the corner of the room. "Corporal Ramirez?"

"Who wants to know?" asked the lone drinker before his eyes reluctantly travelled to Stone. "Ah, I know you. The archaeologist."

"The very same." Stone sat.

"Last time I saw you, you were in one of the cells." Ramirez took the offered beer and placed it on a coaster next to his partially empty drink.

"A lot's changed."

Ramirez finished his beer and looked around the room. "No cops tailing you now. So what do you want?"

"I want to offer you a job."

"I already have one."

"But who doesn't want to make a little more money on the side? I pay well."

"I'm listening."

"Have you heard of the Unwanted?"

"I'm not an idiot."

Stone sipped at his beer. It was cool and bitter. He hated the taste. Stone was a wine drinker, nothing better than a Chilean cabernet sauvignon. "I didn't realise that those who entered illegally were left to fend for themselves. I want to go below and see these people, speak with them."

"Why?"

"I came here to explore, and in my current predicament I can't go outside the walls of the city."

Ramirez regarded him for a long moment. "No, Doctor. I can't help you."

"Can't or won't?"

"It's run by gangs down there. Red Aquila has a working relationship with the New Worlders and Peacemakers. We don't get involved in each other's shit."

"This is important."

"Look, Doctor. I've worked for people like you all my adult life. You're used to concessions from rules and laws, protected by money and institutions. But you go down there, you'll die. Those people have run out of options, and they've carved themselves out a corner in Uriah's Hope. They'll protect it no matter what it takes."

"So that's it? Your final word?"

Ramirez sniffed heavily. "I know a guy. But to get him won't be cheap."

"And I suspect an introductory fee is mandatory, paid to you?"

"Of course."

"So this guy? He'll do what I need done?"

"He takes idiots like you to the Undercity, protects them and gets them back to The Hope in one piece."

"When can I meet him?"

"He'll be in touch tomorrow, as long as I get paid. Now finish your drink and leave like nothing happened."

***

Stone's door chime sounded. He woke and brushed off his latest sleep-deprived fantasy of cutting off his hands. They burned constantly. He blew gently at his fingertips. It gave no relief. Stone threw back the covers and crossed to the entrance.

"I'm Jericho Lees." Lees was an unassuming man. Neither particularly tall nor heavy set. A dusting of freckles marked his pale forehead. He wore his mousey hair tied high into a small ponytail. Quick, blue eyes danced over Stone. "Ramirez sent me."

Stone stood back from the door, allowing him entry.

"My fee for three days." He pushed a folded bit of paper into Stone's hands then dropped a long bag on the floor.

Stone unfolded the note. "You better be worth the money. Cash or digital?" Cash was still used in Uriah's Hope. The Esworth pound and pence. Digital transactions were more common, but every establishment would still accept physical currency.

"Cash." Jericho opened up the bag and pulled out a bulletproof vest. "Get dressed and put this on. It'll save your life if we're getting shot at."

"I don't plan on getting shot at."

"You never know."

Stone pulled on a pair of jeans and yesterday's t-shirt. The armour was heavy and cumbersome. He fiddled with the straps, finally managing to buckle it in place.

Jericho chuckled. "Try this on for size, too." He passed Stone a small pistol.

Stone turned the weapon over in his hands. He'd never used a gun before, never had the need. It felt heavy and unfamiliar, just like the body armour.

"You aim and pull the trigger at the thing you want to die." Jericho pointed at a pocket in the front of his body armour. "That's your holster."

"Tell me, have you ever heard of The Pilgrim of Hate?" Stone clumsily inserted the pistol into the holster then pulled on a coat.

Jericho grabbed an apple from the bowl on Stone's table, and sniffed before returning it. "I've heard of him, yeah."

"Him? I thought they were a gang?"

"He's some kind of preacher with a following. Maybe a hundred people turn up to hear him speak down in the Undercity."

"Speak about what?"

Jericho shrugged.

"I'd like to meet him."

"Difficult. Not impossible. There's no schedule to help us find him. He appears and people congregate through fast word of mouth."

Stone pulled on his gloves. "What else should I bring?"

"Money. A thousand should be enough. I've got food and canteens of water. Safe drinking water is an issue down there. Some of the supply is tainted. Other than that, nothing. You ready to go?"

The unassuming mercenary did not instantly fill Stone with confidence, but he knew men of violence came in all shapes and sizes. He opened his safe and counted out the mercenary's fee.

"Your money. Half now, half when I return. Fair?" He handed half the fee to Jericho and returned the remainder to the safe.

Jericho nodded and secured the wad of cash in the confines of his long coat. He bent down and pulled one final item from his bag. It was a long-barrelled weapon, designed for use with one hand. He clicked a switch on the side of the weapon. It hummed to life throwing out a red light. Direct energy weapons were expensive and deadly. Even Stone knew that.

"You don't mess around, huh?" said Stone.

"No, I don't fuck about." Jericho secured the gun into a holster on his left side beneath his coat.

Stone caught sight of a long knife on Jericho's belt and another holster strapped to his chest above it.

"I can usually tell why people want to get to the Undercity. Whores. Drugs. Murder. But you, I can't place." Jericho halted at the door.

Stone considered telling him to mind his own business, after all, this gun for hire was nothing but a tool. But something in him made him speak, as if providing a reason would make more sense to himself. "I'll indulge you, Jericho. Do I call you Jericho?"

"You do."

"I'm interested in the people."

"The people?"

"I understand it's like another world down there, and recently I made a discovery here, out of the city. Something buried under the ground, and it cost many lives. I can't explain it, but I have a feeling I might find something down there to help make sense of it all."

Jericho seemed to consider this for a second then nodded. "I don't judge. Just like to know what kind of shit I'm getting myself into."

***

Captain Olivia Scott, Eris, Esworth Orbit.

Captain Scott sat before her computer in her dark stateroom. She had stripped off her uniform, untied her hair and slipped into a nightgown. The computer was the only source of light, and over and over she switched from studying the movement of the creatures on Esworth to watching the footage of the last encounter. No matter how often she played the footage, her mind analysing every frame, the horror refused to dilate. She blew out a heavy sigh and grabbed a framed photo of her and Hal Hastings taken before they departed for Esworth.

"What would you do if you were here?"

The ghost of Hal Hastings did not answer.

She wiped the glass covering and yawned heavily. "What did you know about this place? Something's not right and I don't know what I should be doing."

A call connected to her computer. She accepted the audio call.

"What is it?"

Holopainen spoke. "Captain, we've got a situation here. It's Remus Station. They're no longer broadcasting status updates. We can't raise them."

"An equipment failure?"

"Before communication ended we received multiple reports of weapon fire on the station."

"Get comms back on. We need to know what's going on there." Scott gathered up her discarded uniform and pulled it on.

"We're trying. And Captain, their last communication was a message, text only. I'm forwarding it to you now."

Scott zipped up her uniform, tied her hair and opened a second window on the screen.

London Bridge is Falling Down,
Falling Down, Falling Down
London Bridge is Falling Down,
My Faire Lady

"Captain?"

"I see it." Scott pulled on her boots. "I'm on my way to the bridge. Keep trying to establish a link with Remus. Send a priority warning to the other ships in the Fleet. Bring the crew to alert."

Scott tripped over the nightgown tangled at her feet. She swore, kicked it off and left.

***

"Report XO?"

Holopainen stood clearing a way for Scott to reach the captain's chair. "Ship and crew are at full readiness, Captain. Remus is changing trajectory. Still no communication."

"Ideas?"

Holopainen scratched his chin, eyes on the viewer. "Everything would suggest that it's a deliberate act."

"If so, who?"

"Islamists?"

"Out here? I don't think so. Besides, none of them would be able to operate Remus."

"Hostages? Maybe they're forcing them at gunpoint?"

"Perhaps," said Scott, leaning down and pulling the tongue of her boot into proper position.

Both Romulus and Remus were permanently aimed at The Gate. Should any unwanted ship come through unscheduled, the mighty rail cannons would deal with the threat. Remus was now positioning away from The Gate, breaking all symmetry between the two combat stations.

"Any signals coming out of Remus?" asked Scott.

"Comms?" Holopainen aimed his question at the bank of communication stations.

"Negative. Remus is dark," came the reply from the duty officer.

"The hangars are open," said Scott, studying Remus magnified. The habitation complexes, which ringed the base of the massive cannons, housed several large hangars with blast doors wide open exposing the compartments to the void. "We need to find out what's happening on that station."

"You thinking of sending marines?"

"The hangars are open. They wouldn't have to breach."

"What if the defensive systems are operational? It's bristling with defensive weapons."

The Romulus-pattern Station was a ship killing cannon first, and defensive installation second. It was designed to work with an attending fleet providing additional protection however formidable the station's defences, with missile pods, point defence turrets and reinforced armour sections on critical systems.

"Get Colonel Hopkins online. I want her predictions for a marine landing on Remus. I also want shipping manifests. I want to know who and what has been transported to Remus over the last two weeks."

Holopainen leaned in close and whispered, "Captain, we may have to fire on Remus to disable their weapon systems if we lose control."

"I know, XO."

"What if it's those things? What if they're on Remus? That's one of our most powerful weapons platforms."

She couldn't believe that events at the Esworth Chamber were resulting in this. No, the answer had to be something more mundane. She hoped for a systems failure but the reports of weapons fire on board and the movement of the station made it more unlikely.

Thrusters fired aboard Remus tilting it slowly, the barrel of the rail cannon turning like the hand in a giant clock, moving toward the planet.

"Link me to Director Garcia. Now."

***

Agustin Garcia, Uriah's Hope, Esworth.

Scott's face dominated the viewer in The Hub. "Director, at present we have lost contact with Remus. It's burning thrusters, altering its trajectory toward Esworth. It is my recommendation that you engage all defensive measures."

"Captain. Is it them? Is it the demons?"

"Unknown at this point. Raise the shield, Director."

"Captain, I know little in the way of military matters, but should Remus fire at my city, will the shield protect us?" Agustin knew enough to know the shield would protect against direct energy weapons, but suspected a kinetic round fired from Remus would annihilate the city, with or without a shield.

"It won't come to that, Director. You have my word."

Agustin nodded. "Keep me informed, Captain. God help us all."

The link ended. Agustin stood and turned to his staff. "Ladies and gentlemen, you've all heard the brief from Captain Scott. Remus is not responding to command. I'm authorising the Hope's shield activation until Fleet has resolved the issue. Make it so."

"Director," complained Stacey Palumbo, chief of the defensive team in The Hub. "We've still not solved the power consumption issues. The shield cannot remain active for longer than twelve hours."

"I am aware of that. Raise the shield. I'll be on my PWD if you need me." Agustin left The Hub and climbed the stairs to the viewing platform.

He stood at the long windows, hands behind his back watching the city. Darkness cloaked the visible buildings. Thick beams of light illuminated the power relay plants above ground. Henrietta Hall always stood out, the jewel in the crown, spiralling arches, appearing like a grand cathedral.

Lightning flared above the walls, bursting into fantastic strobes of blue. The energy shield suddenly materialised, crackling with unseen force, encompassing the entire city. The hairs on Agustin's arms stood on end. Protection like this was usually only available for capital ships. Twelve hours. That's how long Scott had to resolve the situation. After that, the batteries would die and so would the shield.

"Twelve hours," said Agustin, looking up to the distorted sky. Everything beyond the shield now appeared hazy and blue.

What the fuck was going on up there? Demons running around outside the perimeter defences of the city. An orbital cannon, capable of levelling cities, gone rogue.

"Oh, Tanya." He blinked hard.

He needed more coffee.

***

Calis Grundy, Remus Station, Esworth Orbit.

Remus, Romulus' mighty twin, had gone mad. Calis Grundy wasn't exactly sure when things went from bad to worse, but it happened within hours of his decision to get off Remus Station. He had been aboard for months, working in the dark sections, crawling into vents and tubes fixing electrical faults. He was a large man and regretted ignoring his burgeoning size, for the workspaces were not generous. But he was due to rotate back through The Gate on the next opening. That now felt like an impossibility.

At first he'd thought the disturbances were riots. He heard the din of the crowds from deep in his maintenance sections and investigated stepping foot into the public sections. Crew and staff took to the corridors and retail sector. Commander Bei ordered the garrison out to halt the disturbances. But things worsened. They fired on the protestors and caused panic. Grundy then decided to get back to his quarters, and pack and leave when he could.

Grundy now sat in his quarters, the door barricaded. He'd disabled the lock mechanism so that only he could open it. He could hear people wailing, their cries punctuated by occasional gunfire. The comms terminal in his room was dark. Grundy stabbed a finger at the screen, but nothing reacted. He didn't expect any. Communications had failed for some time now. His mind carried to the possibility of being trapped for days. He looked at the paltry collection of ration bars piled on his bed. If he was frugal, very frugal, he could make them last for three days.

More gunfire came, much closer than before. Angry voices, distorted by the wall separating his quarters from the corridor. Gunfire, blasting directly outside his apartment. Grundy threw himself to the floor, hands over his ears. The sounds died down, the voices ended and Grundy pushed himself from the floor.

The room smelled heavily of sweat and oil. He thought he was used to it, but at that moment his nostrils caught rancid air. His quarters had a small arrow-slit window looking out to Esworth. He peered out. Esworth appeared larger than usual. Had Remus Station moved? The artificial gravity systems on Remus ensured occupants would not detect movement of the station. But if the cannon was to fire, it would be like being stuck in the middle of a sudden and violent earthquake.

Far beyond the station sat the Terran Cooperative Fleet. Lights blinked from the collection of ships. They were drawn up, close in an unfamiliar formation. Was that in response to whatever was happening on Remus? He scratched at his itchy chin. Flakes of skin flicked away. Would Fleet destroy the station if they deemed it a danger? Run, warned a voice in his head. Get off Remus!

Grundy grabbed an industrial wrench from beneath his bed. He weighed it in his hands and gave it a test swing. It would do enough damage if required. He stuffed the ration bars into his pockets, grabbed his maintenance keys and pulled the screwdriver out of the door's mechanism.

The corridor was a scene of anarchy. The dead lay in piles, three or four high, killed and left to lie where they fell. The sounds of violence echoed some distance away. Grundy gave one final look back to his room then ran.

Remus Station was a warren of corridors, levels and sections, and there was only two ways to get off Remus that Grundy could think of. One was to hijack a shuttle or lander from the hangars. The other was to enter an escape pod and eject. He knew the way to both.

Grundy turned the corner. A member of the station garrison was slumped against the wall, a knife protruding from his side, his helmet in his lap.

"You got the same idea as me." The fallen man threw his helmet to the ground. "I was trying to get to the escape pods, too."

Grundy knelt on the floor and studied the man's wound. The knife was deep to the handle.

"I hate to be the one to tell ya, buddy, but they won't let you off the station. They've cut the power to the launch mechanism. None of the pods will launch."

"What's happening?"

He winced and wiped a trail of blood that spilled from his mouth. "Do I look like someone who knows what's going on?"

"I'm guessing you know more than me."

He breathed heavily. "The medical centre reported an outbreak of people suffering from headaches and hallucinations. Next thing we know, Commander Bei was ordering us out. It's like a madness. People we know, screaming this and that. Purpose. Purpose is a word they kept saying."

"Does Fleet know?"

"I don't think so."

"Can you move? I'm headed for the hangar."

"No."

"Try." Grundy stood and offered an arm.

"You need to go. They're coming. Go. Go! Now!" His head lowered.

Grundy charged down the corridor. He needed to ascend two levels to get to the right floor, then a five-minute run to the hangar. One of the crew, stripped to the waist, bleeding from several wounds to his torso, ran toward Grundy.

"The Pilgrim has come. The Purpose. I am filled with Purpose."

He heaved the wrench up, holding it like a baseball bat and swung, aiming for a homerun. The impact shot a tremor up his arm. The crewman left his feet, landing hard on his back. He clutched his chest and whimpered. Grundy raised his weapon high, poised to strike again, but the thought of killing someone was repulsive. Grundy wasn't a killer. He just wanted off this godforsaken station. The pathetic figure at his feet posed no threat. He moved past him, dashing to the access point.

He slotted his key into the lock and opened the door to the maintenance room. The shaft upward was tight for him. He needed two hands to climb the ladder, so dropped the wrench, cursing the need to do so. He climbed, pulling himself up rung by rung. Dim lights were mounted in the wall behind the ladder every ten feet. His grunts echoed in the confined space. He climbed two levels and stepped off into the maintenance shaft to catch his breath. His lungs laboured and he promised himself a strict regime of exercise and healthy eating if he was to get off Remus and survive.

He crawled, dodging pipes and levers and vent markers, and pulled with his elbows until finding the exit hatch. He slipped down the ladder and continued along a corridor. Every step cracked underfoot. He passed rooms, moving like a spy in a movie. Many doors were closed, but those open revealed empty chambers. The sounds of violence were far off, perhaps a level below, but engines revved ahead. He moved faster and faster.

The hangar usually stored Remus Station's complement of shuttles and cargo landers, large craft used to transport freight from the surface to the station. Only one shuttle remained and one lander. The shuttle was prepping for launch, engines hot and the rear ramp down. A collection of people made their way on board. Three of the garrison kept a small group of twenty away from the craft. They were desperate, begging and crying to be let aboard but the soldiers held them at bay with weapons raised.

Grundy ran from his cover. "What are they doing?"

"Bastards are leaving us behind," shouted one man.

"Let us come through, Commander Bei," screamed a woman in medical scrubs. "You're supposed to protect us."

Commander Bei? Grundy could not see Bei amongst those boarding the shuttle.

"Hey," Grundy yelled, moving to one of the armed garrison soldiers. "Get Commander Bei back here!"

"Step back, shit face!" The barrel of the rifle was pushed forward inches from Grundy's face.

"We all need to get off here," protested Grundy, hands raised.

"This shuttle's for staff and garrison only. Step back! I won't ask again."

"We're being left here to die?"

"Shuttles will return for the rest of you."

"Let's go!" yelled another soldier.

The rear ramp began to lift.

The crowd surged forward, Grundy too, enveloping the three soldiers before any shots were fired. The soldiers tried to run but couldn't break free of the crowd's collective grasp.

"I'm sorry," begged one of the soldiers. "I was just following orders." His helmet was ripped off and someone struck him hard in the face. Another soldier was lying on the floor, a woman straddling his chest, pushing a knife deep into his neck.

Grundy snatched a rifle from an unconscious soldier. The shuttle's hatch closed, the engines revved and the craft lifted. A wave of heat pushed him back. Grundy aimed the rifle at the shuttle and fired. What could small arms do to a shuttle? Nothing. He lowered the weapon and the shuttle left the hangar.

The crowd wailed. Grundy shouted over them, asking for quiet but was ignored. He raised the rifle and fired one shot into the ceiling. The gathering ducked for cover and fell silent.

"I'm Calis Grundy," he said. "I'm getting off Remus Station."

"How?" asked one now wearing the helmet of a garrison soldier. "They've taken the shuttle. The escape pods are deactivated. We're stuck here and there's still the garrison troops going round shooting folk."

"The lander," replied Grundy, pointing over to the ship. The large craft would make a sorry lifeboat but it might just work.

"It's for hauling supplies and equipment. The cargo sections have no atmosphere and we wouldn't all fit into the crew compartment."

"Yes we would. Just. We don't need to fly it to Esworth or one of the ships. We just need to get beyond Remus Station and use the comms to link in with Fleet. They'll come to our rescue. Can anyone fly this thing?"

A woman dressed in torn overalls raised her hand. "I think I could."

"Pilot?"

"My husband was. I think I can do enough to get us out of the hangar."

"What about the others? There's still good people on this station," the nurse asked Grundy.

He considered this a moment. "There's nothing we can do for them. We've got a chance to get off Remus. Us, here and now. Nobody else." He didn't like it. That's just how it had to be.

***

Captain Scott, Eris, Esworth Orbit.

"So, you're advising me there's been no arrival or departures from Remus for five days?" Captain Scott asked her XO.

Holopainen scanned the screen. "It would appear so. And I agree, it's unusual. It seems Commander Bei suspended all arrivals and departures five days ago, but didn't mention it in any report. And the status updates didn't hint at anything wrong."

"Captain, a shuttle has departed Remus." Lieutenant Rowland, the officer of the watch, cast the image to the bridge's main viewer. "Commander Bei is aboard the shuttle and seeking priority clearance to dock on Eris," she added with incredulousness.

"Patch him through to me. Now," ordered Scott.

"Remus weapons lock activated." The bridge's weapons officer was a petite thing with a quivering voice. "Remus is targeting Bei's shuttle."

"What the hell is happening?" said Scott.

Remus' turrets opened up on the shuttle. Bright streaks of light struck the small craft, ripping it apart. There was a moment of collective silence in the bridge. Ensign Kay turned from her console and looked back to Scott.

"The shuttle has been obliterated," advised the assistant weapons officer, his tone calm.

"Battle stations," ordered Scott.

Noise returned to the bridge.

"Shields up," she added. "Bring all weapons online. XO, I want a battle readiness report from Fleet."

Holopainen tapped at his tablet.

"Who is in control of Remus?" asked Scott, not expecting an answer.

"Captain, another ship has launched from Remus," said Holopainen.

"Identify the craft."

"It's adrift. Audio signal coming in."

"Loudspeaker."

"This is to the Terran Cooperative Fleet. We're survivors from Remus Station." The audio quality was poor. "We've killed our engines and are drifting. Request immediate assistance."

"Where's Commander Bei?" said Scott.

Static returned from the speaker. Silence. More static. Silence, and then, "He was on the other shuttle. It's been fired upon. We suspect no survivors. Please, the life support on this tub wasn't designed for twenty, and I don't know how much longer we'll last."

"This is Captain Scott of the Esworth Defence Fleet. Who am I speaking to?"

"Calis Grundy, Captain. I work maintenance on Remus."

"What happened on Remus?" Scott cut her microphone and spoke to Holopainen. "Check his credentials."

The XO nodded. Scott activated her microphone again.

"I don't know what to tell you, Captain. The people weren't themselves. Some kind of madness took hold. Five days of rioting and murder. Commander Bei locked down the station. He didn't inform you?"

"Grundy checks out, Captain," informed Holopainen.

"Five days?" Scott questioned Grundy.

"Five days, Captain. I'll be happy to chat more but you're going to have to come get us."

"Stand by, Mr Grundy. We'll get to you ASAP."

Scott cut the communication. "Five days and not one attempt of communication from Bei?"

"None, Captain," said Holopainen.

Scott thought for a long time. What was happening out there? Who was the enemy? What would Hal do? What should she do? Options? Risks?

Holopainen spoke low. "Captain, may I suggest destroyers Renown and Hermes form a defensive screen between Remus and the lander. Destroyer Furious can do the intercept."

She nodded. "Make it happen, XO. I want those people brought to safety."

"Yes, Captain."

The main viewer showed the drifting lander. Scott leaned back into her chair, pursed her lips and chastised herself for her hesitation. Holopainen's suggestion was the obvious resolution. Those people were depending on her. Their lives were in her hands.

"Fleet formation, Captain?" asked Holopainen.

"Yes," she said, pulling her thoughts from her self-absorbing moment. Scott gave orders to reorganise Fleet, bring the formation into a tighter grouping to respond to the departure of the three destroyers. Erebus would be the centre, Eris and Colossus flanking, and the rest of the destroyers would provide a screening force ahead.

"Renown is not moving, Captain," warned Holopainen.

"Get me Captain Quinn of Renown."

The screen showed Hermes and Furious responding to orders. Renown remained in Fleet formation.

"They're ignoring our communication, Captain."

"Try again," ordered Scott.

Hermes and Furious continued moving away.

"Nothing, Captain."

"Damn! Send Lanzhou in Renown's stead. But raise Captain Quinn. Goddamn her."

The battleship Erebus, destroyers Renown, Warspite and Cassiopeia moved away from the main body of The Fleet, creating a wedge formation. Erebus in the centre, Renown before her, and Warspite and Cassiopeia on either flank. The small formation powered their engines and pulled away.

"Incoming transmission from Erebus, Captain," informed an officer.

"Goodsir," hissed Scott. "Allow."

Goodsir appeared on the main screen. He looked immaculate in his uniform, groomed to perfection as a Captain of the Terran Cooperative Fleet should. He stood from his command chair, and straightened his uniform. His face was set in stone, grim but determined.

"Captain Scott and all the sailors of the Esworth Defence Fleet—"

"Your intentions?" interrupted Scott.

"I intend to bombard the Esworth Chamber, destroying the threat to our planet."

"You will not!" ordered Scott.

"Be assured, Captain, when the current crisis has been dealt with we will submit ourselves to a full review."

"Commander Goodsir, I order you to—"

"We will be found to have acted in the best interests of the people of Uriah's Hope and the Terran Cooperative. Do not send forces to stop us, Captain Scott. I will brook no interference. Erebus out."

The screen returned to depicting Remus Station, still tilting, thrusters burning. Tension in Scott's neck and forehead ached. She grabbed her console and tapped in the codes required to neutralise Renown and the other defiant ships. *'Failed'* flashed across the screen. Scott tried again. *'Failed'*.

"The command override isn't working."

"Goodsir must have found a way to block it," said Holopainen.

Scott called up Colonel Hopkins in Marine Command and Control. "Colonel, we have an issue. Contact the marines on Erebus, Renown, Warspite and Cassiopeia immediately and have them take the senior officers into custody."

"Captain?"

"For dereliction of duty and disobeying orders. Now!"

"Are we permitted to open fire, Captain?"

"Colonel, you're authorised to take control of those ships using whatever force you deem necessary. I want those ships brought back in line."

"Yes, Captain." Hopkins vanished from the screen.

The coolness of a gun barrel pressed against Scott's head. Holopainen leapt from his seat. Scott glanced sideways. It was the weapons officer. Her hand shook.

"Give me that weapon, Ensign Lysate, and return to your post," said Scott, slow and calm.

"I can't do that, Captain." Lysate's voice trembled. "Please step away from the bridge until Captain Goodsir has completed his mission. You won't be harmed."

"That is your Captain," spat Holopainen. "Don't be a goddamned fool."

The assistant weapons officer pushed back from the consoles. He stood, his movements lazy. He pulled a weapon up and aimed it at Holopainen. "Commander, please step away from Captain Scott."

Unlike Lysate, Ensign Kay looked resolved, almost taking pleasure in the situation. "I won't ask a second time."

Nobody moved.

"I know what you're thinking," said Scott. "Really, I do. I get it. You're scared. Worried that what we face down there could be the start of something more. Captain Goodsir is well respected. He inspires loyalty and he's proposed a bold plan to tackle the threat. But that is not how we do things in Fleet."

"It's not up for discussion, Captain," said Ensign Kay.

"You are violating the chain of command."

Kay waved his gun. "You were never meant to take control of Fleet. Step toward the lift, please. Both of you."

The lift doors opened. A squad of armed marines emptied out into the bridge, rifles aimed at Kay and Lysate.

"Your mutiny is over," said Scott. "Stand down. Now!"

Ensign Kay's aim moved from Holopainen to the marines. The marines opened fire. Kay's body flinched violently at every bullet then ragdolled over the console before sliding to the floor.

Scott raised her hand and shouted, "Hold your fire."

Ensign Lysate dropped her firearm and raised her hands in the air. She was arrested.

Scott ran to Kay's side.

"You know you're about to die, don't you?" Kay whispered.

"I think it's you that's about to die. Shame. I'd like to see you hang."

Kay gurgled, blinked twice and stopped breathing.

"Captain, Remus Station is powering up to fire!" cried the officer of the watch.

The barrel of the Remus super-weapon glowed on the screen. Stabilising thrusters fired from the rear and flanks, ensuring the recoil be absorbed as best it could.

"Trajectory?"

"It's not firing at Esworth!"

"Orders to Fleet. Break formation. Evade."

The lethal projectile tore from the cannon, travelling twelve-thousand kilometres per second, hurtling at her ships.

CHAPTER 8

Atlas Drinkwater, Erebus, Esworth Orbit.

Atlas trusted Owl and Luna were searching for him. Atlas could be an asshole but doubted either of his team members would believe he'd gone AWOL. His cell provided a view into the security area of the brig. A guard was alone, busy clipping her fingernails. The battleship suddenly groaned. The guard stood. Erebus rocked as the engines came to life pushing the ship into movement.

"Hey! What's going on? Why are we moving?" He thumped at the glass barrier futilely, knowing that the sound would be nothing more than a dull thud outside his cell.

The guard moved from her seat fast, but suddenly stopped and raised her hands. Owl and Luna burst into the security area, long rifles aimed at the guard. Owl looked furious. She wore a tank-top, combat trousers, and looked ready to kill. Luna laughed, pointed first at the guard and then the cell.

Owl removed the guard's pistol from her holster and snatched the lanyard from her neck. She threw it to Luna.

The cell door opened.

"Atlas!" Luna bowed gallantly, weapon in one hand and keycard in the other. "We humbly request the honour of your company."

"Took your time." Atlas ducked through the doorway of the cell. "But I didn't expect a jailbreak."

"We have to move, Atlas." Owl homed the site of her weapon at the guard.

She had never looked more dangerous or attractive to Atlas.

"You planning to push the panic button once we're gone?" Owl asked.

"You fuckin' Leviathan idiots are as dumb as the marines if you think you'll get away with this."

Owl nodded. "Everyone has a right to an opinion."

Owl threw a fast kick at the guard's chest. The guard doubled over and Owl kicked out again. The guard's nose split. She moaned and held her face.

"Sharp." Luna dragged the guard into the cell and locked the door.

"What happened to you, dude?" Luna asked Atlas.

Owl gave Atlas the guard's pistol. "You poked your nose where it wasn't wanted, right?"

"What's been happening since they put me in here?"

"A shit storm," said Owl. "Erebus and three destroyers have broken off from Fleet. Goodsir plans to bombard the planet to destroy the Esworth Chamber."

"It's not a bad idea," said Luna, following Atlas and Owl from the security area.

"They're sitting on a huge heat source. See any problem with that, idiot?"

Alarms blared, signalling Erebus was now at battle stations.

"What's the rest of the Fleet doing?" asked Atlas.

"Holding position, as far as I can tell," said Owl. "What's our play?"

"We could intervene and take back control of the ship," said Luna. "Not many people are going to mess with us if we march in there in our Leviathans."

Owl rolled her eyes. "You reckon the Leviathan suits can just stroll down narrow corridors?"

"Probably not."

"This isn't our problem to fix," said Atlas. "Let's get to our suits then to a shuttle and make for one of the battlecruisers."

The trio rounded a corner and met a group of marines. They all raised their weapons.

"Drop your weapons and identify yourselves!" the sergeant yelled over the alarms.

Atlas raised his hands and nodded to Luna and Owl. They all placed their weapons on the ground.

"I'm Atlas Drinkwater, Leviathan operator."

The sergeant pulled off his helmet and wiped down his brow. "Should have known from the size of the three of you."

"What's happening here, Sailor?" asked Atlas.

"Goodsir isn't following orders. We've orders to seize control of the ship. You've caught us trying to set up choke points on the approach to the bridge."

"We can help," offered Owl.

"No," ordered the sergeant. He gestured to his team, and the Leviathan operators' weapons were collected from the floor. "Sorry, not leaving these with you."

As the marines headed away, Luna said, "So what do we do now?"

"Fuck. Let's go," said Atlas.

They continued further, moving deeper into the ship. Three sailors lay dead beside a marine, gunshot wounds to their torsos.

Erebus rocked violently, throwing the three Leviathan operators upwards, slamming them against the ceiling. A booming explosion followed, deafening, like the sound of a world ending. Atlas fell back to the deck. The air burst from his chest and he clutched his ribs. The ship trembled and a new alarm replaced the battle alarms. Atlas pulled himself up, tasting blood in his mouth. He spat.

Owl rubbed her forehead. "Damn, my head is rattling. Everyone okay? Luna!"

Luna lay on his front, unmoving. Owl rolled him onto his back pressing two fingers to his neck. "He's out cold."

Secondary explosions ripped through the ship some way off, but enough to rock them violently again.

"We need to get to the suits, Owl."

"Fleet firing on us?"

"Maybe. Lead the way, I'll take Luna."

Atlas heaved Luna onto his shoulder. He managed to keep up with Owl as they moved toward the Leviathan section of the ship. Explosions and tremors followed them as they ran. The corridor's light flashed from life to death, plunging them into darkness. Emergency red lighting flickered to life on the wall panels. The Leviathan bay doors were jammed closed.

Atlas laid Luna down against the wall and scanned his card, but the reader didn't respond. "Power failure."

"Shit. How long before we lose life support, too?" asked Owl.

Luna moaned and mumbled.

"I've always wanted to do this." Owl slapped Luna across the face. And then did it again.

"Alright," said Luna, groggily. "Enough. I'm awake."

"Help me with the door, Owl."

Owl pulled out a flashlight and tinkered with the cover to a small circuitry hatch to the left of the door. "There has to be a door release for when the power fails." The cover sprung open and she pushed at buttons.

The door jerked open, not fully, but enough for one person at a time to move through. Owl went first, easily sliding between the door. It wasn't so easy for the two men.

"Diet after this," Owl said after they successfully manoeuvred through, then pointed her flashlight at the suits. "You all right to do this, Luna?"

"Are you kidding me?"

"We're linking in hot," she warned. "We got power, Atlas?"

"Different source in here." Atlas crossed to the control panels and clicked all the switches he could find until the control lit. He hit the activation keypad. The Leviathans woke, power humming through them. The armour opened at the rear, ready to accept their operators. They climbed in.

The internals of the suit tightened around Atlas' body, providing a powerful exoskeletal carapace. The armour closed and the interface hot link commenced. Pain ripped through Atlas' head. He let out a yelp. Through the hurt, he could feel the system come alive. Visuals first, then the HUD appeared, indicating the Leviathan was operating at maximum capacity. Atlas saw the world from the Leviathan's optics.

"Owl? Luna? All good?"

"Come on, meds!" said Luna.

"All good here," said Owl.

"That's it. I'm good to go," said Luna.

The ship staggered violently. Two empty suits broke free of their clamps and chains and slid across the deck. Atlas' sensors indicated life support was failing.

"I'm patched into the ship's comms," said Owl. "They're abandoning ship."

Atlas disengaged the clamps.

"Remus has fired twice at Erebus."

"We can't make it to the shuttle," said Atlas. "We'll use the drop pod."

"There's nobody here to guide us down," said Luna. "We'll smash into Esworth like a bug on a windshield."

"We're not going down to Esworth. We just need to get off Erebus."

Luna and Owl disengaged their clamps and followed Atlas. The ship tilted and groaned. Explosions boomed near the bay.

Atlas remotely activated the winch. The crane arm swung around securing Luna first, lifting him from the deck into the drop pod. Owl next.

"Owl, get control of the drop pod," ordered Atlas.

"I'm trying."

The winch lifted Atlas next. He swore every few seconds, expecting the ship to break apart or explode when they were so close to escape. The winch lifted him down and into position. A warning symbol flared on his HUD, warning of a fire in the Leviathan bay.

The drop pod closed around them. The central column of the drop pod interior had a screen for each operator to see vital information. Speed. Location. Holographic information of exterior objects and ships. Atlas shifted the view on his screen to the external sensors.

"Come on, Owl! The fucking ship is breaking up," said Luna.

"Got it! Firing in five, four, three, two, one."

The drop pod fired from the launcher. The jolt sent Atlas back in his brace.

"I'm putting enough distance between us and Erebus," said Owl.

"Did anyone else get off?" asked Luna.

"I'm a little busy now," shot back Owl. "Okay, I'm slowing our burn."

The craft slowed, pushing back against the irresistible force.

The sensors showed a confusing picture. The Fleet was scattered before Remus. Three destroyers were positioned in close proximity to the station. Erebus and three attending destroyers had moved some way off. Erebus lurched out of the small formation.

"The fuel reserves on the pod aren't substantial, Atlas. It's not designed for cruising."

"Aim us toward Eris."

The drop pod's thrusters fired, pushing it in a wide angle around Erebus.

***

Agustin Garcia, Uriah's Hope, Esworth.

The chicken and noodle dish was saturated in a greasy additive. Agustin twirled his fork, captured a small amount of noodles and spooned them into his mouth. He chewed and the macerated food sat high on his tongue as if waiting. Waiting for what? He swallowed then grabbed a piece of chicken. He chewed and swallowed again without pleasure.

Agustin looked to his PWD lying on his bed. For a week he had willed the PWD to bleep with news of Tanya. A constant ache bled into his every pore, churned and whizzed and spun and poked. He washed down the food with the last of his beer.

The PWD beeped and for a moment he believed the sound to be a figment created from his own longing. It beeped again.

A video message from Isambard Stone. The man responsible for his pain. The man responsible for Tanya's ... death.

Agustin cast it to the main screen. Stone was seated in his apartment. A thin smile appeared, unfriendly, perhaps a nervous greeting. What the hell did Tanya see in this man, this periphery archaeologist? He wasn't particularly handsome.

"Hello, old friend. Well, I suppose we were never friends, were we? Anyway, with recent events I've been feeling a little obsolete. I've been cooped up here wondering what I can do to help. And, I have a plan. I have become aware of the Unwanted, desperate people existing on the fringes of the law, unregistered and somehow surviving. There's not too much that happens here you don't know about, so I can only guess their plight is known to you. And it goes without saying you'd be aware Red Aquila is somewhat responsible for their existence, receiving fees in return for their transport here. I had a chance to talk to a woman who sheltered two Unwanted children. I'm no humanitarian, Agustin, but what's happening down there is beyond the pale."

"You hypocritical prick!" Agustin grabbed another beer.

"Did you know the kids are trafficked? Young kids. Boys and girls, Agustin. We have to do something about it." Stone sniffed heavily and looked high. His jaw tightened. "But I don't know if it's real or imaginary. Since the Esworth Chamber I've felt different, and now I feel a pull, some connection between the chamber and the Undercity."

"What are you up to, Stone?"

"I've become aware of someone calling himself The Pilgrim of Hate, a preacher of sorts. We need to find him, Agustin, if nothing else but to get some answers about Tanya. I've hired a fellow by the name of Jericho Lees and we'll be leaving soon, so I'll be gone by the time you receive this message. But from what I understand so far, he won't be enough. Agustin, I'm begging you. Send people after me. I'll leave a trail as best I can."

The message ended with a frozen image of Isambard Stone leaning toward the camera. In that halted moment he looked vulnerable, none of his usual bluster or innate confidence.

***

"You should've kept him under a tighter leash, Agustin." Rebecca Reid wasn't exactly shouting, but then the Chief Constable of the Uriah's Hope Municipal Police didn't have to in order to intimidate. She sat behind her office desk and glared.

"He's not a dog, Rebecca. I can't just chain him up and hope he'll stay put."

"You realise he's signed his own death warrant going down there? It's not like here, Agustin. Not one bit. The New Worlders and the Peacemakers will swallow him up and he'll just be another one of humanity's lost souls. And for what? Because of a feeling?" She adjusted her uniform collar. "I've little affection for the man. Tell me why I should risk more of my officers rescuing a fool from a situation he created on his own."

"I wouldn't be coming to you to ask this favour if there was no benefit to us."

"I'm waiting, Agustin, and I'm impatient."

"He was right about the Esworth Chamber. He seems to have some unnatural ability connecting him to whatever is happening here."

"And I was right about not winning the Terran Lottery. Doesn't mean I'm a clairvoyant."

"I think we need him. I think we need to follow him, see what he digs up."

She raised a finger. "You don't know what it's like with the Unwanted. The gangs are entrenched in a warren of tunnels that are forever changing down there. We've been down there, tried to map out the place but our people disappear. We tried to infiltrate the gangs, and again our operatives disappeared."

"So, you're refusing me?"

"If he's got himself a gun for hire, someone that knows how the world is down there, then that's the best protection he could hope for."

"It might be a chance to save hundreds, perhaps thousands of children forced into slavery."

Reid laughed sarcastically. "Good try. But if you want to help those kids, change the policy for illegals. The Unwanted are forced into the arms of the gangs because Uriah's Hope won't help them."

"I don't set the policy for residency," Agustin said with too much volume. "The Cooperative set the laws."

"Then speak to them," Reid replied with just as mush frustration.

Agustin sighed heavily. He trusted it sufficed as an apology. With a quieter tone he said, "So what do you know of The Pilgrim of Hate?"

Reid shook her head. "I've not heard the name, but I'll put out some feelers."

Agustin stood and tapped her desk. "There's no way for me to help him, is there?"

"I'm sorry I couldn't be of more assistance to you, Director."

* * *

Remus' first shot tore the stern of Erebus, punching through the shield and armour of the great ship. Casualty reports were received. Hundreds were dead. Erebus listed, unable to manoeuvre away from the continued firing. Six explosions ripped through the hull. The distant bursts of flame were quickly choked by exposure to space.

"Captain, we need to give orders to Fleet," warned Holopainen.

"Orders to Fleet," Scott repeated.

Comms patched her to all ships.

"Remus has opened fire on Terran Cooperative Fleet. I want that rail cannon put out of commission. Break formation and fire at will. Disable, do not destroy. I repeat, disable, do not destroy."

Remus fired again. The round tore through the engines of Erebus, sheering the ship in half and continued striking Cassiopeia. Erebus died in a brilliant, brief fire. Cassiopeia's hull blew outward, fragmenting the superstructure into thousands of pieces.

"Pods are launching from Erebus, Captain," said Holopainen. "Sixteen of them."

"We've got a job to do," said Scott, refocusing the bridge crew. "Fire when ready, XO."

Eris rounded on Remus Station. Firing solutions were calculated and Holopainen gave the order to fire. The Fleet accelerated past the mighty station, taking defensive fire but unleashing thunderous ordinance against the orbital guardian. Direct energy batteries opened fire, aiming for the cannon. The destroyers flew in waves, launching ballistic broadsides from their array of batteries. Space was filled with the dazzling brilliance of the lance batteries. Everything felt wrong. They were firing on a Terran Cooperative installation.

Eris sustained a pounding of defensive fire, the impacts causing the ship to shudder.

Scott gripped her chair. "Status reports," she ordered to all the ships.

Captain Keeler of the destroyer Furious appeared on her screen. "We've secured the survivors from Remus and are moving back from the station. Furious has sustained minor damage, no fatalities. Keeler out."

Colonel Hopkins was next to appear on the console. "Captain, my marines have taken control of Warspite. Senior officers in custody. They're manoeuvring the ship out of the area and will power down awaiting further orders."

"And Renown?" said Scott.

"We've lost contact. It's suspected the marines were unable to take control of the ship. I'll keep you updated." Hopkins saluted and the popup disappeared.

"Renown is continuing to burn at full speed away from Fleet, Captain. She's broken orbit and is heading in system," said the officer of the watch.

Renown disappeared from Scott's holographic display.

"Where's Paris Quinn gone?" she asked.

"Turned off the transponder and powered down non-essential systems," replied Holopainen. "She can now run silent. Difficult to locate her."

"Status of Remus?"

"Canon buckled, Captain," said the officer of the watch. "Disabled."

Scott touched her Fleet communication key. "Order to Fleet. Hold fire on Remus and return to formation."

Eris slowed, taking central position of the formation. Colossus moved adjacent, and destroyers took up position as a screen.

Scott turned to comms. "Raise Remus."

"Nothing, Captain."

"Captain? I'm no longer reading an energy signature from Remus Station," said the officer of the watch. "It's as if when we disengaged, the power went off like a switch."

"Show me on the screen," ordered Scott.

Remus appeared and the image magnified. Remus was dark, the lights which constantly shined along the length of the rail cannon and habitation sections were out. It was as if all life had been sucked from the structure.

"Life support?"

"None, Captain. Remus has no active systems. It's dead."

"Did we do that?" asked Scott.

Holopainen shook his head. "No. We disabled the rail cannon but didn't damage any of the critical systems."

"Someone turned off all the systems? But that would be suicide. Or did we hit an energy node that knocked the power out?"

"Couldn't have," explained Holopainen. "Romulus-pattern stations are designed to function even after heavy bombardment. Perhaps Mr Grundy can provide some answers. He and his companions are now the only survivors."

"XO, have Mr Grundy transferred to Eris as soon as possible."

Scott leaned back into her chair. The XO was busy with communications. The officer of the watch tapped away, gathering updates of damage reports. Nothing like this had happened in the history of Fleet. Scott anticipated Goodsir would move against her authority, perhaps worm his way into the confidence of key members of Fleet until gaining enough support to challenge her authority. But not like this. And now Paris Quinn and Renown. The destroyer couldn't operate away from the base of operations around Esworth for more than a few months. Energy reserves and supplies would deplete and sooner or later Captain Quinn would bolt from the hole she hid in. If she was found alive she would be hung as a traitor. If someone had asked Captain Scott yesterday if she trusted her crew she'd have replied with a sincere positive. Well, that trust almost cost her very life.

When she eventually retired to her state room she'd make sure to wear her side-arm. Trust nowadays could get her killed.

***

Marines escorted Calis Grundy to Olivia Scott's office.

"Mr Grundy, I'm Captain Olivia Scott of the Eris. Thank you for your time."

Grundy was a large man, the type that appeared to have been born for skilled labour. His shoulders were wide, arms thick. He looked exhausted, eyes dark and heavy.

"That will be all," she said to the marines.

The men saluted and left.

"Won't you take a seat?" Grundy eased his large frame into the seat opposite. "Have you been assessed by our ship's medical team? Offered food and water?"

"I have. Thank you."

"What happened on Remus?"

"Nothing good, Captain. Nothing good. I work in the crawlspaces of the station."

"I know of your skills and position, Mr Grundy."

"Of course you do, Captain," he said apologetically. "It was disturbances. People in the corridors, rioting. That bastard Bei and his staff took the last shuttle and left us to die."

"What can you tell me about the riots? The people? The actions of Commander Bei?"

Grundy rubbed his chin, ruffling his beard. "It was like the people were driven mad. Not acting like themselves. Prone to bursts of violence."

"Details, Mr Grundy. Think."

"Sure, Captain. I found one of Bei's garrison. He'd been stabbed and was in a real bad way, and he said he'd heard something about Purpose before he died. And that's what I heard some of the rioters screaming. The Purpose or a purpose. I dunno, Captain. It was like a madness had taken over the place. A bloody contagious one at that. And one of them came at me shouting the same, and about a pilgrim. I had to take him down." Grundy looked suddenly worried. "You have to understand, Captain. It was him or me and I had to get out."

"Commander Bei and his passengers died on that shuttle."

"Wasn't me—"

Scott held up a hand. "Remus opened up on the shuttle. There were no survivors."

Grundy lifted his chin. "Then the bastard got off lightly."

"What else can you tell me?"

Grundy shook his head. "Only that it's made me want to get back to Earth and never leave again. I'm due to rotate at the next opening of The Gate. It's not gonna change anything is it?"

Scott stood. "Of course not. Quarters will be arranged for you on Esworth when we can get you down there."

***

Alone in her office, Scott rolled the words pilgrim and purpose around her mouth, speaking them out loud over and again. Grundy provided little of worth. The riots were unusual, as were Commander Bei's actions. Her first instinct was to allocate blame to another religious group operating on Esworth, but she reasoned that would be almost impossible to establish a group well enough, equip them and exercise an operation to seize control of a powerful installation like Remus.

She felt like a detective, working on an impossible case. It made sense to contact Uriah's Hope and gain their perspective on matters. Scott first called Chief Constable Reid however was told she was unavailable. She next called Director Garcia.

His weary face appeared on the screen at her desk.

"Did I catch you at a bad time, Director?"

"It's all I seem to have at the moment. What can I do for you, Captain?"

Scott made a pyramid with her fingers. "I need to update you on the situation. You're not going to like it."

Agustin nodded along as she spoke, his eyes closed for the most part. She finished with Goodsir's plan.

"What the hell is going on up there?" He leaned closer to his screen.

Scott didn't offer a reply. She assumed one wasn't expected.

"So, we've lost the most powerful ship in Fleet, almost all our Leviathan support, and the orbital defences have been cut by half. And we still don't know what happened aboard Remus?"

"Tell me, Director. Have you had any unusual occurrences in Uriah's Hope?"

"You'll need to be more specific."

"Crowd disturbances? Outbreaks of violence? That kind of thing. One of the survivors talked of a madness taking over the station."

"How can a rabble take over a Romulus-pattern Station?" The director sat back in his seat.

"They were shouting about a purpose. And something about a pilgrim."

The director picked up a mug off screen, sipped heavily and the mug remained at his lips.

"Pilgrim. That means something to you, doesn't it, Director?"

He placed the mug down. "Something from the Undercity. An archaeologist has headed down there to find out more."

"Alone?"

"Close to. He's gone in search of The Pilgrim of Hate, whoever that is."

"Can't be a coincidence."

"Perhaps. I don't suppose you'd consider sending some marines down after him?"

"I'll look into the possibility. What if the intelligence down there knew what Goodsir planned? What if they attacked before Goodsir could?"

"Intelligent life?"

"Yes."

"I've seen the creatures."

Scott blew out a loud breath. "I think you need to tell me more, Director."

***

Beeps ripped Scott from a nightmare. Her breath was fast. She grabbed the pistol from under her pillow and hit the light switch.

"Yes?" she blurted.

"Captain, it's me," replied the XO.

She was naked, sweat sliding down her chest. The nightmare was so real and the whispered words at her ear were still an echo. "I'm coming."

A soft conversation ensued on the other side of the door. Scott grabbed a gown and tied it tightly.

A young marine straightened as the door opened. "Morning, Captain," he said, eyes forward and focused on nothing.

"The marine your idea, XO?"

Holopainen breezed in and the door closed behind him. "I thought it wise, and so did Colonel Hopkins. But it looks like you might not need any help." He nodded to the pistol in her hand.

She put the pistol on her desk and poured herself some water. "What's on your mind, XO?"

"I'm scared, Captain."

She turned and studied his face. It was the look of a man embarrassed to confess a weakness.

"We're all scared."

"We've lost a lot of people and we're no closer to understanding what's happening."

"How are the crew?"

"All talk is of the betrayal."

"Without Goodsir, they won't act again."

"You think that's the end of it?"

Scott emptied her glass. "I'm not sure of anything, and more and more I find myself asking what Hal Hastings would do."

"He always seemed to have an answer. But he's no longer with us, Captain. You're in charge, and I don't think the trouble's ended, not by a long shot."

Holopainen's tone suggested he was reminding Scott of her position. Had he thought she'd forgotten?

"We've got to wipe those things out. And we've got to do it smart," he said.

"No argument from me."

CHAPTER 9

Doctor Isambard Stone, Undercity, Uriah's Hope, Esworth.

Something lay ahead. Jericho held up his hand gesturing for Stone to remain where he was then pulled out his energy weapon. It hummed and glowed red as the power charged. Not brilliant for night fighting, guessed Stone, but then it was not built as a weapon of subtlety.

The object was some fifty feet away. Jericho moved quickly. Before long Jericho whistled, shrill and sudden. Stone guessed that to be a sign all was okay. He stumbled forward, following the dim light from Jericho's gun.

Stone caught up. A stench clung to this part of the tunnel so pungent that Stone held a hand over his mouth and nose. Jericho switched on a flashlight. A female body lay in the halo of light. Pale skin was in the process of blackening. The flesh on her exposed arms and legs appeared tight over her bones, like a victim of famine.

Jericho squatted by the body. "These tunnels are too warm to guess how long she's been dead."

"What do you think happened to her?"

"No recent signs of violence. Hunger? Thirst? One of the two."

"What's she doing here?"

Jericho pointed to the black glyph on her neck. "The symbol of the New Worlders. Learn it well. She is property down here."

"I've seen that mark before, Jericho. On a woman's neck. She was property, too. Doesn't seem right, does it?"

Jericho powered down his weapon and returned it to its holster. He lifted the woman's left hand, studied the palm then the back of the hands and the fingers. "Not a nice way to spend your last hours, lost in the dark, alone, breaking your nails on the rock trying to claw a way out."

"I wonder if she had a name?" asked Stone, suddenly thinking of Tanya.

"Doesn't matter how poor you are here, everyone has a name."

Stone nodded and dumbly followed Jericho, deeper into the Undercity.

***

Agustin Garcia, Uriah's Hope, Esworth.

"I'm telling you this is a bad fucking idea, Agustin." Twomley paced about the office, not settling in one spot. "Even someone as ridiculous as Stone must've known the Undercity is no place to go. And now what? He expects us to send people down to pull him out? Who would we send? Cops won't go. I'll tell you that for nothing."

"I've already asked Chief Constable Reid."

"I bet she said no in a flash. And marines will say the same. And Captain Scott won't be keen to go to his rescue."

"Calm down, Dale," said Agustin. "I just wanted your opinion. And sit down for Chrissake. You're making me dizzy."

Twomley stopped his pacing. "We should've kept him in jail when we had the chance. I can't help but see him as the catalyst for every bad thing happening here. And Tanya would still be here if not for him. You know that, don't you?" He sat on the side of Agustin's desk.

Agustin sighed heavily and ran a hand through his hair. "And yet, he might end up being our best hope to finding some answers."

"Or cause more problems. Just condemn him to his fate. He's more trouble than he's worth. And right now, he's either dead or in a shitload of trouble. Now, can we get on with other business?"

Agustin spread his hands. "Of course. Go on."

Twomley pushed off the table and sat into a chair. "The weather has deteriorated again so we have little satellite cover and the drones are being pulled back. But we know the creatures are still digging or excavating or whatever the hell they're up to. Hundreds of them. We need to think about being honest with the residents of The Hope. Red Aquila will talk sooner or later."

Agustin nodded. He knew that they were barely keeping a lid on everything. Press were already sniffing about and it wouldn't be long before the wrong thing was said in the right ear. "I'll have our people start drafting up a statement. I want it made clear that it's business as usual."

"We need volunteers. Consider that in your statement."

"Why?"

"We apprise The Cooperative Council of events when The Gate opens, ask for additional resources to deal with the issue. It'll take them six months to send anyone. We can't expect to fight with the numbers we have."

"Six months?"

"Could be longer if they can't marshal enough troops and ships."

"I pushed for a garrison of the Cooperative Army to be stationed here."

Twomley nodded. "Yep, and that got us nowhere."

"If the creatures come against the city, Fleet is essentially useless. They can offer limited fire support but the fighting will be done down here. Shit! I have certain emergency powers but never thought I'd actually have to enact them."

"Who'd have thought coming to a new world like Esworth would be anything like this. I'm going back to Earth and never setting foot here again. Even in my most paranoid dreams …"

Agustin stopped listening. When Tanya arrived on Esworth he expected to make Uriah's Hope his home. There was little back on Earth waiting for him. But now, there was little of anything anywhere to pull him one direction or the other.

"Agustin. Agustin? I said, do you think there's the slightest chance we could beat these creatures, these monsters or whatever they are?"

Win? And what would he win? What could such an accomplishment bring to his life? Agustin moved to pour a fresh coffee. "I don't think we have enough to hold them back for six months."

"Pour me one too."

***

Isambard Stone, Undercity, Uriah's Hope, Esworth.

Jericho Lees pushed Stone along another low passageway. Gunfire cracked from behind. Bright, streaking tracer fire shot past. The rounds created little avalanches of the Esworth rock. Jericho thrust Stone to the ground, spun around, his long coat billowing like a cape. He pulled out his weapon, powered it up and fired back down the tunnel. The energy weapon popped with each shot, sending streaks of red fire back at their pursuers.

A man screamed out. "My arm. My fuckin' arm."

Jericho fired three more shots. Stone held his breath.

"I think they're gone."

"You think?"

"Or they're dead." Jericho powered down his weapon and hauled Stone to his feet and turned on his flashlight.

They wandered back until they found a body. Jericho's weapon had severed the right arm from the shoulder. The wound still smoked and the hand of the unattached arm still clutched a handgun. Another shot had speared the man square in the chest, burning a complete hole.

"Peacemakers." Jericho pulled out a knife and slashed the throat.

"Was that really necessary?"

"Half these mongrels are off their tits on drugs. I've seen them get back up too often."

Stone grunted. "His arm's off and there's a bloody great hole in his chest."

Jericho laughed. "It serves as a warning not to fuck with us." He switched the flashlight off and continued down the passageway.

"I can't see a thing," complained Stone.

"I can."

"How?"

"Corneal implants. Gives me a degree of night vision. It makes the headaches worth it for times like these. Just keep moving."

"How well can you see?"

"Three times better than you can right now. Something like that. Keep quiet. We'll be coming up to one of the Unwanted slums soon."

They continued through to a narrower tunnel. Jericho took point and Stone walked behind. The air was fetid. Breathing it in was like swallowing a lungful of glass. A light appeared at the end of the tunnel, dim and flickering.

"What is it?"

"I told you to shut up."

The light grew stronger as they approached.

"We're nearly there."

Some distance on, Jericho placed a hand on Stone's chest. "You keep your eyes low, you don't speak, and you don't draw attention to yourself."

"We're new. Won't that be enough to draw attention?"

"Just do as I say. If anyone speaks to you, don't acknowledge them. If someone asks for help or grabs your hand, don't react. You might see some shocking shit but you have to ignore it. Understand?"

"What are we walking into?"

"A large group. This is their home and they'll protect each other with their lives."

"The one that died, the one without the ..." Stone indicated his arm.

"Probably a New Worlder tunnel rat trying to pick off a stray."

"Sounds like animals in the wild."

"Not much different really."

"How do they survive?"

"There's nothing down here, so they have to chance the tunnels for supplies. Hence the tunnel rats. It's like they're living in the eighteen-hundreds."

"Ah, a student of history?" asked Stone.

"A student of poverty, Doctor. I grew up outside the Terran Cooperative. We didn't have the post-Night tech to make life better. This is life for those outside the Cooperative. This is nothing except a very real reminder of childhood. Come on."

They stepped closer to the light source. The tunnel opened into a vaulted cavern. It looked like a naturally formed fissure in the rock, improved and widened by human hands and crude tools. Holes had been hacked further into the rockface. Sleeping pallets and torn curtains made for makeshift sleeping wells. Oil lamps were bolted to the wall. Candles burned in the cave homes. A sea of tents was erected in the centre of the room, haphazard with no order to their layout. A small fire burned in the middle. The Unwanted sat, speaking softly in small groups. They were a desperate sight. Huddled together, uniformed in their cast-off clothes and abject misery. On noticing the arrival of Jericho and Stone, mothers snatched up children and held them close. Two men pulled out long knives. Jericho moved forward, threw off his hood and withdrew something from his pocket. The men looked to each then back to Jericho then took the offering.

"What did you give them?"

"I bought a thirty minute rest. They know me, so we might get a little longer. Wait here. Don't speak to anyone."

"Where are you going?"

"Get some info about this person you're chasing. I won't be long."

Jericho disappeared through the camp.

Stone hunkered down on his backside next to the cavern wall. He stabbed his fingers into the soil. It felt like soft sand. The Unwanted kept eyes his way. A woman with dreadlocks turned a plump rat on the spit.

"Didn't I tell you to stay the fuck away from us?" came a voice some distance away.

A woman marched towards him. "What are you doing here? How'd you find us?" Salina stood with her coat open, one hand resting on the handle of a knife tucked into her belt. Her neck and jaw were heavily bruised under layers of dirt, her top lip cut and swollen.

Stone remembered Jericho's orders. He didn't answer.

"I asked you a fucking question!"

Stone raised a hand to his mouth to conceal his lips moving. "I'm not here for you, Salina. Honest."

Salina pulled the knife free and pointed it at his neck. "I told you that you couldn't help, and yet here you are."

He dropped his hand and whispered, "We're just passing through."

"We?"

"Yes, we." Jericho appeared behind Salina. "Why don't you run along, Unwanted, before you get hurt?"

Salina turned. Jericho slapped the blade from her hand. It landed at Stone's feet.

"Jericho. Why bring him here?" Salina pointed at Stone. "He's trouble."

"He pays." Jericho put away his blade. "We're passing through. Where are the kids?"

"The New Worlders got them." Salina collected her knife.

"Then they're lost to you. Plenty of other desperate bastards down here that could use your help."

"But what about the kids?" said Stone.

Jericho hauled Stone to his feet. "I told you to shut up, Doctor, so shut up."

A group of Unwanted formed a circle around the two men.

"We're going," said Jericho.

No one moved.

Jericho pushed his coat aside, revealing his weapons. "We've got an understanding and it'd be a shame if that were ruined."

"Let them go," said Salina, not looking back.

"Move," Jericho said to Stone.

Jericho selected one of the many tunnels leading from the chamber as if confident with directions. No one stopped their exit.

"You know her?" Stone ducked beneath a low hanging rock.

"Salina and I have a history."

"Me too."

Jericho laughed. "I bet you do."

"Is there anything we can do for the kids? They made quite a—"

Jericho rounded on Stone, pushed him against the rock face and grabbed him around the neck. "You're not paying me to help any kids."

Stone grabbed hold of Jericho's wrists. He studied the man's face, waiting for a sudden recognition of burning to his skin. But none came. "I just thought …"

"Anyone caught by the New Worlders is as good as dead. Get it?"

"Okay, okay," Stone mumbled.

Jericho released his hold and silently moved on. They had only progressed perhaps five-hundred metres. Jericho stopped, studied a small alcove in the rockface, looked back from where they'd come then announced, "Make yourself comfortable. We're here for two days."

"I'm only paying you for three days."

"Things are more complicated than I thought. I need to contact someone. I'll be gone for a few hours or so. Do not move from here."

"And don't talk to anyone. I get it."

Stone backed into the alcove, settled and listened to the silence.

***

Agustin Garcia, Uriah's Hope, Esworth.

Agustin petitioned Red Aquila, requesting to join an armament run with their patrols. They accepted.

Yuji Sanada watched with some amusement as Agustin sidled into a seat in the Esworth Track.

"It's been too long since I've been outside the walls of the city, so I thought I'd accompany you." Sanada reached for the safety belts, crossed them over Agustin's chest and buckled him in.

The Esworth Track rose and fell like a ship on a wave. His previous experience had been gentle and slow. Nothing like now. It was only the strap that kept him in his seat.

They travelled in silence for the most part. Agustin got the feeling that patrolling outside the city walls was a job nobody wanted anymore. Before, it was simply part of their day, no real danger other than the weather.

"It wasn't like this the last time," said Agustin. "The bumps I mean. Feels like we're at sea."

Sanada looked up from his silent contemplation. "It gets worse the closer we get."

Agustin nodded and returned to his own introspection. Twomley argued a little at his plan to leave but he understood the need. The city was suffocating Agustin. Each update or crisis brought on a crippling helplessness, one he found more difficult to shrug off. He'd even considered making a trip to Romulus Station, a way of both assuring those aboard and resting his own mind, but Twomley advised against it. Security couldn't be guaranteed up there. Out here didn't feel that much safer except that they were behind a line of automatically tracking weapons.

Agustin brought his PWD to hand and removed it from his wrist. He had been cornered. Press were asking questions. He flicked through the speech his office had prepared. The contents were mostly truthful. Truthful enough without causing panic. Creatures was the word used in the report. It made them sound like mindless animals. Demons. Evil and supernatural. They needed an appropriate name. He had sequestered one of the scientists to come up with something and he was still waiting.

The rolling of the vehicle ended.

"We're here, Director Garcia."

Agustin looked up and found the smiling face of Ramirez.

"I was up front."

"How is it out there?" asked Agustin, lowering his voice.

"Quiet for the most part. Some people swear they can here whispers on the wind. I've heard nothing. The demons give the guns a miss now."

"Demons."

"You don't call them demons, sir?"

"Not sure what I call them."

"Well, looks like they've learnt their lesson. There was talk of trying to bring one of their bodies back, but nobody's been that far out. You know that archaeologist guy wanted to hire me to get him down into the Undercity?"

"No I didn't."

"Stupid asshole, I say."

The rest of the Red Aquila team unbuckled, checked their weapons and secured their survival gear. The team leader walked the length of the Esworth Track issuing orders, her voice loud and leaving little doubt over each member's role.

"Another day in the office," Ramirez said, giving a thumbs up. "Watch yourself out there, sir."

Agustin strapped his PWD to his wrist and readied himself to disembark. Survival gear was fastened, masks fitted, packs and communications checked, and thumbs up were shared indicating all were good to go. Agustin stood at the back of the line leading to the rear ramp.

Ramirez lowered the ramp, exposing them to Esworth. A wind punched through Agustin's protective layer, stealing his breath. The troops pounded out of the vehicle, boots stomping down the ramp. Agustin made to follow but Ramirez halted him with an outstretched arm.

"Wait please, sir." Ramirez's voice was loud in the mask's communication system. "Let us secure the immediate area first."

The team moved with weapons raised and formed a rounded perimeter. Radio communications buzzed through Agustin's helmet. Some of the team moved forward, their formation becoming more like the point of an arrow.

"Ready, sir." Ramirez nodded.

Agustin trudged out into the wilds of Esworth, arms folded, trying to trap any amount of warmth. Snow fell in such volume that footprints of those in front filled within seconds. The picket line of automatic turrets waited two-hundred feet ahead; a long line of small fortifications which scarred the landscape. The speed at which marines and Red Aquila erected the defences was a testament to their logistical skills and professionalism. Three Esworth Tracks arrived, rumbling to a stop, their rear hatches opening, spilling out more Red Aquila operators.

Each turret provided an enveloping field of fire so that there were little to no gaps in the defence. Each of Agustin's steps sank deep into the snow, and he busied his hands wiping his visor free of falling snow. The trail inclined upwards and he slowed even more. His breath worked hard, his lungs threatening to burst. By the time he reached the turret, the marines had dug small hollows into the snow to house the weapons. The weapons were belt fed, the ammunition feeds protected from freezing by a sleeve. A large power pack was positioned at the rear by the base of the turret, designed to be switched on and let them do the work. A camera bolted above the barrel constantly scanned for movement. This section of the line had suffered the heaviest influx of the creatures pushing against the defences. He could see little more than fifty feet ahead.

"There's a storm heading our way, Director Garcia." The sound of Sanada's voice was sudden and loud in his ear. The Colonel of Red Aquila stood to Agustin's side.

"Heading our way? What would you call this?" Agustin looked up at the featureless sky.

"The beginning. The worst is yet to come."

Communications ran fast in his ear. Sanada pointed forward. From within the storm, three columns of darkness materialised. The longer Agustin focused, the more substantial the columns appeared.

"Why aren't the guns firing?" He ducked into the hollow where the nearest turret was housed.

Sanada broadcast to the team working around the weapons. "Everyone to the line." To Agustin he said, "It's functioning like it should."

The Red Aquila team transformed from maintenance crews to a combat patrol. They rushed forward, throwing themselves down against the snow barrier.

The three columns resolved to actual figures, each clothed in black capes or coats. Their heads were avian in form, large black holes for eyes and a small beak, like that of a skeletal owl. They stood still.

"Is everyone seeing them?" asked Agustin, unable to draw his eyes away.

"Everyone is seeing them," confirmed the Colonel of Red Aquila.

Sanada motioned for the closest operator's weapon. He dutifully passed it over. Sanada readied the assault rifle, knelt up, braced and fired two rounds. The sounds echoed then were stolen by the wind. One of the figures blurred like a picture out of focus then returned to normal. Sanada fired again blasting almost a full magazine. The figure blurred again, and again returned to normal.

"What the hell is it, Sanada?" asked Agustin.

"I don't know."

Sanada returned the weapon to the operator. Communications were short and succinct. As a well-trained team, all together they left their covert places in the snow and fell back in good order. Agustin was swept up in the rush. They ran for the most part, back to their Esworth Track. Two soldiers jumped up onto the ramp and helped everyone else board. Ramirez counted the heads.

"Ramp clear," Ramirez said through the comms system.

As soon at the hatch closed and Agustin pulled his protective mask off, he asked, "What were you shooting at?"

Sanada moved to one of the internal monitors. "Patch it into turret 22-E. I want to see what it's seeing."

Ramirez tapped at its keyboard. An image appeared. "It's just snow. Lots of it."

"That can't be," said Agustin. "We saw them. We all saw them."

"Saw what?" said Ramirez.

"Whatever you want to call those fuckers," answered Sanada casually. "Ramirez, get us back to the Hope. I want all patrols back double quick."

The Esworth Track rumbled to life. Agustin scrambled to his seat. Sanada sat down next to him.

"What the hell was that out there?"

"I don't have any answers for you, Director."

Agustin fumbled with his safety belts. "They didn't seem to be aggressive. They just … watched. Watchers in the night."

"Watch the Night," said Sanada, repeating the phrase that became the Terran Cooperative's mantra after the war. They both looked at each other. "You're going public with all this?"

Agustin shrugged. "God help us all."

"I don't think there's any Gods on Esworth, Director Garcia."

CHAPTER 10

Director Agustin Garcia, Uriah's Hope, Esworth.

The broadcast team set up a camera a short distance from Agustin's desk, and checked and double-checked connections and microphones.

Agustin scrolled through his speech, making last minute changes, deleting the odd word here and there and tapping in a replacement. He procrastinated on the correct noun. Aliens, monsters, extra-terrestrials, giant creatures, demons, any was bound to induce severe panic, and his job was to avoid that at all costs. His small office in The Hub was more opulent rather than functional with a tall series of bookshelves full of antique tomes. Atop the bookcases were several contemporary sculptures, abstract and brightly coloured. A long couch lay off to the right and a low glass table with carved legs before it. He stood, stretched, heard his back offer two relieving cracks, then patted out the creases on the Terran Cooperative flag draped behind the desk. The flag was a new fixture. New for the media release. He had mixed feelings about the flag and what it stood for, but at that very moment he believed in the power of props.

"If a garrison had been installed here the situation wouldn't be so dire."

"Sorry, Director. Were you speaking to us?" asked one of the cameramen.

Agustin turned and held up a hand of apology. "Sorry. Thinking aloud." Agustin felt constricted in his best suit. He straightened the tie first, then the Terran Cooperative lapel badge.

"We're ready for you, sir."

"Then let's get this over with. Standing or sitting?"

The camera operator looked through his lens. "Sitting."

Tiredness came to Agustin like waves rolling in from the ocean. He sat, straightened his tie again and cleared his throat.

The crew linked up Agustin's speech to a small screen under the camera.

"Quiet everyone," yelled one of the crew. "And Director, on five, four, three, two."

Agustin joined his hands on the desk. The teleprompter began to scroll.

"Citizens of Uriah's Hope and the Terran Cooperative. Brave service men and women of the Fleet and Orbital Defences, I am Director Agustin Garcia and I come before you now due to matters of the greatest importance. We came here to begin a new chapter of human discovery and endeavour. We are the pioneers of the new frontier, and at no time did we believe this enterprise to be easy. It is a heavy responsibility but one we bear with gratitude and a firmness to commitment. Such a duty does not come without risk." Agustin opened his hands. "We are not alone on Esworth. We have initiated first contact with a previously unknown species. A species with human-like intelligence and believe this species was disturbed by mining activity outside the city. I regret to inform you that the interaction was violent and there have been losses. We have established a defensive perimeter and to date, no further contact has been made. Our top academics are working on a means of communication. All efforts to resolve this situation peacefully will be undertaken. Peace by choice, conflict if forced will be our motto."

Agustin waited for the teleprompter to catch up. "Furthermore, it's my solemn duty to report that there has been an accident on Remus Station. Remus suffered a catastrophic equipment failure which resulted in power failure and all life support shutting down. A direct consequence of this is that the battleship Erebus and the destroyer Cassiopeia have been lost. It is a black day for all."

He steepled his fingers. "My fellow citizens, I come to you today with a request, not for me but for Uriah's Hope. While we hope to resolve all issues with the unknown species peacefully, we cannot afford to assume that this will be the outcome The Fleet and the valiant Marine Corps will do all they can to protect us. So too, our diligent Municipal Police and staunch allies in Red Aquila. But The Gate is not scheduled to open for three months, leaving us cut off from all support from Earth. I beg of you, if you are between twenty-one and fifty years old, in good physical health, please join us, volunteer and receive appropriate training. Join the Uriah's Hope Militia. As I have said, confrontation may not come to be, but we must prepare. Together as one, we can overcome any hardships which come our way. I will come to you with further information over the coming hours and days. Uriah's Hope. We will overcome."

***

Isambard Stone, Undercity, Esworth.

The oppression of the darkness rendered the calculation of time almost impossible. How long had Jericho been gone? He flipped his gun from hand to hand imagining a New Worlder had tracked him to the small alcove, intent on revenge. No one approached him. Footfall on stones scrunched by. But in his mind he practised over and again whipping the gun into place, finger on the trigger and aiming. The aiming part would be difficult. Aim at what in almost complete darkness? He quietened his mind and listened for noise. A distant cough. Then a scratching close by. Which direction? Left or right? Left and low. He pointed the gun and imagined that threat to be blown to pieces. The scratching came again.

Stone fumbled deep into his pocket and pulled out his mini flashlight. He placed a palm over the end, then switched it on. The sudden ignition of light, as dull as it was, powered through his eyes. He squeezed his eyelids closed, turned his face away and waited for his eyes to become used to the new light source. Eventually he managed to look. His fingers glowed. The scratching moved to the right.

Stone released the fullness of the flashlight sending a thin beam out of his hollow. A rat sat tall on its hind legs, and sniffed at the air with a twitching snout.

"How did you get to Esworth?" Stone said quietly to the air.

He had not sighted a rodent since arriving on Esworth. Quality control had failed. And it seemed all the undesirables ended up in the Undercity. It was a scabby creature with patches of fur missing revealing pale skin, and plump enough to suggest there was ample pickings down in the tunnels. Food would not have been plentiful for the Unwanted. Did the fat little bugger feed off the dead down here? Stone scooped up a handful of rocks and threw them at the creature. The rat scampered away.

"There you are." The voice came out of the darkness and was followed by shadows. The accents were thick African he guessed. Three figures charged into the hollow swarming over Stone before he could let out a cry for help. The flashlight was knocked from his hand. The beam of light aimed away and cast a confusing dance of shadows on the wall. Stone lost the gun before he thought to even use it, wrenched from his hand with little resistance. The group punched and kicked at Stone. He covered up as best he could, but kicks got through, digging into his ribs. Stone moaned as each kick found its mark. Two men hoisted him up while the third threw punches, knocking the air from his lungs. He tried to beg but the violence robbed him of a voice.

Hands went around his neck. "Maybe we cut you down here, eh?" The close voice brought a wave of decay.

Something pressed against his crotch. A blade.

"How about that, piggy, eh?"

The pressure at his neck ceased. Stone coughed and gasped. His head fell forward and he threw up.

"The piggy wants to speak. Speak piggy. You is trespassing on our land. The sentence is death."

"I'm … rich … a rich … man … ransom," said Stone.

One of the trio opened up a lantern. Stone threw his head back, the brightness threatening to blind him.

One grabbed his chin. "You look at me when I is talking to you, piggy."

Stone blinked and blinked. His eyes adjusted. The man holding his chin was coloured, his naked torso glistening with sweat and deep scars crossed his arms and chest. His face was thickly tattooed with lines and symbols.

"You see this?" He moved his head left then right showing Stone the full coverage of tattoos. "This is power down here. So, tell me why I should not cut you and leave you for the rats?"

The other two dropped Stone to the ground. They, too, bore heavily tattooed faces, and guns were tucked into their waistbands.

"This place belongs to the New Worlders, piggy," said the nearest. "You're trespassing. It is a crime and the sentence is death. Everyone knows that. Why are you here?"

When Stone didn't answer in time, a punch came to his temple.

"Answer!"

Stone wiped blood from his nose and spat on the ground. "I'm a doctor. I work for the New Seattle Institute of Off-World Archaeology."

"That is a lot of words, piggy."

Stone held up his hands. "I'm here to do research. I study things. I like to discover things."

The speaker knelt down. "You have found something, piggy. You found us. You now belong to New Worlders."

"I can get you money."

"Money," he said with a crackling laugh. "Maybe we ransom you. Maybe we kill you and feed the rats. Maybe something better waits for you. Your life up there is over now. Understand, eh? You belong to the New Worlders."

The speaker threw his head forward, headbutting Stone. Stone fell back. He had the sensation of movement but soon lost it to the dark.

***

Atlas Drinkwater, Eris, Esworth.

Atlas, Owl and Luna waited in the conference room. Luna leaned back in the chair and looked ready to sleep. A small bruise darkened his forehead at the hairline. Owl stood at the window gazing out at the planet below. Atlas alternated between watching his team and the door. They'd been summoned, marched there by marines after their wayward drop pod was recovered.

Outside a pair of destroyers moved at a leisurely pace. Their engines burned a fantastic blue.

"Are we at war?" asked Owl.

"You saw what the creatures did down there," said Luna. "If that's not war, I don't know what is."

Atlas had not considered that possibility. The loss of lives was simply a collateral element of his job.

"Did we start it?" asked Owl. "We came to a planet, claimed it as our own and didn't have the savvy to make sure nobody else was in the neighbourhood. Perhaps they're just defending their homes and we've been kicking a hornets' nest and not expecting to get stung."

"It doesn't matter who started it. We don't get paid to think too much about these things. We're weapons. We get pointed in a direction and told to kill."

The door opened. Captain Scott's hands moved to her hips and her stare settled on Atlas. She looked him up and down before her smile transformed her face from stern to pretty. She looked far too young to have so much responsibility heaped on her shoulders.

"Captain Scott," said Atlas, standing. He was sure the last time they met she was unarmed.

Scott sat. Owl moved to the long conference table. Luna nodded a silent greeting but remained seated.

"Nobody will tell us anything," said Atlas. "Did anyone else from our project make it off?"

Scott looked at all three in turn. "I'm afraid the three of you represent the sum of what is left of the Leviathan Project here on Esworth. Erebus was destroyed so quickly that a proper evacuation was impossible."

Atlas could see his two team members in his peripheral. None moved. None commented.

"Your losses are keenly felt by all, I can assure you," said Scott.

"A battleship doesn't just die like that," said Atlas.

"Tell me what you know."

"Captain Goodsir's people locked me in the brig when I discovered his plan. Luna and Owl got me out and that's when the ship was hit. I made the decision to get to our Leviathans and get off Erebus."

"We've lost the rapid insertion drop pods with Erebus. How are we supposed to get down to planet, Captain?" asked Owl.

"Shuttle."

"And the demons?" asked Luna. "Any update?"

"You chose an apt label, Luna. We have them under surveillance. For now, they're staying away from our defensive positions. They occasionally approach the perimeter but shy away before we fire."

"What do you need us to do, Captain?" asked Atlas.

"Tell me what you know about Goodsir's plan."

Atlas blew out his cheeks. "From what I overheard between Goodsir and Quinn and what the captain told me himself I gathered his plan was to bombard the planet and eliminate the threat to Uriah's Hope. He seemed absolutely convinced of his actions and that if he were judged he would be found to have acted in the right. They spoke about other ships and captains having to be removed."

Scott chewed at the inside of her mouth. "You did exceptionally well to get off Erebus. The Leviathan Project has been our best defence against the creatures."

"Still is," said Luna, and finished with a delayed, "Captain."

"And now?" said Atlas.

"Ready yourselves for another deployment. We have engineers standing by to create purpose-built housing for your suits. They'll need your input."

"What about Remus?"

"Colonel Hopkins is preparing an expedition to Remus to ascertain what happened. We're facing a lot of unanswered questions. Any more questions?"

"Point us to those engineers."

***

Agustin Garcia, Uriah's Hope, Esworth.

"Sixty-nine? That's it?" Agustin sat in The Hub studying the list of volunteers.

Twomley straightened his glasses. "You're surprised?"

"Ten-thousand people and only sixty-nine have balls."

"There's some females on that list."

Agustin shot a loud breath into the air.

"People are scared, Agustin. We might have to sweeten the deal."

Since Agustin's announcement to the city there had been minor riots. Businesses along The White Way were ransacked, and the latest protest was underway at the subterranean entrance to the space port. The UHMP were moving to disperse the rioters. At present the port was not currently operating. No traffic from Uriah's Hope to the orbital facilities was taking place.

Agustin brought up a live stream of the protest. "They'd rather linger in the holds of the freighters than stay down here."

"What about Stone?"

"What about him?" Even hearing his name made anger flare.

"You think he's dead?"

"How many people go into the Undercity and come back?"

"I take your point. But what if we're wrong? What if he's the one who can find a solution?"

Agustin's PWD bleeped. An incoming call from Captain Scott. "I'll take this in my office."

Agustin crossed to his office and closed his door. He accepted the call before he sat. "An update, Captain Scott?"

She looked tired, her eyes more sunken than before. "The creatures are on the move again, digging further west from the previous location."

"To what end?"

"We first thought they looked to outflank the automated defences, and Colonel Hopkins readied to deploy ground forces. But they've stopped short."

"Forgive my ignorance, Captain."

"Sir?"

"In the first engagement we were almost slaughtered, and now we're sending more out to meet the same end?"

"Other than fleeing the planet, Director, we have no other option when confronted with such hostility. How did you go with volunteers?"

"Less than a stellar response. Anything else?"

"CID is reporting cell activity in the city."

The Cooperative Internal Division was a higher echelon organisation which in crises wielded power above governing bodies. The organisation was cloaked in shadows, surrounded by rumour. A cell of the CID would be deployed to a region or agency to ensure that it ran concurrent to the ideals and practices of the Terran Cooperative. They were the watchmen of the Cooperative, funded by back channels and staffed by the best.

"And the activity? Are they looking to take power? Command of Fleet?"

"No, they won't come after Fleet." It sounded like a confident hope from Scott.

"So it'll be Uriah's Hope? The UHMP?"

"No threats have been received. It's simply a warning of activity. Your office and Fleet are working well together, probably for the first time. It would be a shame if that were to change should the CID become involved."

Agustin nodded. "At this point, we can't afford to fracture."

"Just under three months, The Gate will open and we'll be able to send word back to Earth."

"Three months, Captain. I appreciate your warning." Agustin gifted Scott a tired smile. "If you come to planet, you'll have to join me for dinner."

Scott returned the smile as if acknowledging Agustin's exhaustion and the offer of a small olive branch to apologise for his shortness. "Perhaps I will, Director."

The call ended.

Agustin settled back into his chair. It creaked as he shifted his weight.

Another call connected to his PWD. Dr Lydia Kim. He touched the panel for her ID. A pretty face on a long neck. He couldn't place her right away. Hydroponics!

"Doctor Kim. How can I help you?"

Lydia Kim was beautiful, but her frown was heavy, a veil of worry. "Are you able to meet me in Hydroponics, Director?"

"My schedule is full for some time, but—"

"Pardon my brashness, Director, but there's little time to waste."

***

Agustin had been a little surprised to find Chief Constable Reid waiting at the transit station. She was in civilian clothing yet still armed. They rode in silence through the transit system, passing the city in a blur, then took a private elevator down into some of the lowest points of the city. Agustin never had cause to visit Hydroponics before now. Nothing there had ever required his direct attention. He checked his PWD. The depth of Hydroponics would cease his uplink to Fleet Net. Esworth's rock and ice kept secrets well hidden. The irony wasn't lost on the director.

Out of the elevator and along a corridor, Agustin stopped.

"Okay, I give up."

"Director?"

"Why are you here? And why are you out of uniform?"

"Is it unsettling, sir?"

"A little."

"I just figured you should have some company," she said seriously.

"You could've sent one of your cops."

"You could've told your security detail where you were going," Reid fired back. "But instead, here we are."

Neither said another word for a long moment.

"Then lead on, Chief Constable."

It was a quiet walk, their footfall the only sound and it came with a rhythm as if they were marching. Ahead were closed vault doors.

"Hydroponics?" said Agustin.

"Yes, sir."

They stopped at the doors. "What are they trying to keep out? Or in?"

The straight-faced cop didn't reply. She scanned the area they'd come from.

"Maybe we should knock?"

The vault door boomed loud. Agustin jumped. His minder stifled a laugh. The barrier lifted slowly, the rumble of hydraulics echoing. Light slipped from beyond. A single figure materialised, walking swiftly, ducking under the still rising portal.

"Thank you for coming." Dr Kim's handshake was firm. She wore a white lab coat, her hair tied back, no makeup, but Agustin knew she'd still turn heads had she walked down The White Way.

Kim looked past Agustin.

"My constant companion," he explained. "Chief Constable with the Uriah's Hope Municipal Police. She likes to ghost."

Kim held out a hand and shook Reid's quickly. "I'm afraid you won't be permitted to enter all the way, Chief Constable. But we have a waiting room."

Agustin halted the cop's protests with a wave. "That'll be fine. Thank you."

They followed Dr Kim. The corridor was brightly lit and opened into a cavernous room.

"Our vaults stretch for miles with every square foot dedicated to growing and maintaining the environment necessary for production," Dr Kim explained unnecessarily, and with no emotion in her tone. "The temperature here is artificially manipulated to benefit the enterprise of agriculture. We are a small team despite our work being integral to self-sustainability here at Uriah's Hope. And so we have not reached our goal, but in the next few years we should be able to feed the entire city. It's an exciting thought, don't you think?"

Agustin didn't respond. He knew the doctor wasn't waiting for a reply of any type.

"You'll be able to help yourself to refreshments here, Officer." Dr Kim gestured to a low couch and a trestle and kitchen bench.

Beyond stood a glass wall, a secure partition of sorts. A team of six in white laboratory coats and face shields fussed over saplings and pots and garden beds, and tapped notes into small screens. Another two, also in typical scientist wear, studied gauges and flashing monitor boards. The room stretched away into darkness.

"I'll be watching from here," said Reid.

Agustin smiled. "Thank you."

"Follow me please, Director Garcia."

They walked away along a short corridor, away from the saplings and away from Reid.

Dr Kim scanned the card in her lanyard and the door opened with a hiss. "This is my personal lab."

It was a small, sterile room. A large workstation dominated the centre. A computer was linked to a powerful microscope. Tubes stood in racks and lighting shone from behind various leaf samples. There was only one chair.

"So why am I here, Doctor?"

"Gloves, Director, if you please." Kim handed Agustin a pair of disposable gloves.

They both gloved up.

"This." Dr Kim directed Agustin's attention to a glass box on the counter.

Inside lay a fragile plant, little more than a sapling, green at the tips of the leaves. The roots were spread out like tiny, delicate fingers.

"A sapling?" said Agustin.

"Do you notice anything unusual about it?"

Agustin looked closer. "I wouldn't know what to look for. My understanding of fruit and vegetables is when they're on my plate."

"We detected something wrong two days ago." She reached into the display case and pulled out the sapling. "The stalk and leaves are perfectly healthy."

"And?"

"The roots. Watch." Dr Kim touched the roots gently. They crumbled, falling like powder. "If a plant can't receive nutrients via its root system, it dies."

"How much is affected?"

"Ten percent of our current crop."

"Could it be something from planet? Something native to Esworth?"

Kim shook her head. "I can't yet explain it. If we fail to isolate this blight and it spreads ..."

"And you're in the process of isolating?"

"We are."

The severity of the problem was not lost on Agustin. "What do you need from me?"

"Rationing."

"Rationing? Doctor, I could do with some good news."

"I saw your media release and I saw the riots. I know this is not timely."

"How long have we got?"

"If we've caught it at ten percent loss, we can manage if minor rationing is implemented. If it spreads quickly we could lose a high percentage of the output."

"How high?"

"Eighty percent. Tight rationing will see us last into the next Gate opening."

"Can you guarantee no more than eighty percent?"

"No."

"Doctor Kim, in your opinion, could this be a deliberate contamination?"

Kim returned the sapling to the display case. "Deliberate? Who'd want to destroy the city's food supplies? If we fail here, we all suffer."

CHAPTER 11

Doctor Isambard Stone, Undercity, Esworth.

Sleep was a period where Stone could be oblivious to his plight. And in that pleasant state he was lying naked with Tanya, in his bed back in New Seattle. Talk was absent but gentle touching provided communication. Her smile was childlike and everything was calm. Waters trickled beneath their bodies. The level grew and he began to float. A muscle in his back twinged. Someone had inserted a tracking device beneath his skin. A radio clicked to life and the sound of a car horn became an alarm. Tanya asked for more water, rolled over and floated away. His belly heated and air suddenly turned acrid.

Stone opened his eyes and instantly wanted to return to his dream. The warmth he'd felt was piss. He was curled on the floor of a cage and wasn't alone. Air was hard to come by. It was sweltering.

A woman wept. "Please. Water. We're dying in here."

Stone sat up, pushed himself back against the rusted bars and drew his knees to his chest. Seven bodies. Seven stinking people squatted in a cage barely large enough to house a pig. Others took up the call for water. His throat burned. Lamps leaked a dull, yellow light. More cages were packed into the hollow as far as he could see.

A lone figure cut a leisurely path between the cages. A rifle hung from his bare shoulder. What the hell had happened? Why was he in a cage? Where was Jericho?

"Hey, over here," rasped Stone.

An equally dry voice from behind cautioned, "Don't. They'll hurt you."

Stone ignored the advice and waved. The guard kicked the cage, silencing his pleas.

The tattoos twisting along the guard's arm, up his neck and under his eyes marked him as a New Worlder. The guard knelt down at the side of the cage bringing his face level with Stone.

"What you saying to me, piggy, eh?" He smiled, revealing a mouth missing three front upper teeth. "What you want, eh?"

"Water." Stone couldn't keep the word in. He'd never been this desperate for water. "Please."

"Ah! You thirsty, piggy? You want something to drink, eh?" The question was loaded and Stone knew better than to reply. "I'll give you something to drink."

The guard dropped his trousers, pulled his penis free and pissed before Stone could even think about moving away. The guard laughed.

"Don't shout again or I shoot you, leave you to rot in there." The guard raised his rifle and aimed it at Stone, the barrel a few inches from his face. The guard laughed again then resumed his patrol.

"You were lucky." His cellmate was bald, dull eyes hanging over a large nose. His body was skeletal, his skin pulled tight over protruding bones. A small paunch in his stomach looked out of place but Agustin had seen similar in the videos from Hyderabad where famine took hold. "They've killed people for less than that."

"Who are you?"

"I was a cop. Up there." One finger moved. "They were sending us down here to investigate the gangs. But it was like they knew we were coming."

"Do they bring water?"

"Every second day. Meat too. Not enough for everyone."

"How long have you been down here?"

"Months and I've not been out of the cage. I don't think I can walk anymore."

Stone looked at the man's bare legs.

"The cage isn't tall enough to stand."

A distant boom echoed. Stone shifted his feet and squished human waste.

***

The lights never dimmed. There was always noise. Groans and sobs. Cage doors slammed. People screamed as they were taken away. Hours grew to days and then to an immeasurable period. His mind raced to chase memories, anchors to hold him from floating to desperation.

His memories played in greyscale. None were of positive times. Regrets came like a reel of highlights. Tanya featured heavily. He used her to get what he wanted. At the time, he didn't see another option. Yes, Stone regretted what happened to her.

Maybe he should pray? No. He had too much sense for that. His father was a devout male, someone who managed to find a balance between faith and science, a feat Stone himself never managed. And despite his father's prayers, cancer robbed the world of the discoveries he was destined to make. Destined? Who had a destiny? So what did it mean to die? Stone understood cellular death but the Esworth Chamber gave him pause to reconsider what was possible in the universe.

A hand from behind suddenly covered his mouth. Stone didn't resist. He relaxed, allowing his head to be pulled back, exposing his neck. If it was his time to die, so be it, and it surprised him how accepting he was of what was about to come. But a blade did not cross his throat. A second hand did not hold his head readying to snap his neck. Nobody else in the cage moved or was aware of what was happening. A voice sounded in his ear. Whispering, almost like a distant echo.

"I'll get you out of here. Be patient and don't eat the scraps. Things have changed. Drink only and say nothing."

Jericho's hand slipped away and a small bottle was forced to Stone's mouth. The water was warm and salty. Reclaimed probably. He didn't care. He gulped at the water and sucked out the last drops. Stone's chest heaved as he fought to catch his breath.

"I'll come back for you when the time is right. Stay alive."

Jericho was gone. The weary moans of prisoners were the only sounds to come to his ears. Was it a fevered dream? Stone licked his lips and felt moisture there for the first time in so long. A long absent smile cracked his dry lips.

The cop's eyes caught him. He had watched everything with those dull eyes. Stone waved a weak hand. The cop closed his eyes.

***

The locks rattled and the cage doors were wrenched open.

"Out! Out! Get out, piggies." New Worlders kicked at the cages. "Up, piggies. Up."

The prisoners stirred slowly for legs refused to obey with any speed, and hands and elbows struggled to prompt bodies into a crawl. Another kick to the cage came. Stone rolled to his stomach and used his elbows to drag his way to the open door. Arms and knees climbed across his back. Three bodies at the door caused a jam.

"Move," he encouraged, not certain the word had fallen from his mouth.

"Move," echoed another with more urgency.

Stone wriggled and pushed at a leg, then a foot. The jam freed up and he was out, but a swift kick made its target and his ribs cracked. He rolled to his back. Standing over him was a female with the snaking tattoos that marked her as a New Worlder.

"Move or you die. They all die. You understand, eh?"

Stone crawled back onto his knees, his breaths short and raspy.

The New Worlder pulled a firearm from her waistband and aimed the pistol at Stone. "Help him or you die."

A prisoner lay still on his left, emaciated arms limp at his sides. How was he to help another when he couldn't fathom where the minute strength came from to have him get out of the cage this far?

"Last chance, piggy. Your choice."

Stone climbed onto one elbow, clutched at his chest and collapsed to the ground.

"Bad decision, piggy."

Bang!

Stone felt a curious wave of relief. He was about to die. Pain and misery would be nothing as soon as he took his last breath. He waited for peace.

Bang! Bang! Bang! Bang! Bang! Bang!

His ribs still ached and the sound of grunting prisoners behind him had stopped. Seven lay dead.

Another New Worlder snatched the gun from her hands. "What you doing, eh?"

"They were weak. Worthless."

"You fucking no better than those piggies." His huge hand came down across her face.

She slipped to one knee and pulled a homemade knife from her boot. "You'll pay for that, Killow."

The man called Killow cocked his pistol and aimed. "Whether you live or die, doesn't matter to me."

She bared her teeth and growled like a panther.

"Titan will make you pay for this. The Pilgrim needs two-hundred."

The woman seemed to surrender and pushed the shiv into her boot. Killow grabbed Stone's hair and hauled him to his feet. Stone grabbed Killow's hands.

Killow released his hold. "You're touched?"

"Yes," he rasped.

"Get up. Come with me." The man's voice was suddenly worried.

"I don't have the strength," Stone stammered.

Killow reached into his pocket and pulled out a brown flask. "Drink."

Stone took the flask without thought and gulped. It was a thick, syrup-like substance, bitter and it prickled his tongue. He studied the man, a wretch like the others but with a sternness in his eyes. "What is it?"

"It help. It hydrate you."

Stone drank more and simply hoped it was a poison that would take him quickly.

"Up now," said Killow.

Life flooded back into Stone's arms and legs. He dropped the empty flask. "What is it?"

"No time. Up." Killow threw a dirty length of material around Stone. "You must get up. Quick."

Stone climbed to his feet.

Killow pushed his pistol to Stone's neck. "Say not one word." The man looked worried.

"You're helping me?"

"No talking. Move." Killow forced the barrel of the gun into Stone's neck harder and propelled him forward. "Get out the way. I've got a piggy here."

They turned out of the prison cave and down a long tunnel with such infrequent light Stone could have closed his eyes and not noticed a difference. They turned again. The rest of the tunnel was narrow and low. Stone felt his hair brushing the roof as they moved.

"Stop," Killow ordered in a whisper.

Stone made out the sound of material being moved aside.

"Get low and crawl. Now."

Stone felt for the walls around him. They had stopped at a hollow.

"Go."

Stone lowered to his knees and crawled. He could hear Killow follow. Nobody could see in these conditions. Stone guessed Killow moved by memory alone.

"Stand."

Stone got to his feet. Killow sparked a single flame into existence, lighting a candle mounted in a hollow. The weak light was enough to see a few feet away, but no more. They had arrived in a small chamber.

"We're safe here. It's a place I come to be away from people. Nobody comes here." Killow's speech had altered. It no longer cracked with the crude annunciations of a New Worlder. He spoke like an educated man.

A short pile of supplies sat at his feet. Killow grabbed a can, ripped off the top and offered it to Stone. "Eat this."

Stone dug into its contents and scooped out the mush. Fish. He ate greedily. "Where are we?"

Killow popped the magazine free and sorted through the bullets. "How did you come to be touched?"

"In a mine." Stone upended the can. The remaining oil and juices ran into his mouth.

"A mine?"

"A chamber, really."

"How?"

"I touched something I shouldn't have."

Killow handed Stone another can of fish. "Give me the details, and from the beginning."

"Touched is a curious choice of words but I suppose no less appropriate." Stone suddenly realised all consequences of the neglect and abuse over the past several days had dispersed. "What was in that flask?"

"Answer my questions first."

The two men eyed each for a long moment.

Stone nodded then ate the contents of the second can. "My name is Isambard Stone. I'm an archaeologist with the New Seattle Institute of Off-World Archaeology. I came to Esworth to prove myself right. I heard rumours of ruins or something buried beneath Uriah's Hope. I thought it would be the missing link between us and the Nights." Stone waited for some kind of response or direction.

"Continue," Killow encouraged.

"Miners were drilling test shafts and encountered a subterranean structure."

"Which company?"

"Deeproot Drilling. The team got sick, refused to work and the site was closed until further investigation was carried out. I bribed my way there with my assistant. We found the chamber. Something happened to her."

"What happened to her?"

Stone shook his head. "I have absolutely no idea. But I saw a creature down there. I touched these statues and since then my hands ..." He held them up. "My hands are permanently cold yet they burn people."

"Anything else strange?"

"Yes. At the back of my mind I have this desire to be somewhere else. I thought it was down here."

"And it's not?"

"I don't know."

Killow sipped from a flask, swirling the liquid around his mouth before swallowing loudly.

"Do you have a story?"

"Everyone has a story. Things back on Earth went badly for my wife and I, so we bought our way here. Three years ago. Not registered, no permits. Do you have any concept what it's like outside the Cooperative for a former citizen?"

Stone shook his head. "How much did it cost? To get here I mean."

"We used the last of our money and paid the smugglers to get us aboard a freighter. We arrived with nothing. As soon as we reached Esworth we were brought down here and that's when things went badly for us."

"Brought here by who?"

"Red Aquila, I think. They never identified themselves. We were starving. We avoided the gangs for as long as we could. Two years scraping out a living down here and then my wife attended a meeting of the Unwanted. They sat in the presence of The Pilgrim of Hate."

"I've recently heard that name."

"She would talk about him when she came back here. He promised much for those who followed. A purpose. He kept talking about a great purpose. My wife slowly grew distant and spent more and more time out in the tunnels on her own. I confronted her one day and she burned me when I touched her. Exactly like you did. The same feeling. The same pain. The last words I spoke to her were hot, full of anger." Killow looked down.

"What was her name?"

"Sammy." A hint of a smile appeared on Killow's face but disappeared as quickly as it appeared. "She ran into the tunnels and I never saw her again."

"Never?"

"Oh, I searched, put myself at risk. But the New Worlders caught me. I was caged like you."

"So how …"

Killow lifted his chin as if daring judgement. "I saw how things were and I took a chance. There were five of us in a cage. I overheard the plan to move us out the next morning, so I strangled the other four during the night. When they found me the next day, their leader took it upon himself to bring me into the fold. They respect strength. Reward it. I did what I needed to."

Stone studied Killow and decided that lifted chin was more an attempt to block out all self-loathing.

"Why save me? Because I'm like your wife?"

"People like you are the key. I've never stopped searching for Sammy. Even now. I will find her. The New Worlders and the Peacemakers were the strongest factions, but now the Peacemakers are gone."

"What happened to them?"

"The Pilgrim of Hate's followers have absorbed them. Titan, our leader, struck a deal with the Pilgrim, one that allowed us to continue without interruption."

"What kind of deal? What does the Pilgrim want?" Stone already had an unsettling suspicion what the deal would require.

"People. Captured Unwanted or the outcasts from the New Worlders. Anyone from the city above who is stupid enough to be caught down here."

"Why does he need people?"

"All I know is things are only getting worse. If the Pilgrim can absorb the Peacemakers, how long until he's got the New Worlders, too?"

Silence descended upon the two for a long moment.

"I'm sorry about your wife." Stone's voice felt loud and out of place in the confined place.

Killow raised a finger. "Don't speak like she's dead. I'd know if she was."

"Of course," Stone conceded politely.

"They made me give up my wedding ring. I will find her."

More silence.

"The Undercity must be massive," said Stone. "So far it's little more than a confusing maze to me. Must be difficult to search alone."

"I'm doing what I can, but if the New Worlders knew what I was doing, they'd kill me."

Killow offered another can. Stone took the fish with a nod.

"So why are you down here?"

"Something is happening on Esworth, outside the city. I think it's something dangerous and I had a feeling that down here, I could get at least some of the answers I'm looking for."

"From the Pilgrim?"

"Yes. I can't explain this feeling, but I'm sure this is where I have to be. Well, not with you, but down here."

"And you came alone?"

"I hired a mercenary to keep me safe and make an introduction."

"But we got you first?"

Stone nodded as he ate. "Things happened and I ran when I should've stayed."

"So we're both looking for people."

"Seems that way. So what now?"

Killow poked at the dirt with his boot. "Sammy had a feeling she couldn't explain, too. A need to go to these meetings. They were never advertised. She just knew, knew when to go and where to go. She called it a feeling."

"I don't hear voices telling me to go somewhere or anything like that. I'm blundering in the dark. It's a hunch thing."

"I think it's more, and I believe you can help me find Sammy."

***

Agustin Garcia, The White Way, Uriah's Hope.
The Uriah's Hope staff transit trundled along at a steady pace, rumbling as it moved high above The White Way. Agustin watched out the window, his reflection distorted in the

glass. The sea of shops, eateries and entertainment facilities passed below in a blur. His protection officer sat across from him, her eyes, a curious shade of dark brown, never left him. She'd appeared outside Hydroponics, a replacement for Reid, all six feet. He wondered what she thought of him. Did she think he was handling the situation well? Or poorly? Did she resent having to protect him? Did she think of him as a father who couldn't protect his own daughter?

"What is your bloody name, Officer? You never did tell me."

She pushed a finger at her ear and held up a hand to ask for quiet. She stood, unfolding to her full height and pulled her pistol from the holster hidden by her long coat.

"Trouble?" asked Agustin.

"Vedad. Officer Vedad is my name, Director. Now, if you'll do me a favour and move away from the window. Now, sir."

Agustin stood and did what was asked. The transit slowed as it pulled into a private station. They were fifty feet above an unused habitation complex, unused and awaiting future citizens of Uriah's Hope. These sections of the city were powered down until such a time as there were citizens to fill them. The UHMP patrolled when they could, trying to keep out gangs of criminals, and their drug dens and brothels.

Lights far below snaked between the habitation blocks, appearing, flickering then disappearing.

A hail of gunfire shredded the window. Vedad hauled Agustin backward and to the floor like a wrestler performing a suplex. Vedad rolled and came to a knee in one perfect motion. Heavy thuds hit the underside.

"Stay down!" Vedad approached the far side of the carriage and fired at the glass. The pane shattered and she used the butt of her gun to remove the remaining shards from the frame. "Get on the comms, Director, and get us moving."

Vedad popped her head out, aimed her weapon and fired a salvo. Spent casings hit the floor with a metallic clink. "Get us moving, Director. We can't win here."

Agustin dialled a priority call to Twomley. "Dale, get this fucking carriage moving! We're under attack. They're shooting at us."

Vedad leaned out and fired again. A heavy impact struck the bottom of the monorail and punched a hole through the floor. The carriage rocked. Vedad reloaded, leaned out to fire but a burst of rounds sent her back and onto the floor. She clutched at her face.

"Vedad!" Agustin crawled over to her. Glass protruded from her temple and forehead.

She moaned.

"It's okay," he said, not certain he was telling the truth. "It's only glass. Don't touch it."

"Get backup." Her voice shook.

"Dale!" he yelled into his PWD.

"We're trying to locate you on the transit system. Hold on."

"I can't open my eyes," said Vedad.

"Keep them closed. My people will get us moving."

"Grab my gun. They'll be coming for you."

"Where …?" He looked around the floor. Her gun had slid beneath her legs. He grabbed it. "Got it."

"Just aim and pull."

"I can do that." He activated his PWD again. "Vedad's hurt."

Gunfire drilled into the side of the carriage. The carriage juddered. Agustin lost balance. Pain tore up his arm. The carriage lurched into movement. Blood seeped the length of his arm.

***

One medic attended Vedad on the floor of The Hub's station while another cleaned Agustin's wound.

"A clean slice, Director. A few stitches and you should be okay."

"I've got no time for stitches. Make sure Vedad gets all the care she needs." Agustin grabbed a wad of gauze and pressed it to his upper arm where the blood continued to seep. "Get one of your team to dress this at my office."

Agustin marched to the lift that would take them to the surface.

"Director, let me tend to your arm." She was a pretty young girl, raven hair and alert eyes. She wore the green scrubs synonymous with the health services of Uriah's Hope.

"Then follow me. Hope you can walk fast."

***

"Holy shit, Agustin," said Twomley.

"I'm fine." Agustin breezed past.

"You're dripping blood on the floor."

The young medic shrugged at Twomley and followed Agustin into his office.

"Jesus. Would you sit down, Agustin, before you fall down."

Agustin fell into his chair, fetched a bottle of his expensive Scotch from a drawer, bit into the lid and tugged it free.

"Hold your arm still for me, Director," said the medic, placing a bag on Agustin's desk.

Agustin drank heavily.

"Should he be drinking?"

"One glass shouldn't do any harm." The medic went to work on Agustin's arm.

Agustin sucked in air and grimaced. "What have you got for me, Dale?"

With his eyes on Agustin's injury, Twomley said, "The UHMP are going through the scene as we speak. Reid's there, too."

Agustin looked down at his arm. The cut was ugly and bled as soon as the medic applied pressure. She dabbed at the wound with a swab which burned with each depression.

"Tell them to go over everything twice. Three times if they have to."

"Reid thinks it's a professional hit."

Agustin took another swig.

"Hold still please, Director."

"Sorry. So what are we facing, Dale?"

Twomley removed his glasses. "The way I see it, there's only two possibilities. The first, and I hope more likely, is that it was a random attack. You know, wrong place at the wrong time bullshit."

"Or?"

The medic began stitching the wound.

"Shit!" said Twomley. "Don't you have a machine to do that or something?"

The medic looked up with half a smile. "Show me one and I'll gladly hand over."

"Or what?" said Agustin.

"Or we've got someone selling information about your movements."

"Why?"

"That is the question. And until we know more, you can't go out into the city alone."

"Unacceptable. People need to know that the Director's Office doesn't cower to attacks like this. We don't give into terrorism."

"And we're done," said the medic, removing her protective gloves. She grabbed the bottle from Agustin and passed it to Twomley.

"Hey," complained Agustin.

"Rest the arm. Have it checked tomorrow. And now, if you don't mind, I'll find some patients who don't make me chase them."

Twomley sniffed the bottle then took a mouthful. "Damn, that's good."

"Lydia Kim brought my attention to a blight taking hold of our crops in Hydroponics."

"You're shitting me?" Twomley returned his glasses to his nose. "When you said something was wrong at Hydroponics, I never thought it could be something like that."

"Where'd the blight come from?"

Agustin shrugged. "She'll let me know."

"What are they doing about it?"

"Everything they can."

"You think they can handle it?" Twomley replaced the stopper in the bottle and laid it on Agustin's desk.

"Doctor Kim is impressive. She's worried but I've got faith in her."

"Well, if they have it under control, go get some rest." Twomley raised a hand. "Doctor Kim is doing what she can, the UMPH is doing what they can, and all we can do is wait."

Agustin took the lift to The Hub accommodation level and made his way to his apartment. He knew up here, away from the general population, he was safe. Not least because of the intense security measures in place, but the very terrain of the city worked against any would-be trespasser. They would have to brave the inhospitable weather and scale several hundred feet of icebound mountain.

The tunnel from the lift to the dome was translucent. Far off, lightning cracked the skies.

His last few thoughts before sleep took him were of Earth. He wondered if he'd ever see the place again. It wasn't so much that he missed Earth or the people and its politics. Whatever else Agustin was, he was an Earther. Born and raised. And he suddenly realised just how much he missed the gentle breeze of a cool, spring morning in the countryside. He missed Tanya.

***

Captain Olivia Scott, Eris, Esworth Orbit.

In the time since the destruction of Remus Station, Captain Scott fended off passive attempts to undermine her position and comments designed to spread uncertainty. It too often felt like her time and energy was directed at tugging on her reins, steering and shushing disgruntled subordinates all while the destroyer Renown and Captain Paris Quinn were still out there.

The Esworth system was made up of six planets and several moons, none capable of sustaining human life, and so, were bypassed by the pioneer ships. Small orbital stations were left around each planet. Their purpose was twofold. A forward base of operation for any future missions to the inner planets, and listening posts. So far none of the stations detected Renown.

The majority of the captains favoured sending a strike force after Quinn, imprisoning the rogue and her senior crew. Some declared being vigilant and reacting when Renown reappeared to be the more prudent solution. Scott was in favour of chasing Renown and bringing the ship back under her control. To do otherwise would show weakness and in these times of crisis she couldn't afford to let herself be viewed as weak.

The chime to her door sounded. Scott grabbed her service pistol, checked it was loaded and proceeded to the door. She flicked on the security system. Captain Reece Tyler of the Colossus waited outside the door.

"Jesus Christ," she muttered, scrambling for some clothing. She threw on her sweats and a hoodie before opening the door. "You could've sent word you were coming." Had it been anyone else, there would've been genuine annoyance in her voice.

Captain Tyler scratched at his greying beard. "Expecting someone else?"

Scott moved aside and placed the weapon on the shelf by the door. "I'm no longer willing to take chances." The door slid shut with a suppressed hiss.

"You've less to worry about than most. Your marines were very thorough in their search before they let me near your state room." He made a face and squirmed.

"How thorough?" she said through a tired smile.

"Let's just say it tickled."

Scott indicated Tyler should sit at her dining table. "How long has it been since you and I sat and shared a cup of coffee? Off duty, I mean?" She poured two cups, cleared the table of her paperwork and sat down across from him.

"When are we ever off duty?" Tyler sipped at his coffee and leaned back into his chair. "And barely time to eat and sleep."

"I hear you." She hiked a thumb over her shoulder to the pile she'd been studying before his arrival. "But you're not here for small talk."

"You've known me too long." The casual composure Tyler wore slipped and he looked pained. "How are you sleeping?"

Scott raised an eyebrow. "With my eyes closed. Not brilliant and not long enough but I'm getting by."

"You have to promise me you won't repeat this to anyone. Promise me."

"We've been friends for long enough. You shouldn't have to ask me."

"Olivia, please."

"I promise, Reece."

"For the last few weeks, every time I wake up I hear voices, all in that horrible moment between sleep and awake. They're like an echo. More than one. I can't make out what they're saying."

"You think you're going crazy?"

"No," he chuckled. "I'm far from that."

"Well, you're not the only one. I've heard similar reports. Something about the planet down there, what's happened recently, the losses we've suffered. We're facing a lot of stress."

"I don't believe it's stress. I don't look forward to sleep anymore. It's like I'm in a constant state of alert, expecting something terrible to happen. Then there is this. May I?"

Tyler indicated Scott's work screen and brought his PWD to life. He streamed the pictures to the monitor. "I've taken the lead on the drone missions trying to get accurate pictures on the excavation site. We've lost more drones than I'd like to count with the weather. They've got a nasty habit of simply dropping out of the sky. But less than thirty minutes ago I received these pictures. It's where the creatures have been digging. It's … it's serious, Olivia. If any of us thought we had a handle on the situation, we need to rethink."

She zoomed in. "It can't be."

The creatures had dug through the permafrost, a hundred feet or so. And jutting out of the pristine whiteness of the Esworth ice at the base of the excavation were statues on plinths. She could make out five. All had an arm raised in the air, the claw-like open hand reaching upwards.

"Taken when?"

"A few hours ago. Olivia, everything about this makes my skin crawl. And if I may, nobody is critical of the fact Hal Hastings chose you. Well, anyone who was is dead or under arrest. But what I'm hearing now is we're simply waiting around when we should take the fight to them."

"You think we should be sending more marines to their deaths? You saw what happened. Those creatures are hard to kill."

"I'm not talking about sending marines down a hole again. Order a limited fire mission. Destroy the area from orbit. Send a small task force to bring Renown back. Give me a couple of destroyers and I'll bring her back."

Scott tapped at the rim of her cup.

"We cannot afford to lose the initiative."

"And if we probe too far, we may unleash another Night War." Scott returned her attention to the images. "Those statues, what do you think they are?"

"When I am lying in bed, watching the light flicker over the roof of my stateroom, my thoughts are on that question. I'm not qualified to make anything other than guesses, but when you look at the creatures, do you think them capable of building something like that? I certainly don't which leads me to assume another intelligence was responsible for the architecture and possibly the creatures. We're in the Esworth System thanks to the Nights' Gate. Esworth obviously held some significance to them otherwise there wouldn't have been a Gate. Did the Nights build the statues?" Tyler shrugged. "Despite their difference in physiology, they share similar traits to us. They need ships to travel, have similar tolerances to extreme temperatures. If this is or was a Nights' planet, where's the evidence? The statues, despite their unusual construction material and energy properties, resemble something more human. What they are I don't know."

"A third party?" Scott sipped at her coffee.

"A fourth party." Tyler held up four fingers. "Nights. Creatures, us and whoever were the progenitors of Esworth."

"I can't shake the feeling that we're being led along a certain path. How much of the Esworth situation has been planned? After the Nights left, we started tinkering with the leftover Gate tech. They dialled out until one responded. And here. Why here? Chance? Maybe. Or we're being fed a breadcrumb trail. We're too busy gobbling up the pieces to see what's at the end."

"Shit, Olivia. You're not the only one to say that. You heard criticism in the media back home that we're progressing too slowly out here. Ours isn't the job to question, only to follow orders from Fleet."

"I just can't help but think all this isn't as random as we're assuming."

Tyler's eyes bored into her. "Let me take some of the burden from you. It's not easy going from Captain of a battle cruiser to Acting Commander of the Fleet. You need to start delegating. Hal Hastings relied on you. So why not rely on me, Olivia?

"There's no double play. I'm not looking to gain influence. All I see is one of my friends in need of a little assistance. What issues can we fix right away? Bombard the excavation site closest to the defensive line. Give me two destroyers to progress in-system and bring Renown back."

Scott knew the benefit of having someone to rely on, but she wasn't sure he was the right one. She looked at her coffee.

"What's your reluctance?"

"Why do you think there's any reluctance?"

"It's written all over your face."

Scott had been too long in Fleet and too long in the Scott family to reveal her feelings so easily to people. It just wasn't something that you did. The fighting Scott family were a hard family. They bled for the good of Earth and humanity against the Nights. It worried her that Reece Tyler was able to gauge her feelings so easily. Too much work. Too many hours lost to stress and not enough sleep. She wouldn't take being pressed over matters, not even by Reece Tyler.

"Risk assessment, Reece. What if the bombardment's ineffective? What if we provoke the creatures into attack before we can summon reinforcements from Earth? What if they can summon numbers our automated defences and the marines can't handle? What if they get into Uriah's Hope? We have only three Leviathans left. It'll be a slaughter."

"Your job is to decide which options minimise loss. You'll be investigated at the end of all this, both your decisions and your hesitations will be questioned."

Scott frowned. "I'm open to counsel from all my Captains, Reece. But I won't be pushed into a decision. Now, if there's nothing else, it's been a long day."

Tyler waited a time before speaking. "Of course, Captain. I won't keep you any longer. I'll be getting back to Colossus." Tyler stood and saluted.

Only when the door closed did Scott let her shoulders sag. She cleaned away the two cups, retrieved her weapon and went to bed. Sleeping with a gun under her pillow was a new experience.

***

Scott spent the first hour of her morning drafting orders to dictate Fleet's actions from now until the next opening of The Gate, and on completion, walked from her state room to the bridge. The corridors of Eris felt calmer. Even her marine escort could not disrupt the tranquillity. Of course, it wasn't the ship that was different. Eris rumbled with the usual frequency she was so accustomed to. It was her confidence, newly buoyed by exacting her commands formally.

Holopainen was already on the bridge and offered a quick salute as she entered. With a curious smirk he whispered, "You look ready for the day ahead, Captain."

"Correct, XO. Things are about to change. Renown will be brought back and Paris Quinn will be taken into custody."

He nodded with the proud approval of a parent.

"Two-hundred marines are being deployed to the surface to create a temporary forward operating base on the defensive line closest to the excavation site."

"Now?"

"They'll be departing in the next half hour."

"Who are you sending?"

"You and I," she said with a curt nod, indicating she did not wish to discuss the matter further at present.

"Shall we watch the proceedings?" He moved aside with a gallant gesture.

Scott slid into her seat and swivelled the console over her knee. "Officer of the Watch, you have your orders?"

"Yes, Captain. Marine shuttles launching, Captain."

Scott cleared her throat. "Your attention, everyone. Eris, Aberdeen and Halifax will hunt down Renown. We'll be travelling deeper into the system which isn't covered in our mandate. However, we cannot allow Renown to roam freely. Our fellow sailors are on that ship, many victims of Quinn's treachery and we will not abandon them."

"Captain," acknowledged Holopainen, and other crew members repeated the address.

"I want the ship brought to readiness, and I know I can rely on you to get the job done. Eris and her crew will complete the mission."

"Captain," came the repeated acknowledgement again.

More than a few smiled and congratulated each other. It was a common desire for sailors to go further than the immediate location around Esworth. While their job was vital for the security of Esworth, until recently the deployment was seen as a cakewalk. Sure, they got to see Uriah's Hope and set foot on a world not in the Terran System, but other than that it was not unlike a prolonged drill.

The general quarters alarm sounded and the crew of Eris responded bringing the ship to full readiness. Holopainen handled the reports from each deck and department. Scott fired out orders like she was firing a weapon. Captain Shellenberger of the Aberdeen and Captain Hale of the Halifax both acknowledged their orders and made preparation to leave in formation.

An incoming private call from Captain Tyler flashed on her screen. Scott activated her electronic privacy shield. It distorted the immediate area allowing a private conversation.

"You shouldn't be going, Captain Scott. You're too important to lose out there." Tyler's face was red like he'd spent the last ten minutes screaming.

"I've no intention of being lost out there. You have your orders. I expect you to keep a lid on everything until I return."

"You shouldn't be going," he said again. "Send me."

"To your duty, Captain. Eris out." Scott cut the link and deactivated the privacy shield.

"Problems?" asked Holopainen.

"Always. Speak with the ship's quartermaster, figure out exactly what stocks were on Renown before Quinn fled."

"What are you thinking?"

"If she's planning to run for a long period, she'll need new supplies. And not having the firepower to return here, she'll have to make for the listening stations."

"Of course. If she's planning to remain out there she'll need to raid the stations."

"I've ordered waking."

Holopainen brought up the holographic chart of the Esworth System. He manipulated the angle of the chart, highlighting each station in turn. "Castor and Pollux would be the logical choice first."

"What's their status of waking?"

Holopainen scrolled through his console. "Activation codes were sent but so far we've had nothing in response. The automated systems should be back online by now. The problem is we don't know what is normal and what isn't. They've not been activated since they were first constructed and tested."

"Helm, I want a course for Castor plotted and readied for immediate execution."

"Castor, aye. Estimated period of transition thirty-six hours and forty minutes at best speed," replied helm.

"What if she's already there and deactivated the automation? She could have free reign on the two stations. What about the other stations?" asked Holopainen.

"What about the other stations?"

Holopainen continued scrolling through his information. "Phoebe, Hilaeira and Leda have all sent back activation confirmation. Castor and Pollux is where we'll find Renown. She's going for the supplies held on those stations."

"Find out what she will be running low on. And get schematics from our engineers. I want to know everything about those stations."

"Yes, Captain." Holopainen left the bridge in search of the quartermaster for Eris.

The separation from Esworth would be good, Scott felt. Esworth was nothing but an anchor of problems and she decided to travel in system partly for her own wishes and partly because she wouldn't send anyone else out there. It was an unknown factor. Captain Tyler surprised her in that he didn't argue further for bombardment. She considered it over and over. Hell, she even saw the merit in it. The issue, one she did not wish to share at present, was that when Captain Goodsir made his intention clear to bombard the planet, events conspired to ensure that didn't happen. Remus destroyed his ship and halted any chance of attacking Esworth directly. Scott dared not risk further losses if she could help it.

Scott placed a call to the office of the director of Uriah's Hope and activated her privacy shield. The screen opened up, not with Agustin Garcia but his deputy, Dale Twomley.

"Assistant Director? I was expecting Director Garcia."

"Captain Scott," said Twomley. "Director Garcia is unavailable. There was an incident yesterday."

"An incident?"

"An attempt was made on his life."

"Why wasn't Fleet made aware?"

"The director was wounded but is fine. His protection officer wasn't quite so fortunate."

"I'll ask you again, why wasn't Fleet contacted?"

Twomley held up his hand. "With all due respect, Captain, a report will be sent to you at the appropriate time. Can I assist you?"

"This is simply a courtesy call," said Scott, unable to keep the venom from her voice. "I'm taking Eris and two destroyers in system to bring back Renown."

"This is most irregular. There is no mandate for this. Your primary concern should be the protection of Esworth."

"I'm giving us a mandate, Assistant Director."

"With the recent losses and the destruction of Remus, surely you need to keep your fleet here?"

Scott held up a hand imitating Twomley's previous action. "With all due respect, we cannot have a rogue warship operating unchecked."

Twomley pursed his lips.

"Captain Reece Tyler of the Colossus will take charge of the attending ships remaining at Esworth and coordinate with the Director's Office should the need arise. You've been briefed by Colonel Hopkins on the marine deployment to the line?"

"I have."

"Pass on my best to Director Garcia."

"And I wish you good hunting, Captain. Twomley out."

"Pompous prick," she muttered, before dropping the privacy shield.

An hour later, Scott ordered Eris, Aberdeen and Halifax to break formation. Their mighty engines powered up, and pushed them away from the pale planet, leaving behind, at least for a time, the troubles of Uriah's Hope. Scott set her vision to the distant points of light. First, the planet of Castor and the Castor orbital station. If nothing there, then onto Pollux. She promised herself they wouldn't return without a resolution.

"Helm, take us to Castor. Best speed."

***

Atlas Drinkwater, Eris, Esworth Orbit.

Luna appeared in the bay clutching three cans of cola. "Look what I found. You remember the last time we had one of these? Months ago, I reckon."

Owl leapt down from the scaffolding around her Leviathan and landed almost without sound. "That stuff will rot your teeth." She smiled and poked a finger at her pristine teeth.

"Fuck you then, Owl," said Luna, with a laugh. "You don't need to drink it."

Owl snatched up one of the cans and Luna threw the other to Atlas.

Following a quiet clink, froth rose from Atlas' can. He studied the tiny mountain of bubbles. Work on the Leviathans was pretty much completed. The crews were gone after putting in monumentally disproportionate hours, long days he suspected were to complete the job in record time and escape the whip tongue of Owl. She wasn't shy in telling people where they were failing. Atlas knew it would only be a matter of time before he, Owl and Luna would be called upon, and it would likely be a short and brutal deployment without backup. This understanding lodged at the back of Atlas' mind, ghosting his every move, making a sullen mood his constant companion.

"Where the hell did you find this?" asked Owl, studying her can.

"It's all about who you know." Luna raised his can in salute.

Owl mimicked his movement. "For an idiot you do some good stuff sometimes."

"Wait," said Luna comically. "Is that Owl complimenting Luna?"

"Don't get too excited. I called you an idiot." Owl sipped from her drink and kicked Atlas' leg. "You're quiet."

He pointed to their Leviathans with his can. "Just thinking. We're as ready as we'll ever be."

Owl burped. "So what now? We wait?"

Luna followed with a louder burp.

Atlas flopped into a chair. "That's exactly what we do."

In fact, waiting could prove to be a potential saviour. The Gate would open in a matter of weeks and with that the arrival of a fresh contingency of Leviathans and operators. Atlas, Owl and Luna were due to rotate back to Earth, but he was under no misapprehension that the departure would be delayed given the circumstances.

"I know how to get you out of your mood," said Owl.

"My mood?"

"Want to go workout?"

He wasn't sure if she meant heading to the gym or to their quarters.

Luna let out a ripping laugh. "Don't worry about me. I'll amuse myself."

"Amuse yourself too much and you'll go blind," said Owl.

Luna pulled up his sleeve and flexed his bicep. "You wanna kiss this, Owl?"

Owl drained the last of her drink, crushed the can, and threw it at Luna. The tinkering of the can echoed in the hollow bay.

The general quarters alarm broke the merriment.

"It's time, boys," said Owl, heading toward her Leviathan.

"No!" Atlas' stern order cut above the blaring alarm. He wasn't keen to put their bodies through an unnecessary hot link. "If they want us they'll come and ask, and until then we do nothing."

Luna stood. "Would it hurt us to make a start?"

"It's the general quarters alarm," said Owl, turning toward her Leviathan. "They're bringing Eris to combat readiness."

"If they want us, they'll come and ask." Atlas leaned back into his chair like he was sitting on a beach expecting water to lap at his feet.

Eris' main engines rumbled to life. The whole ship seemed to groan in protest. It was impossible to not feel a difference when the ship was in full movement. The door to the bay slid open and Commander Holopainen walked in. He raised a hand, a gesture to the operators to remain where they were. He looked the machines up and down, then nodded his appreciation of the mechanical giants.

"First time seeing them up close, sir?" Atlas stood.

"They're quite something. I didn't think they'd be so big."

"Are we needed, sir?" asked Owl impatiently.

"No. The ship is moving to an alternative position. There's no immediate threat."

Atlas speared Owl a look. She returned the 'told you so' with a roll of her eyes.

"Have a closer look, sir," said Atlas. "Follow me. The scaffolding is temporary. We'll take it down today."

Holopainen whistled as he touched the armour. "I was only young when the first prototype was unveiled, and back then I dreamed of being a Leviathan Operator."

"But you didn't?"

"A childhood fantasy, nothing more. The call to Fleet was too strong to resist."

"It's not for everyone, Commander."

"Hundreds apply each year and less than three percent of the intake make it through the training. But I'm telling you nothing you don't know."

"The requirements are rigorous."

"All for good reason. Is this your Leviathan?" asked Holopainen.

"It's mine." Owl scooted up the scaffolding and propped herself on the top level, legs hanging over the edge.

Holopainen looked up then around. "Captain Scott asked me to brief you personally. We're breaking from Fleet and moving in system for Castor."

"Why?" blurted Owl.

"We're pursuing Renown and bringing the ship back."

"Why?" added Luna.

Holopainen smiled curiously at both Owl and Luna, and then to Atlas he said, "We believe Captain Quinn is stripping the orbital stations above Castor and Pollux of supplies. Eris, Aberdeen and Halifax will bring the ship back and Paris Quinn will be arrested."

"And our orders?" asked Atlas.

"Captain Scott doesn't feel that you'll be required to deploy on this mission, however she would like you to work with our marine detachment to progress a closer joint working relationship."

"How long until we get to Castor?" asked Owl. "Is she expecting a battle? I've already been on one ship that was shot out from under us."

Holopainen fixed Owl with a stare. "Eris is the finest ship in the Fleet. There is no chance of anything other than a complete success of our mission."

"Owl meant nothing by it, Commander. I apologise. How long until we reach Castor?"

"Thirty-six hours. I've asked the marine contingent to make themselves known to you."

"And if the creatures on Esworth attack the defensive line? We won't be in a position to intervene."

"Captain Scott and Colonel Hopkins agree that they've stabilised the defensive perimeter. Marines are now deployed to the location, too. Your absence, while regrettable, wasn't deemed unreasonable."

Despite Holopainen's words, Atlas suspected Captain Scott did not want to surrender her ace card, the Leviathans, to another Captain. There were certain rivalries in the Fleet and plenty of animosity since Captain Goodsir led his revolt against Scott's authority.

"Then we look forward to receiving the marines, Commander."

Holopainen left.

"Great, mixing with marines," said Owl.

"Know much about Castor, Atlas?" asked Luna.

"A desolate place apparently and rich with mineral resources, but extraction won't commence for many lifetimes." Atlas had studied other planets in the system as part of his deployment orientation. He came to believe Castor was the kind of area you'd go to with the intention of disappearing.

CHAPTER 12

Doctor Isambard Stone, Undercity, Esworth.

Life in the Undercity was almost always brutal. Long periods of suffering ended in a moment of absolute violence. The unifying factor was darkness. So often the tunnels were alive with miserable inhabitants. You could hear them, smell them. But see them? Killow no longer needed to keep Stone shackled. He had no idea where to run and possessed nothing of value to purchase that information. Credit was the only commodity he had to bargain with but he suspected if you couldn't eat it or use it to survive, it was redundant. Only out of necessity, Stone's movements had become more proficient. He was getting better at navigating in absolute darkness. His head no longer suffered heavy bumps. His knees no longer suffered heavy falls. They travelled through the warrens as slaver and slave. Stone kept quiet and followed all instructions. They crawled through claustrophobic tunnels, side by side.

"Do you have a plan?" The tunnel was quiet enough for Stone to risk speaking.

"Taking you to meet the Pilgrim."

"You are?"

"Not for your sake. For mine. You can help me get Sammy back."

"I'm no hero. No fighter."

"They see me alone, I'm dead. But now I have you, someone touched, and I'm returning you to them."

"I can't be returned if I've not met them."

"They'll recognise one of their own. Then once we're in, I can take Sammy back."

"What if they don't recognise me and we're killed before you can explain yourself?"

"Do you have a better plan, Doctor Stone?"

"Well, no."

The tunnel grew thinner. Stone dropped back. A pinprick of light in the distance destroyed the complete blackness.

"Up ahead the tunnel drops down into one of the main arterial tunnels. It's the boundary between ours and

Peacemaker territory. Neutral ground, but the old laws don't apply. Once we pass through, I don't know what to expect. So be ready."

The tunnel, as Killow predicted, emptied down into a larger tunnel. Stone swung his legs out, dangling them over the edge and dropped down the five feet to the main tunnel.

"Keep low and say nothing," said Killow.

The tunnel was illuminated by a lantern system, lights bolted to the roof at fifty-foot intervals. Secondary tunnels were frequent and of varying sizes. Some little more than natural formations. Others were deliberately hacked, dug by human design. Some of the walls glittered with mineral deposits in the faint light.

Killow held up a hand. Stone stopped. They both listened for sound, searched for movement. Stone thought he sensed a shift in Killow, perhaps the presence of fear.

No sound. No movement. Nothing. Killow waved Stone on. The tunnel widened and the men were able to stand tall and manoeuvre their way at speed.

Stone's feet caught a low obstacle. He tripped and fell heavily. Air burst from his chest and he coughed hard. "I can't breathe."

"Get up," ordered Killow.

"Help me," gasped Stone.

Killow reached down then withdrew his hand. "You'll have to get up yourself. We can't linger here."

A blur of motion appeared behind Killow, resolving to a figure. A sudden, terrible red light appeared with the familiar hum of an energy weapon. Jericho Lees pushed the barrel of the weapon into Killow's neck.

"New World scum," seethed Jericho. "I'm gonna blast your brains to the roof. One less fucking snake down in this shithole."

"Jericho! No!" He couldn't deviate from his course now. He had to meet the Pilgrim. "Don't kill him."

"He's scum." Jericho pushed the barrel harder at Killow's neck. "The things he's done, they've done. They don't deserve anything but death."

"He can help us," said Stone, trying to climb to his feet.

"Somebody's coming," warned Killow, flatly. "The tunnel to your left. Light, moving this way."

"Shut up, scum."

"Jericho, he's right. And we can't be discovered here."

Jericho's peripheral vision worked hard. He pulled Killow's pistol and knife from his belt. "Today's your lucky day, snake."

Killow opened his palms. "As you say."

"Time to go, Jericho." Stone leaned on the wall.

"Don't try anything or I'll leave you for the rats," said Jericho. "And the rats start from the feet up with a preference for live meat."

"Jericho."

"Move," said Jericho.

They moved.

"I know you," said Killow. "You work with us, bartering for free passage yet you talk to me like we were born enemies."

"I use your gang like I use this gun. Nothing more."

The trio ducked into a small tunnel which steeply dipped once inside. They pressed themselves into the concealing darkness.

Stone leaned close to Jericho's ear. "What do you see?"

"Three men. New Worlders. They're wounded. Bleeding. One has an arm useless and hanging. They're hauling ass down the tunnel."

"This way?"

"Shh."

They waited for a long time. The three men remained as still as poles. Their breaths began to find the same rhythm. Stone concentrated on the cadence to take his focus away from his need to gulp in air and cough. His eyes were closed. He heard no sound from the tunnels, but they stood rigid. Stone suddenly felt Jericho's tension slip to the ground.

"Jericho," whispered Stone. "I won't turn back."

"You're mentally ill."

"It's not mental illness," Killow interjected.

"Did anyone ask you, fuck face?" Jericho shot back.

"Sammy was the same," said Killow without pause. "For her to go like she did wasn't in her nature. It's this place."

"Who the fuck is Sammy?"

"His wife," explained Stone. "She's like me."

"Fucked in the head?"

Stone held up a hand. "No, her hands, they burned everyone like mine do."

"You can't trust New Worlders. He says one thing and will do another. I know these people."

The men were still squashed into the small pocket of the tunnel, three sardines in a dimly lit can.

"Jericho, Killow could've killed me a dozen times but hasn't. We both have something each other needs, and we both need to find The Pilgrim."

Jericho stared at Killow for a long time. His glare was full of hate, but his head was full of words and ideas, and Stone couldn't guess any of them.

"You rich folks are all the same," Jericho said to Stone while his eyes remained with Killow. "You all think it's some kind of game, that your money will protect you when shit gets real. That cage should have taught you something."

Stone held out open hands. "Why are you the way you are? What brings you to be employed in such a way?"

Jericho shrugged. "Because people like you pay me."

Stone tapped the back of his head. "You're the same as me. It's like tiny whispers back here telling me to push on and I can't ignore them."

"A weak man using his circumstance to justify what he's done? One more word and I'll cut your tongue from your mouth."

***

Agustin Garcia, Uriah's Hope, Esworth.

"I wish you'd stop fussing." Agustin munched on burnt toast whilst propped up in bed by four pillows. "I'm perfectly fine. I could have burnt my own toast."

Twomley had spent the last half hour bringing Agustin up to speed while preparing breakfast and tidying the apartment. It didn't surprise Agustin that Captain Scott had gone after Renown.

"What else?" Agustin ran his tongue across his teeth, seeking to rid them of crumbs.

"Without Stone, we've been forced to bring together others in the field." Twomley pointed to the screen mounted on the wall.

Agustin nodded and Twomley streamed from his PWD.

"The excavation site closest to the city has been exposed as you've seen. More statues. Drone flyovers have revealed several other sites being dug by the creatures. Thirteen in all.

None of them are uncovered to the clarity of this one." Twomley brought up a still of the area. "Our people are suggesting that the heat source we're detecting is the creatures in such numbers and in a confined space."

"Subterranean dwellers. They'd have to be otherwise we'd have detected them earlier."

"I've spoken to Captain Tyler of the Colossus. He won't enact any bombardment without Scott's say so."

"And the marines are manning the defensive line?"

Twomley clicked through his PWD and brought up a real time feed from the line. The marines were suffering a snowstorm. Occasionally, figures in white camouflage would move from one position to another, dipping out of sight into protective dugouts.

"They report no contact."

"Our official policy has to be defensive. If the creatures are satisfied to leave us be for the time being, we must run with that. If we're lucky, they remain where they are until we can summon enough force from Earth. Show me the other sites."

Twomley streamed a map of Uriah's Hope. Thirteen flashing red dots were clustered to both the north-east and the south-east of the city.

Agustin studied it like a prolific thinker. "These are the creatures? The red?"

"That's right. What are you looking for?"

"A pattern maybe? Something to indicate why they're doing all this."

"Agustin, they're aliens. We don't even know if they're capable of thought in the same manner as you and I. Like the Nights, we just need to accept their ways and react when we can."

"Maybe," Agustin said quietly.

"You don't agree?"

"I saw those things down at the Esworth Chamber. Yes, they're alien but the large creatures, especially the one that tried to grab Stone, there was something too familiar."

"It makes it easier to accept if I think of them as something new, something we can't explain. A problem we just need to solve."

Agustin knew Twomley well enough to realise when he was unnerved. "Any other news?"

"Two murders. Beaten to death in the riots. UHMP moved in but the victims were dead before medics could get to them."

"Is it getting better or worse down there?"

"Hard to say really. The UHMP are doing what they can but people are scared. They're counting down until The Gate opens and some can go home. But, that's a problem for another day."

"I'll come to The Hub later tonight."

Twomley moved to the door. "I'll see you in the morning. If you come before that, I'll have you marched back here. Sweet dreams." Twomley left with a wave over his shoulder.

Agustin would be lying if he said he didn't take a small measure of comfort in being banned from The Hub. It was liberating to let go of the reins, even for a few days of convalescence. He lay back, shifting against his pillows until comfortable, then clicked on the TV. Channel after channel reported on the riots. He stumbled over entertainment channels.

"What's on?" he asked the remote.

Agustin liked the old shows. Frasier was his favourite. Tanya and he would spend hours watching episode after episode, laughing at the brothers, and the father and his dog, and the strangeness of everyday life back in those days. They would debate the advantages and disadvantages of the past compared to the present, and before long Tanya's mother would be included under the umbrella of things in the past.

The ache in his heart burned a little more. Was Tanya also in the past, too? But if she were truly dead, he'd feel it. Somehow. Agustin needed to believe she was alive and that they could get her back. As for Stone, he was probably dead, and that thought made Tanya's loss just a fraction easier to endure.

***

Dr Isambard Stone, Undercity, Esworth.

Once free of the main tunnel travelling became easier. The passage was smoother, wider and lit by the occasional lamp. It was hard to not believe the path was custom-made for them. Jericho's weapon pumped out its red light, casting devil shadows on the walls. A plump rat scurried beneath a boulder, blocking one of the many tunnels. Its tail remained visible as if confident he was out of reach.

A slight incline began underfoot.

"Where is everyone?" asked Stone, looking back down the tunnel. "The Peacemakers. How many of them were there living here?"

"Thousands. Last time I travelled through here the tunnels were teeming. Look at this." He pointed up to a hole in the earth ceiling. "This one's newly carved. It's wider than most. Smell the air?"

Stone and Killow both sniffed.

"It's fresh," agreed Killow. "Fresher than any other tunnel I've been in. If I closed my eyes, I could believe I was back home in Montana. It's strange being here. It used to be death for a New Worlder to set foot in Peacemaker territory. Yet here I am, strolling along and nobody cares."

"Somebody cares," said Stone. "For the last half hour, I've felt something's following us."

"You're feeling them, aren't you? The others who are touched."

Stone not only felt the presence of others, he felt different. He felt stronger. Weakness from being starved and denied water was becoming a distant memory. He was gaining vigour. His hands, for so long permanently cold and lacking much feeling, were resurrected.

"It's called Tunnel Ghosts," said Jericho. "They're common. The lesser used tunnels creak and bang. I've heard it often enough."

"What I've seen lately suggests there's more than we ever thought possible."

"They know we're here," said Killow casually. "Can we slow the pace?"

"Keep up or fall behind," Jericho muttered. "Neither of us will carry you."

***

The Pilgrim of Hate was the natural conclusion to their current path, for Stone heard the voices echoing ahead.

Two figures appeared at the next tunnel juncture, both obviously unarmed. Jericho raised his weapon but Stone held out a hand.

"If they wanted us dead, Jericho, they could've done it hours ago. No weapons."

Stone walked toward the sentries, arms spread. Neither sentry spoke. Something about them wasn't right. Their eyes remained unfocused yet tracked his every movement. Two welcoming smiles appeared artificial as if painted on and were perhaps the only expression they were capable of. They waved the newcomers forward, not quite in unison, but an attempt was obvious.

Jericho and Killow's scrutiny was similar to Stone's, and although his weapon was lowered, Jericho's finger was on the trigger. The sounds of a gathering could be heard, the quiet din of a congregation in patient wait.

They walked through a rudimentary archway. The chamber beyond was huge, hundreds of feet in diameter and height. The walls were constructed of the same blue as the Esworth Chamber. They glistened like a frozen waterfall. Close to a thousand people stood in the centre, orderly, their backs to Stone, and the slight shifting of bodies was the only movement perceived. It was like a crowd waiting for a rock star to appear.

Colossal statues of the creatures lined the walls, hands of stone outstretched, and inert faces raised to the roof.

"What is this?" asked Killow.

"It's like the Esworth Chamber, the one I told you about." Stone held up his hands. "The place I got this."

They stepped further into the chamber. The more he studied the crowd, the more he could distinguish differences. The people at the front looked like the two sentries, still and silent, not communicating with their neighbour. Their chins were raised as if in prayer to statue plinths set back in hollows in the wall. The rest behind seemed restless, both in an excited way and nervously. Eyes turned left and right as if in search of danger and pleasant surprises. Stone glanced back to the entrance. The two guards now stood in the doorway, arms folded across their chests.

"I don't think they're going to let us out." Stone nodded back to the entrance.

"And you paid good money for this, Doctor. No refunds."

"I'm going to look for Sammy," whispered Killow.

"Good luck," said Stone.

"Luck is the only thing we have left, Doc," said Jericho.

Killow moved surreptitiously through the crowd.

The air felt and tasted fresh. It wasn't too hard to imagine a slight breeze seeping through an open window. Stone turned to find the source. Jericho was gone. The mercenary was nowhere to be seen.

Stone moved closer to the crowd. To his right stood a short woman, her face dirty, her long hair matted, and her arms painfully thin.

"What is this place?"

The woman took him in with her peripheral vision. "We're here to listen to the Pilgrim."

"The Pilgrim?"

"We're promised food, safety and a Purpose."

"Safety," he repeated softly.

"Anything is better than the tunnels," she said with impatience. "Shh. Here he comes."

The cavern fell silent. Eerily so. Everything was still. A dead silence. All eyes turned to the same point.

A single figure emerged from a concealed opening in the glittering wall and moved to stand high on a dais.

"Is that—"

"Shh," she hissed.

The Pilgrim wore a simple white robe which flowed past his knees, and dark ankle boots. He appeared an older man with grey hair swept back, curling at the nape of his neck. A salt and pepper beard hung untidily from his chin. Something struck Stone as familiar.

The Pilgrim raised a hand, and his loose sleeve swayed as if caught in a breeze. "Brothers. Sisters. Newcomers. Familiar faces. Welcome." His voice was honey, instantly compelling and carried well in the chamber.

The first rows of the audience dropped to their knees. Foreheads were placed to the ground. The two sentries at the entrance did the same. Stone restrained an urge to mimic the movement and his heart ached for more words from the Pilgrim.

"It's been many weeks since I last stood before you and I come with news. Those who hunger will be fed. Those who have been so cruelly discarded and abused will be given purpose. Those who seek answers will be illuminated. And those who come with treachery will be revealed."

The Pilgrim looked in Stone's direction. Stone dipped his head. The ambrosial words brought an unexpected sense of shame.

"There is one who stands with us now."

That voice silently commanded Stone to look up again.

"He comes with desire and theft in mind. Desperation and longing." The Pilgrim pointed into the crowd, scanning left and right. He closed his eyes and with a louder voice added, "Illuminate this man. Reveal him for judgement."

Stone's knees began to buckle. He wanted to fold into a small profile, become invisible. One of the guards raced past shoving aside those in his way. He moved like a dog with a scent. Another moved from the front and they joined up somewhere in the sea of humanity. Stone lost sight of them. Heads moved and bobbed.

"Get your hands off me, eh? I'll cut you." Killow wrestled with The Pilgrim's men. "I want my wife. Sammy! Sammy, it's me!"

One fast blow to his head quietened Killow and the guards held him tight. They dragged him forward and the crowd parted obediently.

Killow struggled and spat and cursed. "You'll be sorry! I'll pull you apart, limb by limb! Sammy? Sammy, where are you?"

He was lifted from his feet and thrown to the ground before The Pilgrim. Blood dripped from his pulverised nose.

"You cannot take what is not yours, Killow Xavier!" said The Pilgrim. "You cannot take what has never been yours!"

"You have my wife!"

"You come to us with nothing but falsehood and anger. You cannot save someone when they do not require saving. You should rejoice."

"Where is she?"

"Her life is enriched with purpose."

"You know who I am, eh? I'm a New Worlder. You can't fuck with us and get away with it. Give her to me. Now!"

"Enough!" The power in The Pilgrim's voice made Stone step back.

The crowd responded with heads lowering and feet shuffling backward a step. Then a silence and stillness carpeted the room.

"What's happening?" Stone said to the woman to his right.

She did not reply.

"You hear me?" He touched her shoulder. Still no response.

He swung her around to face him. Her body was manoeuvred easily. The thrall's smile split her face. Though her eyes saw Stone, she didn't seem to register his presence.

Left and right he saw the same mechanical smile. Mannequins. No heart. No soul.

"What's happening?" he said to no one.

Four men rushed past him, all panicking and running for the exit point. Stone followed and more followed him.

An Esworth creature blocked the archway. Inhuman eyes glinted like the walls. A serpentine tongue flickered from its mouth across long teeth.

Someone screamed.

"Run!" yelled another.

Those not under the spell of The Pilgrim retreated to the centre of the room. The creature prowled forward. More screams came.

Stone bumped into painted smiles. "What is happening?" he yelled at one, receiving no answer, no acknowledgement, just a carnival-like grin.

"Do not run, my brothers and sisters!" came The Pilgrim's voice. "The Purpose is here for you. All you have to do is accept it. Open your minds. Open your hearts. Welcome the purpose."

Killow was still held on the dais. "Sammy! Sammy!" he screamed desperately.

The creature herded the crowd like a sheepdog and snapped at stragglers. Scuffles broke out as fear catapulted to hysterics. The room hummed with a tangible power. Green, bale light crackled from The Pilgrim's eyes and ran down his face and to his outstretched hand. He touched Killow's forehead. Killow shook. His mouth flew wide, no sound spewing out. The green enveloped him, saturating the New Worlder until he was no longer fully visible. Then suddenly the light dissipated. Killow slumped to the floor of the dais and didn't move again.

"The Purpose comes to this place!"

More creatures spilled from hidden entrances and came to stand beside The Pilgrim. As if on order, they leapt into the crowd and sank their teeth into the crowd.

Stone pressed his hands to his eyes. The screams grew louder and more hysterical. The crunching of teeth into bones speared Stone's ears. He dropped to the ground, covered his ears and screamed into the floor, waiting for his turn.

His mother, Tanya, his first dog Chummy, a Christmas bicycle, all ran through his mind as if a catalogue of his past. Snow boots, a pool, a forked path, university gates, a train station. Stone banged his head on the floor. "No! No! No!" Faint tremors passed up through his body from the floor. The train?

A strange warmth radiated up to his face. The tremors halted. Silence. Was he dead? Stone's heart was beating fast. He opened his eyes. The Pilgrim stood before him with a fatherly smile.

"Rise, brother. Cowering on the floor is no place for one such as you."

The creatures were gone. The floor was a jigsaw of body parts. Stone and the Pilgrim were alone. He retched. And retched again so hard he wet himself. The smell of the chamber was horrid.

"This was a necessity, to bring you and I together, Isambard."

Stone looked up. He wiped dribble from his mouth. "A necessity?"

"Yes, Isambard."

"Are they all dead?"

"Not all. Those who accepted the Purpose have moved on toward enlightenment."

Stone looked to the walls, the covert entrances, the archway. "Are you going to kill me?"

"Kill you? No. You seek answers and I am willing to provide them. But this is not the place for revelations. Come with me." He opened his hand, nodding for Stone to take it.

Stone didn't move.

The Pilgrim shrugged. "Your enquiring mind urges you to accept the offer, no?"

He was right. No matter what Stone just witnessed, his addiction to discovery wanted him to stand and follow.

"Should you refuse, Isambard, you'll walk between two worlds, never to find true peace. It will be a pitiful existence. Ask Jericho."

"Jericho?" Stone turned.

Jericho Lees stood not ten feet away among the dead as if standing in a field, his face expressionless, his hands limp by his sides.

"I don't understand."

"Understanding is with me. Come," said The Pilgrim.

"Answer me one thing. Tanya Garcia, is she alive?"

"Tanya is with us, Isambard. She has a purpose now. She is safe."

"Don't go," said Jericho.

Stone climbed to his feet. "I don't know what the hell is happening here, Jericho. I don't know what you are, but you need to do one last thing for me. Get word to Agustin Garcia. Tell him Tanya is alive and with them."

Jericho did not respond.

"Tell Agustin I'm sorry. But I'll make things right again. And if he finds me, shoot. The rest of your money is in my apartment. Consider that your contract fulfilled."

***

Captain Olivia Scott, Eris, Castor.

Eris approached Castor and dropped to combat speed. The general quarters alarm was sounded as the battle cruiser was readied for conflict.

"Officer of the Watch, anything?"

Lieutenant Rowland shook her head. "Nothing, Captain. If Renown is out there, she's running silent."

"What about Castor Station?" asked Holopainen. "Are we receiving anything from the installation?"

"Nothing, Commander."

"Bring our shields online. I won't be caught unprepared."

Lieutenant Rowland confirmed the order as the gentle hum of the shields enveloping the ship followed.

"Visual contact with Castor Station, Captain."

The screen to the front of the bridge came to life with a real time picture of their approach. Scott swapped between the holographic tactical views of her ship's dispositions. The ship's sensors were linked to the holographic image and would show if Renown could be detected.

"I don't like this," said Holopainen. "She could be luring us in, waiting to hit us."

"Comms, broadcast this to whoever might be listening."

"Broadcasting, Captain."

"To Captain Paris Quinn and the crew of the Renown. I am Captain Olivia Scott, the rightful Officer in Command of the Esworth Defence Fleet. You are hereby ordered to make your location known and surrender Renown to my custody. Paris Quinn, you will be placed under arrest. Do not make the mistake of underestimating me. If you fail to comply, you'll be hunted and forcibly brought to justice. You have three hours to broadcast your location. There will be no further communication from this point."

Scott cut a hand across her neck, indicting communication should end.

Holopainen smiled. "Nicely done, Captain."

"If we're lucky, the crew will take control of the situation and hand her and Renown over. If not. Well, if not we'll take the ship back. Three hours and we'll be within boarding range of Castor Station."

"We've received the information you requested," said Holopainen.

"From the quartermaster?"

"Yes."

Scott fired up her screen. The report was thorough. Renown held enough food supplies for another four weeks. Ammunition and power cells were near full. Food would be the key and Scott guessed that was why she made for Castor. Emergency food supplies were held on Castor Station. She studied the schematics, a standard design that represented the bare minimum for an orbital facility. A small habitation zone. Most of the lower levels were given over to a dock and storage facilities. A small science lab and medical bay were located toward the command hub. It lacked significant defences, relying on its thick armour and defensive turrets.

Three hours passed in silent contemplation. Castor grew in size on the viewer. Scott's every muscle contracted, ready to react to a sudden emergency. The planet was a pale and lonely body. Few people had travelled this far in system before.

"Send the activation signal again, Officer of the Watch."

"Captain, there's no power reading coming from Castor Station. Not even what we'd expect from a station in lockdown."

"Damage to the station?"

"None, Captain."

"Helm, bring us closer." To Holopainen she said, "Prepare a party of marines to board the station. I'll lead the team. If I'm right, Quinn has been aboard and tampered with the station's systems."

Holopainen activated their privacy shield. "Captain, with all due respect, is that wise? Perhaps let me go."

"No, Jan. I will be going. I'll say no more on the matter."

***

Large, magnetic boots made Scott's feet feel five times too large for her legs. She stomped onto the shuttle in the zero-g suit and tested the HUD system in her domed helmet. Scott had probably clocked up more zero-g walks than any of the marines, but it had been some time since she pulled on the suit. Information flashed onto the screen displaying environmental details. A squad of five marines accompanied her aboard. One fastened her to the chair. Internal communications crackled to life inside the helmet.

"Disengage your boots, Captain," said one.

She did and gave him the thumbs up. A high-powered rifle was pushed into her hands, one designed to fire accurately in zero-g situations. She locked it down against her suit.

"You okay, Captain?"

Scott wasn't sure which marine said that last but she gave another thumbs up.

"Stick with us. We'll keep you safe, Captain."

The marines were totally efficient in securing themselves and their weapons. They seemed relaxed and overly familiar with their routine. Yes, she'd be safe with them.

The engines fired and the shuttle lurched from the deck. The marines chatted on the open channel. One offered odds on the time they would return. One complained about missing his early coffee. They could've switched to private but Scott suspected they'd been ordered to keep communications open to her.

She closed her eyes, allowing the banal conversation to float into the background. What if real trouble was ahead? What if she was leading a team on their final mission? What if Quinn rigged Castor Station to blow once they boarded? Perhaps a small ambush waited. Had she allowed her pride to dictate her decisions? Holopainen may have been right suggesting it to be a mistake to go. After all, her place was on Eris commanding the small battle group. But she refused to be cowed by Quinn. She would tackle the rebel personally.

"One minute," said a marine, the voice booming in the helmet.

The shuttle rocked and the engines powered down. The red light by the rear hatch changed to green. Scott disengaged her restraints and followed the team to the hatch.

"Activate your magnetic boots, Captain. Zero-G from this point."

Scott obeyed and the hatch opened. The marines moved off the shuttle with practiced efficiency, weapons ready, laser sights flickering left and right. Scott followed. The shuttle powered up the external lights. Automatic lights on her suit activated, shooting strong beams ahead.

Castor Station's five-port hangar was empty.

"Captain Scott, if you get separated from us for any reason, make your way back to the shuttle. Ready?"

"Yes, let's do this."

"Good. Disengage the magnetic lock on your rifle."

She did.

Holopainen's voice came through the speaker. "Captain, I'm monitoring your live feed from Eris. If anything goes wrong, I'll guide you back to the shuttle. We've got an extraction team suited and ready."

"Received, XO. Keep me updated on any changes with the scans for Renown." She followed the marines into the bleak corridors leading from the hangar.

For a dead station, Castor felt in order. Scott had served on the Aggressor when the gravity field disengaged in error, and hallways became littered with the floating detritus of ship life. But nothing seemed out of place here.

The marines swept forward, one of their number hanging back behind Scott. No interior lights were active. Most doorways were open, but those closed required the manual release engaged and the heavy steel doors forced apart. It was slow going.

"Clear."

"Clear."

"Clear," came the announcement over and again.

The lower levels were all clear. They crept further up through the habitation zone. All the facilities were new and ready to use. Not one bed had been slept in. Not one shower had been turned on.

"Captain, if we turn the power back on progress would be a lot quicker. Lights would help."

"Complete the sweep first. I don't want to give anyone who might be here warning we're coming for them."

They swept the habitation and science lab finding nothing but newness. It felt like walking in fresh snowfall, they were the first since construction to walk in the hallways.

"Only the command section left now, Captain. Ready to proceed?"

"Proceed."

Two of the marines opened the door's circuitry hatch and pulled the disengagement handle. The door bumped open enough for single file. Without power, the main transit lift was out of action, and the only way to move from the habitation zone to the upper command section was up a narrow ladder. One by one the marines disengaged their boots and pulled themselves up the ladder.

"Likewise, Captain. Take hold of the ladder, disengage your boots and pull yourself up. Got it?"

"Got it." Scott secured her weapon to her environment suit and disengaged the magnetic lock on her boots. Now weightless, up she went grabbing every third rung. At the top, she used the wall to turn herself and plant her feet, then activated the boot locks.

"You okay, Captain?"

Scott could see which marine spoke. It was the sergeant. A handsome face looked directly at her.

"This isn't my first time, Sergeant."

"Of course." Smile lines appeared at the sides of his eyes.

They stood in a small plaza. The lift doors to her left were closed and lifeless. Huge blast doors stood before them, shielding the most sensitive section of Castor Station. The doors would only be open in an emergency or to allow crew to move from command areas to other parts of the station.

Scott's lights illuminated the imposing barriers. "Sergeant, you see these doors?"

"Yes, ma'am. They've been welded shut. You can see the burn marks on the metal up there."

"Could that have been caused during construction? An error that was never corrected?"

"No, Captain. Doesn't look like anything other than a deliberate attempt to keep someone out."

"Exactly what I'm thinking. Can we break through to the command section?"

The sergeant inspected the doors closely. "We'd need to bring in cutting equipment. It wouldn't be a quick thing either. These doors are pretty good at their job, and that's holding people out."

"How long?"

He shrugged. "Five hours."

"Get it done in three."

***

Marine engineers arrived soon after.

Four hours later, "Captain, we're about to break through."

A deep gorge had been cut through the armoured door. The marines stood ready, and Scott brought her weapon up, too, while the engineers removed the cutting equipment.

"Small explosion now," warned the sergeant. "Stand clear!"

The area that was cut boomed three times as the doorway was blasted open. Dust clouds filled the air. The five marines stooped to move through the opening one at a time, laser sights leading the way. Scott followed. Inside, the command zone was a scene of confusion. At least one-hundred bodies, all dressed in underwear, drifted like rocks in space, frozen and dead. Dark screens and empty terminals lined the walls. Windows to the outside were covered by further blast doors.

"Check for signs of life." Scott moved between the bodies. The faces were cemented in terror, eyes wide, mouth open in a rictus scream. They didn't deserve this. All of them would have been looking forward to returning back home once The Gate opened. Back to friends and family, children even. It should never have come to pass that they were betrayed by those in the same uniform.

All were frozen and would've died quickly when the station's systems were turned off. The computer linked to her suit scanned the faces as she passed, bringing up names and details. All were crew from Renown.

"You seeing what I'm seeing, XO?"

"Yes, Captain."

"Further orders, Captain?" asked the sergeant.

"Bring Castor back online and let's get our dead back to Eris. They'll be laid to rest in the proper way."

Holopainen's voice crackled in her ear. "Why would Quinn do that? Why not put them in life pods, send a beacon for them? We'd have come for them."

"It's a message, Jan. A message to me. To all of us. I want this bitch dead. Get those engineers in here. I want the station operational and moving for Pollux as soon as possible. I'm returning to Eris."

***

Via the bridge viewer, Scott watched Castor Station resurrect. Lighting at the extreme points was the first sign, then internal lighting.

Soon after came a transmission from Castor Station. "This is Castor Station reporting all systems at maximum operation." Castor lived again.

"Report re supplies," ordered Scott.

"Emergency supplies gone, Captain. We'll be ready to depart at seventeen-thirty hours."

Shuttles moved from Castor to Eris, conveying the dead.

"Officer of the Watch, I want Halifax and Aberdeen made ready for transit to Pollux. XO, I want Eris ready for the return journey back to Esworth once we've recovered everyone from Castor."

The bridge crew moved to their consoles to make Eris ready. Scott couldn't have been more proud. When she stated that Eris was the best ship, with the best crew in the fleet, she believed it. This is what Scott lived for. On Eris, she was master and the crew moved to her command without pause.

A private call bleeped for Scott. Captain Hale of the Halifax appeared on her screen.

Hale nodded in greeting. "Captain Scott, please activate your privacy screen."

Scott activated the distortion shield. "Screen activated, Captain. What can I do for you?"

Hale breathed out noisily. "Halifax has suffered a loss of power translation from our core to the engines. We can manoeuvre but that's about it. Won't be able to keep up with you."

"What happened?"

"All systems were checked before we left Esworth."

"You're suggesting it wasn't an accident?"

"Near on impossible to be an accident."

"How long to repair?"

"Days. Days to get us to speed and longer to get us to fighting capability. Captain, I'm urging you not to depart for Pollux. Not yet. If it's sabotage as I suspect, Paris Quinn's plan is to split us up."

Scott rubbed under her nose. "Time isn't a luxury we have, Captain Hale. Return to Esworth when repairs are completed. Eris and Aberdeen will continue the hunt."

Hale pursed his lips. "May I have my objection noted, Captain Scott?"

"Noted. You have your orders, Captain Hale. Return to Esworth on the completion of your repairs. Eris out."

Scott dropped the privacy shield and relayed the information to Holopainen.

"Christ, what a mess," said Holopainen, rubbing his forehead. "Does it ever seem to you that something more than chance is against us?"

"All the time, XO. All the time."

A short time later, Eris and Aberdeen's engines fired and the ships pushed free of Castor's orbit, making for Pollux.

***

Travel to Pollux took three days. Alarms rang.

"Captain, we have a confirmed sensor reading from Pollux Station. There's a ship in orbit."

"I want that ship identified," ordered Scott, though she knew it could only be Renown. "Bring shields and weapons systems online. Sound general quarters."

"Renown confirmed, Captain. No movement from the ship," said the officer of the watch.

"Comms, let me talk to Renown."

"Communications established, Captain."

"This is Captain Scott of the Eris to Captain Paris Quinn. You're hereby ordered to stand down. Surrender command of Renown and you have my word you'll be treated fairly. Refuse and you'll be met with force." Scott let a moment hang.

Two helmsmen and Scott exchanged glances.

"Dammit, Quinn, don't be a bloody fool. Stand down."

"They're not responding, Captain," confirmed comms.

"They're powering engines, Captain, and activated all weapons systems," said the officer of the watch.

"Course?"

"Intercept course, Captain."

"You've just got a lot of people killed," said Scott, under her breath. "Very well. Bring Eris into intercept course. Order Aberdeen to shadow."

"Weapons fired from Renown!" said the officer of the watch.

Scott dragged her screen close. Holographic representations of the fire flash pulled away from Renown. Six torpedoes raced toward Eris.

"Point defence turrets are online, Captain," said Holopainen, punching a finger at his terminal.

"Another torpedo salvo from Renown," said the officer of the watch.

Twelve torpedoes sped toward Eris, eating the distance between the two ships fast.

Aberdeen, smaller and nimbler than Eris, pulled ahead, breaking standard formation.

"What's Aberdeen doing?" asked Holopainen.

"Putting herself out there to intercept the torpedoes?" offered one of the weapons specialists.

Scott switched her terminal to tactical. Digital circles opened around Eris and Aberdeen indicating the range of their weapons.

"Captain?" said Holopainen.

Scott could've ordered the firing of her own torpedoes, but they were weapons for destroying ships, not capturing and arrest. The first six torpedoes entered the first circle.

Scott gripped the armrests of her chair. "Take out those torpedoes."

The rapid thudding echoed through Eris as the point defence turrets opened, firing their salvo. Aberdeen joined with the defensive fire. The six red indicators disappeared on Scott's screen. The second barrage breached the ship's defensive perimeter.

"Take out the second onslaught."

Again the thudding echoes rumbled through Eris as the point defence turrets spat out uranium tipped rounds. They intercepted the first five missiles. The sixth rocketed through unimpeded and crossed further circles on her screen. It thudded into Eris' shields. Eris rocked. A fantastic ripple of light countered the brief explosion.

"Report damage," ordered Scott.

"Minor damage to the hull, Captain," reported the officer of the watch. "No breaches. Shields absorbed the majority of the impact."

"Shield efficiency?"

"Ninety percent efficiency, Captain."

"Captain." Holopainen's voice was hesitant and unsure. "Aberdeen didn't fire on the second salvo."

Aberdeen pulled away from Eris and moved toward Pollux. Scott placed a call to Captain Shellenberger. Instead of Shellenberger's face, one unfamiliar greeted her.

"Where is Captain Shellenberger?" she demanded. The ship's computer brought up the name and service file from the smiling face looking back at her. "Lieutenant Commander Adam Doran."

"So you remember me?"

"Not at all. Where is Captain Shellenberger?"

"Captain Shellenberger is no longer in command of the ship, Captain Scott." Doran leaned into the camera until his face filled the entire view. "Look what you've done to this fleet and the tradition we uphold. If there's any blame, it's on your shoulders."

The link ended only to be replaced by another link with an unkempt Paris Quinn. Quinn was once a pretty woman, but it seemed rebellion invited ugliness.

Quinn's frown was extreme. "Take your ship back to Esworth, Olivia. I won't ask again."

"I'm you're commanding officer. I order you to surrender."

Quinn cackled without humour. "You couldn't command a bunch of obedient show dogs."

"How dare you speak to me in that fashion. I saw what you did to the crew on Castor Station. You're a murderer. Surrender, Paris or by all that's right I'll see you suffer."

"There's more going on here than you know."

"What do you mean?"

"It's not always about you, Olivia. It's beyond an argument of succession after Hal Hastings."

"You're just—"

"Whatever's down on Esworth is affecting people up here. Those left on Castor Station weren't put there because I couldn't trust them, they were there because a collective madness took them."

"You have no—"

"We won't go back to Esworth," Quinn seethed. "When The Gate opens we'll negotiate our surrender and return to Earth. You don't understand and neither do I, but right or wrong, we've been set on different paths. I won't risk the remainder of the Renown crew being exposed to that madness. Tell Shellenberger to turn his ship around or I'll destroy Aberdeen."

The link ended abruptly.

Scott beckoned Holopainen to activate his privacy shield. "What Quinn said about a madness."

"Grundy said similar about Remus."

Scott nodded. "It seems possible."

"She's fearful, not just defiant."

"It seems our friend Doran isn't a welcome associate but merely opportunistic."

"How do you want to handle this?" asked Holopainen.

"No one will dictate to me," Scott answered with heat. "We bring her back, alive if possible, but I will bring her back, and whatever madness she's talking about we'll deal with then."

"If we allow Aberdeen and Renown to fight, it might make it easier for us to subdue them both."

"We can't risk any more ships."

Scott dropped their privacy shield. "I want Aberdeen's weapon power disabled. Leave her some power but slow her down. We intercept Aberdeen then go after Renown."

Where Quinn had removed the threat of a command override on Renown, Scott hoped that Doran wouldn't have had the foresight to do such a thing. It took knowledge of the system and wasn't a quick process.

"Disabler ready, Captain."

Scott punched in her command override. The request stalled. "Come on," she encouraged.

Still nothing. And then an error message.

Scott slammed her fist on the armrest of her chair. "Someone aboard has managed to remove that protocol."

The rear batteries on Aberdeen opened up, firing rounds at Eris. Lance fire streaked out, licking at Eris' shields, each impact rocking the ship and causing a small eruption of colour.

"They're not firing with all their lance batteries," observed Holopainen. "Aberdeen is under crewed."

"So we assume Doran has removed the command staff? They have control but not the expertise?"

"Good chance, Captain."

"I want Aberdeen stopped."

Eris opened up on Aberdeen. Brilliant streaks of lance fire shot between the two ships. Aberdeen's shields constantly erupted in flashes of colour when struck.

"Keep firing. Strip away their shields." Scott switched her view between real time and the holographic tactical map. "Comms, keep broadcasting for Doran's surrender. Assure them if they stand down, they will not be harmed. Helm, I want the distance closed."

Eris' structure shuddered as the engines powered to close the gap.

"Aberdeen's shields are collapsing, Captain." The officer of the watch turned to Scott. "Orders?"

"Stop Aberdeen. XO, prepare a marine boarding party. I want that ship."

Eris drew closer, shrugging off more intense fire from Aberdeen.

"Our shields are down to seventy percent, Captain," informed the officer of the watch.

When the battle cruiser fired, it was surgical. Lance beams tore into the engines of Aberdeen, searing through the casing and rupturing the internals. Minor internal explosions rocked Aberdeen and the engines dulled, dropping the ship's speed. Eris tore past and fired using lance fire to strike at the turrets and Aberdeen's own lance batteries. Eris rocked violently, absorbing fire from the destroyer. Scott was thrown from her seat. Holopainen fell to the floor.

"Report!" yelled Scott, climbing to her feet.

"Captain, three dead and a hole punched through our armour plating," said the officer of the watch. "Lance battery A-16 is out of commission."

"Get repair crews down there," said Holopainen.

"Bring us round for another run," ordered Scott.

"Renown is firing another spread of torpedoes at Aberdeen," said Holopainen. "We've weakened their defences."

"Helm, get Eris into a position to intercept," ordered Scott.

"We're not going to make it," said Holopainen. "We're out of range for the point defence turrets."

Six torpedoes slammed into the hull of the destroyer Aberdeen. The ship split in half. Aberdeen became two sections. The remaining engine banks snuffed out. There was silence for a long moment.

"Did anyone make it off the ship?" asked Scott, finally.

"Escape pods launched but were destroyed by the secondary explosions." The officer of the watch tapped at her screen. "Aberdeen has been lost with all hands, Captain."

"I want every torpedo we have aboard fired at Renown," said Scott, so quietly it could have been a whisper.

Holopainen turned to Scott. "Captain? Are you sure you want to do this?"

"I want Renown blown out of the stars. Continue to close and fire everything."

Eris closed and fired salvo after salvo of torpedoes, the red markers streaking toward their target.

"Twenty-eight torpedoes away, Captain," the weapons system officer announced. "Renown taking evasive manoeuvres and firing counter measures."

Renown entered a full burn, lurching suddenly, moving back toward Pollux Station.

"Quinn's putting herself between the station and the torpedoes," said Holopainen.

The missiles changed course, continuing to track Renown. Point defence turrets opened. Tracer fire streaked out. One torpedo got through and struck Renown, bursting with fire over the shields. Renown turned, exposing her port side. They fired everything at the incoming salvo. Lance and defence batteries struck out. Another three torpedoes were brought down.

"Captain, a pod's been ejected from Renown."

The remaining torpedoes slammed into Renown's port hull and engine housing erupted along the length of the ship. Scott altered her view between holographic battle display and real time, watching the entirety of Eris' torpedoes drilling into Renown. The destroyer crumpled under the sustained attack, breaking into several pieces. Renown blinked out of existence on her battle display.

Holopainen sat back in his chair and blew his cheeks out. "Renown has been taken out."

The bridge crew erupted in cheers.

"We did what we had to do," whispered Holopainen to Scott.

"Yes," Scott said numbly.

"When the investigation comes it'll be clear that Goodsir and Quinn left us no choice."

"Bring the escape pod aboard. Nobody speaks to the survivors but me."

***

Flanked by marine protection Scott made her way to the brig. She'd been told three people were found in the pod, but no names were yet known. Scott approached the nearest cell and saw a female sitting on the bench, head down and hair covering the face.

"Open it," she ordered.

It slid open silently and Scott stepped inside.

Paris Quinn looked up, shackled to a bench, her face crossed with cuts and swelling above her left eye.

"Wait outside," said Scott to the marines.

"You destroyed my ship," said Quinn. "So what happens now?"

Scott waited for the door to close before speaking. "Why?" The single word hung between them like an impenetrable wall.

Quinn straightened. "Because Goodsir should've been in command of Fleet, not you."

Scott marched at Quinn, grabbed her hair and pulled her face closer. "Whether you agree or not, we all follow orders! That's how we survive!"

Quinn flinched. "When Erebus was destroyed, I heard the voices, Olivia. As clear as you are speaking to me now."

Scott released her hold and worked hard to contain her anger.

"I heard them whisper like they were standing next to me. We all did. And many were driven mad by it. Mad I tell you. We had to do some awful things to survive."

"You're a coward," spat Scott. "And a murderer."

"Coward? How can we fight what we don't understand?"

"You deserted your station and disobeyed orders. Your actions led to hundreds of deaths, your actions, you, one who swore to protect and serve."

Quinn shook her shackles violently. "You could've just left us alone!"

"What?"

"At Pollux. You coming here caused this. You knew I wouldn't return. You could have just left us alone, Olivia."

"You'll address me by title."

"Why did you come here if you didn't want to listen?"

"I wanted to look at your face, one last time. All hands died on that ship." Scott pulled her side-arm from the holster.

Quinn backed away until the wall prevented no further retreat. "You can't. Olivia. Please. You need to transport me back to Earth. I'll face the charges there."

Scott raised her weapon, stepped forward and aimed at Quinn's face. "I can't allow that. The records will show there were no survivors from Renown. None."

Quinn screamed for help and Scott pulled the trigger. Quinn remained upright, her eyes dull and empty. She slowly slid sideways, the path of her head painting a lineal arch on the wall all the way to the height of the bench. Scott's hand shook. The weapon lowered as if on its own accord. She was torn between kicking at the dead body and throwing up.

"It needed to be done," she said out loud to no one.

Paris Quinn was the first person she'd killed by her own hands. Scott was glad she did it. Quinn deserved to die, and Scott was her commanding officer, an officer trained to kill the enemy when necessary.

"It needed to be done," she repeated.

Scott left the cell.

A marine waited outside, unmoving. "The others have been taken care of, Captain."

Scott nodded her understanding.

"Some people need killing, Captain." The marine saluted.

"Seems that way."

CHAPTER 13

Director Agustin Garcia, Uriah's Hope, Esworth.

Agustin was welcomed back to The Hub by a round of applause. Despite still being weak from his period of convalescing, his face lit with a grin. It felt good to be back.

Twomley stepped away from Agustin's workstation, and with a flourish of a hand said, "The city is yours, Director."

Agustin sat into his old chair and relaxed into the familiar cushioning. He rubbed his hands together, not to prepare for work, but The Hub was slightly cooler than his apartment. He pulled his terminal to his lap.

Twomley sat into the chair beside him and pointed to the screen. It displayed a real time image of The Gate.

"We've done it, Agustin. In a few hours The Gate will open and we'll be able to send requests for help from Earth."

The influx of ships, supplies and staff would be sorely welcome. They would alleviate much of The Hope's woes, but nothing would get Tanya back. His greatest wish was to see her on a freighter slipping back to Earth. And now, it would never come to be.

"Are all preparations in place for departures?"

"Freighters are at capacity, almost dangerously so."

"Any trouble?"

"Riots, protests, all about the lack of information as to what's happening outside the city. But I think we're past the worst."

"And the creatures?"

Twomley shrugged. "Nothing to report. They seem content to remain where they are."

"And what of Captain Scott?"

"Eris and Halifax should return in the next few days."

"The condition of Halifax?"

"Damaged but mobile. Hence the slow progress."

"And Scott?"

"I've told you all I know. She's not saying much more than that."

Agustin blew out a loud breath. The destruction of both Aberdeen and Renown came as a surprise, and it seemed, avoidable. Scott may be held responsible and face charges once Fleet Command received a full report. Her situation, in his opinion, was untenable. Someone would need to take the fall.

"It could've been worse, Agustin. A lot worse. I'd say all things considered and what we're dealing with, we've been lucky."

"A lot of people died to make sure we stayed lucky," said Agustin.

***

Alarms rang in The Hub and the screens switched to a live stream from Romulus Station. The opening of The Gate always filled Agustin with a certain fascinating dread. The space tore, like a theatre curtain drawing aside and opening to a show, and this show being the Starless Sea. The science and mechanics behind the feat often leant him to believe in miracles, and those mesmerising colours and movements did little to contain his supposition that a magical artist called all the shots backstage.

People more intelligent than Agustin argued over the true nature of the Starless Sea. The most commonly held belief was that it was folded space, a stable wormhole between two points allowing rapid travel over a huge distance. Others believed once you entered The Gate you were taken somewhere else, somewhere humans shouldn't go.

Power transferred to The Gate struts one at a time. The computer display flashed green lights as all thirteen struts reached maximum charge.

"Power transfer complete. Uplink and rift stabilisation in sixty seconds," said the team leader.

Twomley squeezed Agustin's arm. "We've done it," he mouthed silently.

Agustin wasn't ready to share his friend's enthusiasm. There were too many variables.

The seconds ticked away.

"Uplink initiating," said the team leader.

The main viewer showed the energy in the struts discharging, the blackness between shimmering, but The Gate didn't open.

"We have no uplink." The team leader waved to Agustin, his face as pale as the snow outside. "Director. We have no uplink with home."

Agustin stood like the captain of a ship taking command of a wayward vessel.

"Gate team liaise with Fleet and technicians. I want another attempt to secure an uplink executed immediately."

"What the fuck is going on?" Twomley stood, too.

The Hub command team broke into hurried conversation.

"Director, we're getting a lot of calls from the freighters waiting to depart. What do I tell them?" asked Hawker, the comms manager.

"Tell them to stay their course, Mr Hawker," said Agustin. "Give us time to work this out."

"Second uplink attempt commencing."

The Hub quietened with all eyes on the main screen. The remainder of the power reserves discharged again. The space between The Gate rippled but no rift formed. With no power remaining, The Gate struts returned to inactivity.

"Second uplink failed."

"Shut it down," ordered Agustin. If all the charge left the struts it would take days to transfer power again. "Power everything down and have the freighters return to their pre-translation positions."

"Sir?" said the team leader.

"Shut it down. Now." To Twomley he said, "Get Chief Constable Reid online. We're going to have problems with crowd control."

"We're cut off from Earth," said Twomley, still looking at the screen. "How can this happen? It can't happen. We can't be cut off."

"Dale, look around you. You and I can't be seen to panic."

Twomley whipped off his glasses and rubbed his eyes. "What do you need me to do?"

"Coordinate with the UHMP and Fleet. When words gets out The Gate didn't open, the city will tear itself apart."

***

Agustin reined in his bubbling panic and snapped out orders, delegated tasks, and demanded uninterrupted focus. The situation was grave, there was no denying that, but there were procedures in place to deal with situations such as these.

The clock would be reset and scheduled for the next Gate opening.

The door to The Hub opened and Agustin gave only a customary glance. Three new arrivals strode in.

A woman, flanked by two armed soldiers with faces concealed by masks, approached the command chairs. The woman wore an expensive black suit, black tie and knee length overcoat. Her blond hair was pulled back into a tight ponytail and swayed behind her with every step. Red lips broke into a smile as she fixed her icy stare on Agustin.

"Who the hell are you?" asked Twomley, stepping ahead of Agustin. "You can't just come in here. This is a secure area."

"She's Cooperative Internal Division," said Agustin, placing a hand on Twomley's shoulder. "Or am I wrong with that assumption?"

The woman's smile widened. "Director Garcia, you are correct. I am Grace Anderson of the CID. I have orders to assume temporary control of the Directorship of Uriah's Hope until such a time as this crisis is concluded." She pulled a neatly folded envelope from a coat pocket. "My orders, Director. An electronic copy has been sent to all appropriate members of your command team. For now, Director Garcia, I must request that you leave this facility. You will be utilised as a consultant … if we have the need." Those red lips closed.

The two guards flanking Grace Anderson stood a little more rigid.

"That won't be necessary," said Agustin, holding up a halting hand.

"Thank you for your cooperation, Mr Garcia. Your security clearances will be revoked temporarily. We thank you for your service. Assistant Director Twomley, I would like you to remain on staff to ensure continuity as we navigate through this crisis."

Twomley shook his head. "I'll never work for a harpy like you or the CID."

"Dale," warned Agustin.

"No. They want to rip apart the one thing which keeps this city running. I won't be part of it."

Agustin rounded on his friend. "I need you here to keep an eye on her," he said quietly.

Twomley's jaw tightened then he nodded, one sharp movement.

"Well, there's nothing else for me to do here." Agustin made for the doorway, ignored Grace Anderson and left The Hub.

***

Atlas Drinkwater, Eris, Traversing to Esworth.

The call for help never came, so Atlas found the battle to be nothing more than deep rumbling, blaring alarms and the occasional rocking of Eris. He'd heard second-hand that two ships had been destroyed but received no specifics.

Atlas walked Eris' corridor, heading back to the bay where they essentially now lived. Owl came running around the corner.

"It's the CID pricks, Atlas. They cornered me. They were asking me if I was loyal to the Terran Cooperative, asking about you and Luna."

"And?"

"I told the boss bitch to go fuck herself. They're with Luna now."

"Let's go," said Atlas. They bounded through the corridor.

"Watch where you're going," said an ensign almost taken out by Owl.

"Fuck off!" Owl threw back over her shoulder.

The bay door slid open and they dashed inside.

Luna stood by his Leviathan, arms crossed, nodding as a woman wearing a well-fitting suit talked.

Luna looked to Atlas and Owl. "Hey guys, I was just speaking with, well, I never got your name. She's interested in the Leviathans."

"Get the fuck away from him," said Atlas, placing himself between Luna and the woman.

"We were just speaking," she said, smiling. She was beautiful, pale skin, bright eyes and lips that seemed impossibly alluring.

Atlas lifted his chin. "You're done speaking. Get the fuck outta here before I throw you out."

"Atlas." Owl's voice wavered.

A red dot traced down Owl's forehead and hovered over her chest.

The CID woman giggled. "You wouldn't want to do that, Atlas Drinkwater. We're not here to cause trouble, only to talk."

"I doubt that."

"The day will come when you three will be asked one question, the most important question you've ever been asked."

"And that is?"

"Are you loyal to the Terran Cooperative?"

Atlas frowned.

"Think on it and remember today as a day I chose leniency over force." The CID woman turned her back and walked toward the door. She waved a hand in the air and an armed figure detached itself from the dark corner of the bay to follow her out.

"What the fuck was that?" asked Owl. "Those CID pricks think they can come in here and push us around."

"Say nothing to them. Agree to nothing. We're not getting drawn into their political bullshit," warned Atlas. "And if they try anything, we'll be ready."

"Why are you both looking at me?" Luna placed a hand over his heart and feigned hurt. "Just because she was hot, you think I would agree to whatever she asked?"

"We know you," said Owl.

"She wasn't that hot," laughed Luna.

***

Agustin Garcia, Uriah's Hope, Esworth.

Three hours later, Agustin sat in his apartment sipping from his second glass of scotch, whilst flicking through the muted newsfeeds. All news sources pushed the same story of The Gate. Was this to be the end of his career? So what was left in his life? No job. No family. No future.

He dropped another rapidly melting cube of ice into his drink and swirled it about in the amber liquid. Agustin held his glass up, saluting. "Here's to the end," he said, pessimism washing down with the scotch.

A chime sounded on his screen and PWD. An incoming call. He accepted the call. The media feed was replaced with Colonel Yuji Sanada of Red Aquila.

"Director Garcia," he said quietly. "Have I called at a bad time?"

"Not at all, Colonel. And it's simply Mr Garcia now. What can I do for you?" Agustin drained the last of the whisky in a heroic gulp and slammed the glass down on the table. "Not that much anymore, I imagine."

"I've called to invite you to dinner, Agustin."

"Dinner?" asked Agustin.

"Indeed. Now."

"Now?"

"You have anything better to do?"

"I've got a lot of drinking to do, Colonel Sanada. But thanks for your invite."

"Drinking yourself into a stupor will help nobody. Come to the Red Aquila barracks and we'll enjoy a meal together. I find myself in need of the company of someone else who's looked into the unknown. I've been thinking about what we saw out there, those things looking back at us. You remember?"

***

The last time he'd been at the Red Aquila barracks was to interrogate Stone. It felt like a lifetime ago. He'd walked in there as a man of power and influence. Now, he was broken like a useless relic of a past time.

Under heavy escort, Agustin was waved through security checkpoints and secure doors, and directed to the private chambers of Yuji Sanada. Solid carved doors depicted a scene from the Night War. The battle of Tokyo Bay, where the Japanese Defence Forces overran a Nights' position, killing over one-hundred. Under different circumstances, Agustin would've stopped to study it more and contemplate the inclusion of each subject. Perhaps it illustrated Sanada's family, their involvement in the war. Perhaps it honoured nameless faces, heroes of the past. But the great doors split open and Agustin stepped inside. Sanada wore his impeccable uniform, the Night Blade strapped to his side.

"Mr Garcia, welcome to my home. Please, follow me."

The doors closed behind, sealing with a bang. The rich aroma of cooking meat filled his nostrils. He followed Sanada into the dining room beyond. It was laid out like a museum, a parody of a Victorian era dining room with none of the originality. A long table capable of seating ten waited. A man sat there eating. He looked up at Agustin, said nothing and returned to pushing food into his mouth. Rich paintings hung along the walls, portraits of people and places. An oak sideboard stretched almost the entirety of one wall showcasing vases and ancient weapons, swords from Japan and antique firearms.

"Private security pays well," said Agustin. "I've not seen anything like this outside a museum or old movies. Very impressive."

"Please sit, Agustin," said Sanada. "You'll have to forgive my other guest. He's not eaten in some time."

Agustin lowered himself into the chair closest to the door. "Just the three of us?"

Sanada took the chair across from Agustin and smoothed down his uniform. "I'm certain my ruse of a dinner together has been transparent."

"No at all," smiled Agustin.

"Your removal and the takeover by the CID could not have happened at a worse time."

"I'm not of the opinion there could be a good time."

"Of course," allowed Sanada. "But now we have an unstable element in a situation we cannot control. I could not risk talking to you on a call, and so, let me introduce my other guest. This is Jericho Lees."

The name rang a bell somewhere in the back of Agustin's mind. The man called Jericho looked up and nodded to Agustin. His jaw worked fast, chewing on his meal.

Sanada sipped from a tall glass. "Jericho Lees approached us because he could not get to you."

"Me? Have we met before?"

Jericho drained his glass and poured more from a shiny flask.

"Your associate Doctor Stone hired me to take him to the Undercity." When Jericho spoke, his voice was soft yet laced with the prospect of violence. "Things are complicated down there."

Agustin fixed Jericho with a quizzical gaze. "Isambard is alive?"

Jericho spread his hands. "The last time I saw him, yes. And he charged me with one final task."

"Which was?"

Sanada nodded some encouragement to Jericho.

Jericho shrugged. "He told me to find you and tell you Tanya is still down there. She's not dead and he's going to try to save her."

Agustin's heartbeat thundered in his ears. Tanya? Tanya alive? He sat forward, and looked to Sanada, craving verification that this was not a cruel joke. Sanada smiled.

Agustin closed his eyes. "My daughter is alive? And still down there?"

"There's more. Allow Jericho to finish," said Sanada.

"Stone told me to tell you or anyone who is going down there that if you see him again you're to shoot him. He doesn't want to end up like The Pilgrim or his followers."

Agustin stood from his chair, the motion sudden and causing the chair to fall back to the floor. "What are you talking about?"

"We haven't got much time," interjected Sanada. "In summary, we believe The Pilgrim of Hate is an agent of the creatures out there on Esworth. He is human, but altered."

"Altered? How?" Agustin demanded.

"The Pilgrim has powers over people. They follow his commands."

"How is this possible? You're not telling me everything."

"He's telling us enough." Sanada sipped wine from a crystal glass. "The followers of this Pilgrim have managed to destroy and absorb the Peacemakers. They are simply gone. The New Worlders so far have resisted any advance from these followers but we are unsure how long this will last."

"There's a temple below Uriah's Hope," said Jericho. "Larger than the one you found in the mine. Stone and I went there. He was taken, and that's where I last saw him."

"Taken? How?"

"The creatures have uncovered many more such chambers outside the city and we believe each is connected by subterranean tunnels," said Sanada. "Though we cannot confirm this at present."

"I need to go. I need to get Tanya back. If Grace Anderson gets hold of this news the CID will take steps to neutralise the threat. The Unwanted, any innocent, it'll be a slaughter."

"There's already been slaughter down there," said Jericho. "It won't be long before The Pilgrim's thralls move against the

New Worlders, and the Unwanted will be caught up in that shit storm."

"Thralls?"

"Those who have succumbed utterly to the mind poison of The Pilgrim," explained Sanada. "We assume what happened on Remus is the same as what happened down in the Undercity."

"You have a plan?"

"We need to collect more information and a small expedition led by Jericho will gather what we need. I'll be going and, Agustin, I'd like to invite you, too."

"You bet your ass I'm going. When do we leave?"

***

Isambard Stone, Undercity, Esworth.

The Pilgrim of Hate set a blistering pace. Stone followed along tall hallways of the blue metal, passing lines of those who succumbed to The Pilgrim's power. They waited silently, stepping aside and bowing heads when they passed. Men and women. But no children.

"What happens now?" asked Stone.

"You keep following."

"Your ... converts, there's no children. Why not?"

The Pilgrim chuckled softly, the sound almost musical. He guided Stone down a smaller tunnel and suddenly stopped at a doorway. The way was blocked by a shimmering energy, like green rippling waves. It reminded him of when Tanya was taken, the same movement of energy. The Pilgrim raised his hand and the barrier disappeared.

"What is this?" asked Stone.

"This provides the answers you seek, Isambard. Inside is your first step toward finding your purpose."

"Will I be harmed?"

"Nothing here will harm you, Isambard. You're here to learn, and so you will understand." The Pilgrim waved Stone through.

"Are you coming?"

"I am not required. We will see each other again."

Stone took a deep breath as though readying to dive under water. The air was suddenly extremely fresh. He stepped through. The shimmering returned to close the doorway behind. The room was large and lit by green, bale light in the far corner.

"Hello?" His voice echoed.

Stone turned back to the doorway. Was he trapped? He reached out, keeping his hand a foot away from the shimmering barrier.

"Don't touch that, Isambard."

Tanya's voice was so sudden and so close Stone almost leapt into the energy.

"Tanya? Is that really you?"

"It's me, Isambard."

"I came to save you," he said, voice faltering. "I came down here to take you back home."

"I do not need to be saved, Isambard." Her voice grew powerful. "Look at me, Isambard! Turn around and see me for what I am!"

Isambard Stone turned. "My God! What have they done to you?"

The End